# THEY
# WENT
# LEFT

# PRAISE FOR Monica Hesse
## *Girl in the Blue Coat*

∞

**The Edgar Award Winner for
Best Young Adult Mystery Novel 2017**

**An *Entertainment Weekly* Best YA Book of 2016**

**A *Booklist* Best Young Adult Book of 2016**

**A 2017 Indies Choice Awards Finalist
for Best Young Adult Book**

**A YALSA 2017 Best Book for Young Adults**

**A New York Public Library Best Book for Teens of 2016**

**A Notable Social Studies Trade Books
for Young People Selection 2017**

**A 2017 Bank Street College of Education
Best Children's Book of the Year**

**A 2018–2019 California Young Reader Medal nominee**

**2018 All Iowa Young Adults Read**

"*Girl in the Blue Coat* is a powerful, compelling coming-of-age story set against the dark and dangerous backdrop of World War II. It's an important and page-turning look at the choices all of us—including young adults—have to make in wartime. A beautiful combination of heartbreak, loss, young love, and hope."

—Kristin Hannah, #1 *New York Times*
bestselling author of *The Nightingale*

"A tapestry of guilt and acceptance, growing responsibility, and reluctant heroism, Hanneke's coming-of-age under heartbreaking circumstances is a jarring reminder of how war consumes and transforms the passions of ordinary life. Every devastating moment of this beautiful novel is both poignant and powerful, and every word feels true."

—Elizabeth Wein, *New York Times* bestselling
author of *Black Dove, White Raven*; *Rose Under Fire*;
and the Printz Honor–winning *Code Name Verity*

## *The War Outside*

**A *Publishers Weekly* Best Book of 2018**

**A 2018 *BCCB Bulletin* Blue Ribbon Title**

**A 2019 YALSA Best Fiction for Young Adults Pick**

**A 2019 Notable Social Studies Trade Book
for Young People**

**A 2019 Notable Book for a Global Society**

★ "Superb.... A satisfying and bittersweet novel, perfect for those who enjoyed Markus Zusak's *The Book Thief*."    —*SLJ* (starred review)

★ "An extraordinary novel of injustice and xenophobia based on real history."    —*Booklist* (starred review)

★ "A moving book that successfully describes an unjust aspect of U.S. history."    —*Publishers Weekly* (starred review)

★ "Keeps readers guessing through the final pages."
                                    —*The Bulletin* (starred review)

★ "Teens and adults interested in WWII books, especially situations that haven't been written about extensively, will want to experience this story."    —*School Library Connection* (starred review)

"Monica Hesse's *The War Outside* pierces the heart with its exceptional story of family, friends, and country.... Riveting and meticulously researched, this story reverberates with authentic voices as it explores adolescent growth under dreadful circumstances."

                                                    —*BookPage*

"Timely.... [Hesse] again uses a well-researched historical backdrop to tell a powerful coming-of-age story."    —*The Washington Post*

"Hesse's books are like time machines—vehicles that help us explore our past."    —Mashable

# THEY
# WENT
# LEFT

# THEY WENT LEFT

## MONICA HESSE

LITTLE, BROWN AND COMPANY
New York Boston

Copyright © 2020 by Monica Hesse

Cover art copyright © 2020 by Laywan Kwan and Faceout Books; fabric texture © Katsumi Murouchi/Getty Images; city ruins © vicnt/ Getty Images; red thread © Evelina Petkova/Arcangel; woman with suitcase © Ildiko Neer/Arcangel; needle © Mir Basar Suhaib/Alamy Stock Photo.
Cover design by Marcie Lawrence and Jenny Kimura.
Cover copyright © 2020 by Hachette Book Group, Inc.

Little, Brown and Company
Hachette Book Group
1290 Avenue of the Americas, New York, NY 10104
Visit us at LBYR.com

First Edition: April 2020

Little, Brown and Company is a division of Hachette Book Group, Inc. The Little, Brown name and logo are trademarks of Hachette Book Group, Inc.

The publisher is not responsible for websites (or their content) that are not owned by the publisher.

Library of Congress Cataloging-in-Publication Data
Names: Hesse, Monica, author.
Title: They went left / Monica Hesse.
Description: First edition. | New York : Little, Brown and Company, 2020. | Audience: Ages 12+ | Summary: "Zofia, a teenage Holocaust survivor, travels across post-war Europe as she searches for her younger brother and seeks to rebuild her shattered life"— Provided by publisher.
Identifiers: LCCN 2019031255 | ISBN 9780316490573 (hardcover) | ISBN 9780316490580 (ebook) | ISBN 9780316490603
Subjects: CYAC: Holocaust survivors—Fiction. | Brothers and sisters—Fiction. | Jews—Poland—Fiction. | Holocaust, Jewish (1939–1945) —Poland—Fiction. | Europe—History—1945—Fiction. | Poland—History—German occupation, 1940–1945—Fiction.
Classification: LCC PZ7.1.H52 The 2020 | DDC [Fic] —dc23
LC record available at https://lccn.loc.gov/2019031255

ISBNs: 978-0-316-49057-3 (hardcover), 978-0-316-49058-0 (ebook), 978-0-316-54044-5 (intl.)

Printed in the United States of America

LSC-C

10 9 8 7 6 5 4 3 2 1

For Andrew, my own little brother

*THE LAST TIME I SAW ABEK:*

*Barbed wire, rusty metal knots. I was being transferred. We all were, we lucky girls who could still sew and still stand, and as the guards marched us past the men's side of the camp, the men were lining up for roll call. Our eyes scrambled over them, greedy, searching the living skeletons for our fathers and cousins. We were good at whispering without making a sound by then; we were good at reading lips. Rosen? Rosen or Weiss? we girls mouthed, passing family surnames through the fence like prayers. Are there any Rosens from Kraków? From Łódź?*

*His cheeks were still round. His eyes were still clear; I noticed that. The older men must have been giving him their bread. In the beginning at least, we would sometimes do that for the youngest among us. I saw a healthy Abek and gave thanks for all the times I'd given bread to anyone's sister in my own barracks, a barter with the universe that someone else should be doing the same for my brother.*

*"Abek Lederman," I mouthed to the girl next to me. "Third row."*

*She took his name and whispered it through the fence, and on the other side, I saw the men part, reaching for his shoulders and pushing him closer.*

*I knew we would have no more than a few seconds. Barely enough time for me to grab his hand or pass him something. What did I have to pass? Why hadn't I saved half a potato, a piece of string?*

*Ahead of me, a woman stopped to take a rock from her shoe. Stupid. This guard would hit you for such an infraction, any of them would. As soon as the woman bent, the guard brought her mallet down on the woman's back, and she yelped in pain. But as she cried out, she also looked back at me, and I understood this delay was a gift; this delay would give me enough time to speak to my brother.*

*"Zofia!" he cried. "Where are they taking you?"*

*"I don't know," I mouthed. I could already feel tears pooling in my eyes but bit them back so as not to waste time. I reached for his hand through the fence, his little-boy fist that I could still cup my palm around.*

*"Abek to Zofia," I told him.*

*"A to Z," he said back.*

*"When I find you again, we will fill our alphabet. And we will be whole, and everything will be fine. I promise I will find you."*

*This is the version I have dreams of sometimes. Clear as day, sharp as a needle, so I can see every hair on his head. And when I dream this scene, Abek nods at my promise. Like he trusts me, like he believes me. For a moment, I feel at peace.*

*But then something changes. Then dream-Abek's face twists, and his words come out pained: "Something happened," this Abek says. "But we don't have to talk about it yet."*

# Part One

## Lower Silesia, August 1945

L INES. I AM GOOD AT LINES. I AM GOOD AT LINES BECAUSE YOU don't have to think in them, just stand in them, and this line is easy because now only a few people are in front of me, and easy because I understand the reason I am in it, and it's a good reason, and I am good at lines.

At the front of it, an official-looking woman—from the Red Cross, I think—sits behind a table. It's a nice, indoor table, as though it was carried out to the street from someone's dining room. Except, instead of sitting on a rug, it sits on cobblestones, and instead of candlesticks, it's piled with neat stacks of papers and smells of furniture polish, or I imagine it would; it looks like that kind of table. A solitary cup also sits on it, next to the papers at the proper two o'clock of an imaginary place setting like a leftover from the table's former life. A cup of tea for the official worker.

"Next," she says, and we move forward because this is how lines work; they move forward.

I look back toward the door, but the other nothing-girls don't come out to say goodbye. I'm the first one of us to leave the hospital. In the early weeks after the war, there were always goodbyes from the healthier patients, always plans being made. You could look out the ward window almost any time and see a truck grinding past, stuffed with German soldiers on their way home, Polish soldiers on *their* way home. Russians, a few Canadians, everyone traveling in a different direction, and every direction was someone's home, as if the world were a board game and all the pieces had ended up scattered in the wrong corners of the box.

But none of the nothing-girls were well enough then. So we don't have a protocol yet for what to do when one of us leaves. We have no addresses to exchange. We have nothing. We weigh nothing, we feel nothing, we existed on nothing, for years.

Our minds are nothing. That's the biggest nothing, the reason we are still in the hospital. Our minds are soft. Confused.

"Zofia? I didn't know if you wanted to keep this."

I turn to the voice, the little blond nurse jogging out the door, mouth like a red bow. She hands me a letter, addressed in my own handwriting. *Return to sender.* The sender was me; the addressee was—I'm not even sure who the addressee was this time. For months, from the day I was well enough to pick up a pen, I have been writing letters to everyone whose address I'd ever known. *Have you seen him? Tell him to wait for me.* But their addresses weren't their addresses anymore, and the mail wasn't the mail anymore. And I wasn't me anymore, but it became clear I couldn't do what I needed to from a hospital bed. If I wanted to find him, I would have to pull myself out of it.

Even though my mind is still soft, that's why I'm standing outside and the other girls are still in the window.

*Tell him the doctors won't let me leave by myself until I'm better,* I wrote. *Tell him I won't be better until I leave and find him.*

"Here, I also made this for you," the blond nurse says, passing me a bundle of cloth, still warm. Food. The heat feels nice against my stomach. I start to unwrap the cloth so I can hand it back, but she says to keep it.

So now I own this checkered cloth. It is mine, and that will bring the number of possessions I own in this world to six. Later, I can fold it and use it as a kerchief for my hair, or I can cut it in half, in triangles, and have two handkerchiefs; that would bring my number of possessions to seven. I also have a dress, undergarments, a pair of shoes, a donated bill of money in a large denomination, and a document saying I was a prisoner in Gross-Rosen. It's supposed to connect me with relief organizations, help with food rations. The workers who gave it to me said it would be my most valuable possession.

"Next," the official woman says. She's my mother's age, with lines on her brow that have only begun to soften her face. The queue behind me has grown, as more soon-to-be-discharged patients come out. Another worker arrives to help.

The blond nurse, still watching me. "Did you forget anything else?" she asks. *Urbaniak,* I remember. *Her surname is Urbaniak.*

"My shoes. Where are my shoes?"

*Why didn't I realize before?* I've just looked down at my feet, and the brown leather boots I'm wearing are a stranger's.

"Those *are* your shoes. Your new shoes. Remember?" She's gentle, and then I do remember: These brown boots are mine now, because when I was brought to the hospital months ago, I was wearing the shoes the Nazis had assigned to me, ill-fitting and full of holes. My frostbitten feet were so swollen that a nurse couldn't pull them off; she had to slice them at the tongue. The nurses said I cried; I don't remember crying.

It turns out, if you have to lose toes to frostbite, the third and the fourth are possible to lose and still be able to walk and balance.

"Are you sure you don't want to stay longer, Zofia?"

"I remember about my shoes now; I just forgot for a minute."

"You had already asked me about them once today."

I force a smile. "Dima is leaving; he's going to his new post, and he has a car to drive me."

Dima-the-soldier is the one who brought me to the hospital, which was not a hospital then, just a building crammed with cots and bottles of iodine. Dima's Red Army jeep was crammed, too, with people. The Russians had liberated Gross-Rosen three days before, but it had finally become clear that none of us, including the Russian soldiers, knew what liberation was supposed to look like. Hundreds of us were still inside the gates, too weak to leave. Dima found me barely conscious in the women's barracks, he later told me in the broken Polish from his mother. It was lucky I'd passed out, because by the time he stroked life back into my face, all the good rations had been handed out already: waxy chocolate, tinned beef.

Our stomachs were too weak for rich foods. I watched people who'd lived for months on a potato a day eat the beef and never get up again. We were liberated and still dying by the dozens.

"*It's over now,*" the soldiers said to us in February. It wasn't over, not officially, not for a few months, but what they meant was, the SS officers were not coming back to the camp.

"*It's really over now,*" the nurses told us in May, spoon-feeding us sugar water and porridge. We could hear cheering and yelling in the corridor; Germany had surrendered.

What did they mean, it was over? What was over? I was miles from home, and I didn't own so much as my own shoes. How was any of this over?

"Next," says the official woman, and I take another step forward.

A puff of smoke, the growl of a motor. Dima pulls up in his jeep. He leaps out when he sees me waiting, and I'm struck again by how much he looks like a cinema poster, like the film version of a soldier: Square chin. Nice cheekbones. Kind eyes. Dima, who postmarked my letters for me. Who, when I begged him, asked his soldier friends about Birkenau and found out for me that it had been liberated a few weeks before Gross-Rosen. And who repeated the same thing for me again when I forgot, and then again when I forgot again. *Remember, Zofia? We discuss already.* My mind is a sieve, and Dima is how I am allowed to leave this place—because he is leaving with me.

"I would have come inside, Zofia." He places his hands on my shoulders. His hair is shorter above one ear. He must have cut it himself again in the mirror. "You get too tired. You know I worry about you."

"I have to stand in this line now."

"She has to be processed," Nurse Urbaniak explains. "The aid organizations are keeping records."

A tap on glass, like a bird. I look up. In the second-floor hospital window behind me, the nothing-girls have woken; they're touching the glass and waving. To Dima as much as to me; they love him. He waves back.

"Next," the Red Cross woman says. I wait for a minute before realizing it's finally my turn. Her uniform is a single-breasted blue suit. My dress is also pale blue. The nurse who gave it to me said it went with my hair and eyes. *Kind lies.* My hair then was patchy and scabbed over, short as a boy's. It's grown back almost to my chin, but a thin, timid brown instead of lustrous curls. My eyes are still the color of empty. "Miss?" says the matronly woman. "Miss?"

"Zofia Lederman." I wait for her to check me off on her papers.

"And you're going home?"

"Yes. To Sosnowiec."

"And who would you like me to put on your list?" I stare at her, and she reads my confusion. "We're asking if you have any names."

"Names?" I know what she's asking must make sense, but my brain is fogged again; it can't parse the words. I start to turn back to Nurse Urbaniak and Dima for help.

The worker places her hand on mine until I look back at her. Her voice has softened from its clipped, official tone. "Do you understand? We're logging where you're going, but also the family you're looking for. Is there anyone who could be looking for you?"

*Names.* I did this once already, months ago, with some charity workers as soon as I was conscious. Nothing ever came of it, and now his name hurts in my throat.

"Abek. My brother, Abek Lederman."

"Age?"

"He would be twelve now."

"Do you know anything about where he might be?"

"We were both sent to Birkenau, but I was transferred twice, to a textile factory called Neustadt and then to Gross-Rosen. The last time I saw him was more than three years ago."

I watch her make careful notes. "Who else?" she asks.

"Just Abek."

Just Abek. This is why I need to go home. Birkenau was liberated before Gross-Rosen. Abek could already be waiting.

"Are you sure that's all?" Her pen hesitates over the next blank line. She's trying to figure out how to be delicate with me. "We've found that it's better to cast as wide a net as possible. Not just immediate family, but cousins, distant relations. All will improve the chances of your finding someone."

"I don't need to add anyone else."

*Distant relations.* She doesn't mean it this way, but it reminds me of when my old teacher would bring candy to lessons. *Don't be choosy,* he'd warn, walking around with a bowl.

Don't be choosy. You'd be lucky to have any relatives at all; just pick something.

"Look at all these empty rows." The worker gestures to her paper, patient, as you'd talk to a baby. "There's plenty of room to add as many people as you'd like. If you're looking for only one person—one on this entire continent—it could be impossible."

*One person. Impossible.*

I look at her empty lines. There aren't enough of them, not even close. Not nearly enough space for me to tell the story of the people I'm missing. I squeeze my eyes shut, trying to keep my thoughts from leaking, because I know the nurses have been wrong all along: Sometimes it's not that I have trouble remembering things, it's that I have trouble forgetting.

Behind me, Dima shifts his weight, concerned. I can tell he wonders if he should help.

If there were enough empty lines on that sheet of paper, this is how I would start:

I would start by telling her that on the twelfth of August in 1942, all remaining Jews of Sosnowiec were told to go to the soccer stadium. The instructions said we were to be issued new identification. It seemed suspicious even then, but you have to understand—I would tell her, *You must understand*—the Germans had already occupied our city for three years. We were accustomed to arbitrary orders that sometimes became terrifying and sometimes benign. I would tell her how my family had been moved from our apartment to another across town, for no other reason than imaginary boundaries had been drawn on a map, and Jews could now live only inside them. How Baba Rose and I had already made stars to pin on our clothes, cut from a pattern in the newspaper.

Papa had already reported to the stadium once: The Germans made all men report. They were taken, but they were returned, ashen and not wanting to speak of what they'd seen. *They returned.*

I would tell this Red Cross worker that our identification cards were how we survived: Without one, you couldn't buy food or walk in the street. So we had to go, and we wore our best clothes. The instructions told us to do this, which we took comfort in, because maybe they really were going to take our pictures for identification.

But then we got there, and there were no cameras. Just soldiers. And all they were doing was sorting us. By health. By age. Strong-looking into one group; weak or old or families with young children in another. One line to work in factories. Another line to camps.

It took hours. It took days. Thousands of us were on the field. All of us had to be sorted. All of us had to be queried about whether we had special skills or connections. The SS surrounded the perimeter. Behind my family, an old man I recognized from the pharmacy was praying, and two soldiers came over to jeer. One knocked the pharmacist's hat off; the other kneed him to the ground. My father ran over to help him up—I knew he would; he was always kind to old people—even while my mother and I begged him not to, and I thought, *What's the use?*

My mother and I took turns curling our arms around Abek and telling him fairy tales: *The Frog Princess. The Bear in the Forest Hut. The Whirlwind*, his favorite.

Abek was tall for his age, which made him look older. When we realized how the soldiers were sorting us, we told ourselves that would matter. *Abek*, Mama said. *You are twelve, not nine, all right? You're twelve, and you've been working in your father's factory for a year already.*

We made up these reassurances for all of us. We looked at Baba Rose, my sweet, patient grandmother, and we told ourselves she looked much younger than sixty-seven. We told ourselves nobody in Sosnowiec could sew half as well. Customers who bought suits and skirts from my family's business did so because of the embroidery done at Baba Rose's hand, and surely this counted as a special skill.

We told ourselves my mother's cough, the one that had made her weak and gasping over the past months, the one Abek was starting to get, too, was barely noticeable. We said nobody would even see Aunt Maja's limp.

*Pinch your cheeks*, Aunt Maja told me. *When they come to you, pinch your cheeks to make them full of life.*

Beautiful Aunt Maja's face was so pretty and her laugh was so gay, none of her suitors ever cared that she was born with a mangled hip that made her lurch instead of glide. She was much younger than Mama, just nine years older than me. She used to tell me to pinch my cheeks so I would be as pretty as she was. Now it was so we would both be safe.

Darkness fell; it started to rain. We opened our mouths to

catch the drops; we hadn't eaten or drank in days. The water on our now-sunburned skin felt nice for a minute, and then we were cold. Next to me, Abek tucked his hand in mine.

*And Prince Dobrotek crept into the horse's ear*, I said, telling *The Whirlwind* again. I was always good at telling stories. *And when he crawled out the other side, can you remember what he was wearing?*

*A golden suit of armor*, Abek said. *And then he rode the horse to the moving mountain.*

*Pinch your cheeks!* Aunt Maja hissed to me. *Zofia, pinch your cheeks and smile.*

I kept Abek's hand in mine and dragged him with me to the soldiers.

*Fifteen*, I told them. *I can sew and run a loom. My brother is twelve.*

Do you see why there isn't enough room on this woman's intake form for me to explain all this? It would take her hours to write it down. She would run out of ink. There are too many other Jews, millions of missing, whose information she also needs to collect.

Dima steps forward. "Zofia doesn't have more names; she's not well."

"I can do it," I protest, but I'm not even sure what I mean by *it*. I can keep standing in this line? I can be well again?

The official woman adds my records to her pile. Dima extends his hand, and I accept it. I fold myself into the passenger side of his jeep and allow him to arrange his coat over my lap while Nurse Urbaniak makes sure the bundle of food is secure on the floorboard.

What I should have told the official woman is this: I know I don't need to put anyone else on my list, because when the soldiers sorted my family, they sent us all to Birkenau. And when we got to Birkenau, there was another line dividing into two. In that line, the lucky people were sent to hard labor. The unlucky people—we could see the smoke. The smoke was the burning bodies of the unlucky people.

In that line, Abek and I were sent to the right.

On this continent, I need to find only one person. I need to go home, I need to survive, I need to keep my brain working for only one person.

Because everyone else: Papa, Mama, Baba Rose, beautiful Aunt Maja—all of them, all of them, as the population of Sosnowiec was devastated—they went left.

DIMA DRIVES SLOWLY. ON WHAT LOOKS LIKE THE MAIN street of this town, an aproned woman sweeps her stoop. At least, I assume it's hers, I assume it was a stoop. What she's doing is sweeping pebbles into a dustpan, then emptying the dustpan into a bin, and behind her is nothing. Rubble. The waist-high remnants of a brick structure, the vaguest hint of a doorway. It could be new rubble, from the Allies, or old, from the Germans. Poland was invaded twice. Is this Poland? The boundaries keep changing. This is the farthest I've been from the hospital. From the window, I could make out only a half-boarded-up milliner's shop, with no dresses in the window. *What do you think we'll buy when we're well?* the woman we called Bissel had asked dreamily. *I expect we'll buy nothing*, I said. *Because nothing is for sale.*

Dima's Polish is a baby's Polish, one- and two-syllable words punctuated by points and gestures. "Hungry?" he asks when the cobblestones give way to dirt. "Candy, under your chair."

"No, thank you."

"Look anyway," he says proudly. "Surprise."

Obligingly, I feel under my car seat. A paper packet of hard candies, and next to it, something rectangular and smooth. A fashion magazine. American, it looks like. A woman in a smart red hat. The first time Dima visited and I was actually awake, he asked what he could bring to the hospital, and I told him, *lipstick*. I could see he was taken by this, this idea of a scabbed, wasted girl wanting to look beautiful. I didn't tell him I just wanted something to stop the pain in my chapped lips. I didn't think he'd know the Polish words for *beeswax* or *petroleum jelly*. *Lipstick*, I thought he might know.

"Comfortable?" he asks.

"Yes."

"Blanket," he offers, nodding toward the back seat.

"I'm not cold."

"But every day you are cold." He frowns. He was so pleased with himself to have thought of this, and so crestfallen that I might not need it. I reach for the blanket in the back seat and arrange it over my shoulders. Dima smiles approvingly.

"Thank you," I say. "You are very kind."

"Exciting day," he says. "We'll be there soon. This car is fast. Until, you rest."

I lean against the side of the car but don't close my eyes. The road is dotted with debris. Broken wagon wheels, upturned yokes, milk cans with rusted-out bottoms. Each item, I think, is a family that couldn't walk any farther before they were stopped, or taken, or just too tired to carry more. Possessions were left behind this way, the frivolous things first, like music boxes and silk shawls and then everything but what a body needs for its own survival. And since a body can survive on almost nothing, everything was left behind. Broken wagon wheels, upturned yokes, milk cans with rusted-out bottoms. Each item is a family that couldn't walk any farther before they were stopped, or—

*Stop it*, I tell myself, trying to break the loop. *Stop.* This is what happens to my brain now. It trips. It goes in loops. It won't let me think about some things and won't let me stop thinking of others. Sometimes my brain is fine. Getting better. But still triggered by things that I can't always predict, and patchy like black ice.

I look to the other side of the road, toward the rolling farmland, trying to get unstuck. No debris in that direction. But there's a large plot of upturned earth, brown and mealy, and I can't stand to look at that, either.

Sometimes it's not that families got tired. Sometimes they were shot on the spot. Sometimes it was whole towns, into mass graves. I squeeze my eyes shut.

*It's over, it's over, it's over.*

I used to like the smell of dirt. On holiday in the country, Abek and I would draw pictures with sticks; I would teach him the alphabet.

*A is for Abek.*

Is it possible that right now I can smell something beneath this earth, something fetid and terrified?

B *is for Baba Rose.*

"We stop for lunch?" Dima suggests, and I'm relieved at the sound of his voice, breaking up my thoughts.

"Do you mind if we keep driving? I want to get to Abek. Unless you want to stop," I add hastily. This is the longest period we've ever spent together, the first time he's seen me off the hospital grounds. But if he thinks it's strange, he hasn't let it show.

"No, we can drive. I want to take you there, safe. Do you need anything else? Water? Walk your legs?"

"Stretch your legs," I correct him.

"Stretch?"

"That's what you say. It's an idiom. A saying, I mean."

"You need to stretch your legs?" He's pleased with the new phrase; he reaches over and pats my knee. *Lucky*, the other nothing-girls had said. *Be sweet to him.*

I don't know if Dima's posting to Sosnowiec was chance. He might have requested it. I didn't want to ask; I thought it was best not to clarify our terms.

"No, I—could we just keep driving?" I ask. "That's what I'd like best. Maybe you could tell me a story. Or I could try to rest again."

His eyes immediately fill with concern. "Yes. You should rest. You rest, and I'll take us home."

I didn't even mean for my eyes to close; I was looking for quiet, not sleep. But they must have closed, because suddenly I feel the car jolt to a stop.

"Zofia." Dima's hand is on my shoulder, gently waking me.

My eyes fly open, get my bearings. The ground is flatter. The sun is in the middle of the sky; hours have passed. Dima smiles broadly, gesturing through the windshield.

At first, I can't tell what he wants me to see, and then I can't believe what I'm seeing. A wooden sign with painstaking calligraphy.

"Already?" I gasp.

"I told you, this car is good. This car is fast."

SOSNOWITZ, the sign says. The Germans had come into Sosnowiec and given it a German name.

I hadn't meant that the car is fast, though. I meant, *How can we be here? How can I be back home already?* It was easier to imagine the evil things happened far away. On a different continent. But Birkenau, the first camp, was barely twenty-five kilometers from my town.

"This is it, yes?" Dima asks. He's pulled the jeep to a stop and peers at me curiously. I'm not having the reaction he thought I would.

"This is it."

"Tell me where I should go now?"

I swallow, get my bearings. "Home. Abek."

"Which way?"

We're on the edge of Sosnowiec now. Small farms, small plots of land. As we get closer to the city, the houses will cluster and turn into three- and four-story apartment buildings. In the distance, I can make out the factory district; if we were closer, I'd be able to see the soot that the factories create, hovering in the air above the power lines for the trams. Wide, paved plazas. Electric streetlights, lunch cafes filled with rushed workers.

"Zofia?"

I gather my thoughts. There are two addresses I could direct Dima to. The first is in the Środula neighborhood on the outskirts of town, the Jewish ghetto my entire family was forced into when I was thirteen. Trash in the streets. Crumbling walls, vacant lots. Six of us crowded into one room.

The second address is my home, my real one, which belonged to Baba Rose, where my mother was raised and my father moved after they married. Closer to the center of the city.

"Turn right," I decide. Our real home. That was the plan, for Abek and me to meet there. That's what I'd told him. *Repeat the address, Abek. Remember the birch trees outside?* What if he's been waiting there alone for me? *I tried to get better sooner, Abek. I tried.*

Dima turns, and the gravel road becomes a paved one. We pass a few men in simple work clothes, and then we pass more men, but they're in business suits and hats. Dima raises a hand in greeting; one waves back, cautiously, and the others don't acknowledge our presence at all.

"What's this?" Dima points through the windshield at a large expanse of green in the middle of buildings.

"Sielecki Park. Sometimes we would go here on school trips."

"Ah!" A few minutes later, he stretches out his hand again, pointing at something else. "And this?"

He's so excited to see this town, as if he himself were on

a school trip, as if we were on holiday together. At the hospital, they tried to prepare us that it might be strange to return home, but I didn't expect what I'm feeling now. My twisting insides, the shallow, metal taste in my mouth.

"This is a castle?" Dima points toward the most ornate building we've seen yet.

"Train station. There used to be a market there on weekends. We call it—" I break off, because even this inconsequential memory makes me feel a pang of familiarity. "We call it the Frying Pan."

My ugly, beautiful city. Sosnowiec is not an impressive place like Kraków, where Mama would take me for birthday lunches. Sosnowiec is where the industrial barons came to build their mills: iron, steel, ropes, and dyes. It has wide roads, practical buildings, smoggy air. Efficiency, not charm. Who could love a city whose fondest nickname was "The Frying Pan"?

My family did. We had no idea how little the city loved us back.

I know that many people resisted the German Army: the Home Army, the National Armed Forces, the Jewish Military Union all fought against the occupation. I know—or I heard later—that there was a revolt in Warsaw, that the city rose up for more than sixty days to protest the Nazis, and I know that this is why there essentially is no more Warsaw: The Germans punished the city by razing it.

But I also know that when the Germans invaded, a lot of people in my city knew the Nazi salute.

The scenery becomes more personal. We pass the library,

or what used to be. The market where we bought food the week of the invasion. It was summer; our cupboards were bare because we'd just returned from holiday. In the store, staples like bread were already scavenged. What was left behind were delicacies. Paper-thin nalesnikis, waiting to be rolled with minced meat. Bright jars of rhubarb preserves, in rows beside the dazed-looking grocer.

"Buy it all," my mother said quietly.

The first two weeks of the German occupation, we ate like we were having a party.

The jeep circles a redbrick building with limestone archways, and I don't wait for Dima to ask what it is. "Dietel Palace," I say. "Heinrich Dietel started the textile factories in Sosnowiec."

But as I say the words, my heart rate quickens, my mouth is dry. Dietel Palace means we are close to home. My father used to walk this route to get to our own factory.

I look closer. The fabric draped over the palace's front gate isn't the usual brocade representing the Dietel family's fortune, but a billowing red with a yellow star and sickle.

"That must be where you're supposed to go, Dima." I point toward the Soviet flag.

His face lights up. "I think so. I will stop here, and then I will take you to your home?"

My panic rises, my heart pats faster. "No! I need to get to my house first."

His face falls. "It will take only a minute."

I bite back annoyance, and I'm already reaching for the door. "My *house* is only a minute."

"But, Zofia." He's stunned, I think, by my sudden fortitude, and I'm stunned, too.

"You should go. I'm sure you want to check in with your superior officers."

*And my brother might be home already, and I don't want to wait. And I can't have a reunion with other people watching.*

"You'll be safe without me?" he says reluctantly.

"I'll write down the address—you can come over when you're done."

Eventually I persuade him to leave. I wasn't lying. I'm only a few blocks from my home, an even shorter walk if I cut through the alleyways, which is what my feet do by memory, running, running, while my bad foot begins to ache on the stones. I can't run; I've been too weak to run for years, and yet here I am, running while my heart explodes in my chest.

And then I am there, standing beneath a white street sign: MARIACKA.

It's a short road, made mostly of apartment houses facing the team line. Our building is midway down the block. Four stories tall, made of rosy brownstones.

I've rehearsed this moment a thousand times. What I would do if our old doorman was there. What I would do if it were a new doorman who didn't recognize me.

Nobody is standing by the entrance, though. There's nobody to stop me from going in, so I push against the oak door. In the lobby: the same marble tiles. Same flickering bulb. *Home.*

At the row of mailboxes, I stop. Sweeping my hand through the box, I feel a lump of brass: the spare key, taped far in the back where nobody would feel if they weren't looking. The key falls into my hand, heavy and sculpted, Sellotape crumbling into brown flakes.

Maybe Abek is already home, waiting for me. My heart flutters with the possibility as I run up the stairs. A fire on the stove. Clean sheets on the beds.

I've barely even touched the handle when it swings open.

A BEK!" I RUSH INTO THE FOYER. "ABEK? ARE YOU HERE?"
Straight ahead of me in the parlor is furniture, but not enough of it, and not ours. A large area rug too modern for Baba Rose's taste. On top of it, an unfamiliar chaise lounge and a few spindly chairs.

I must be in the wrong apartment, one floor too low. I must have gotten confused again.

But no, from here I can see: The center of the floor is marked with three round water stains. Could the stains have moved, too? *Five years.* I haven't been in this building in five years. I'm not in the wrong place. It's just that this apartment has lived its own life since I was here.

I am home. *I am home.* A sound escapes my lips, something between a bark and a cry.

The air is the same. The heavy heat, which Mama always said was the downside of living on the highest floor. Is it possible

I can still smell the leftover ghosts of Aunt Maja's nightly cigarette? I look down, and without realizing it, I've slipped off
my shoes. I haven't done this in months. Even at nighttime,
I've slept holding my shoes, to make sure they weren't stolen,
to make sure I could be ready to run. *It's because it's Thursday.
Thursday is the day Mama washed the floors.*

My feet remember to take off my shoes, and my hands
remember to deposit my parcel where a credenza used to be.

"It's me," my voice remembers to say, and is it possible
that in this apartment, my voice remembers that it used to be a
higher pitch? That it used to have a sharpness, a bit of wit?

Now, the only response to my voice is an echo.

*Abek's room first.* I try to focus, walking toward the smallest
room at the end of the hall, feet sticking to the polished walnut
floors—*there used to be a carpet runner*—and pushing the carved
door open. Sky-blue walls; the Germans kept those. White
trim, curtains.

But those are the only familiar things. There's no furniture. Even the bed is gone. A pile of rumpled bedsheets sits in
the corner, but I can't tell whether someone used them recently
or whether they were tossed there by whomever stole the bed.
When I bring one to my nose, soft and flannel, it smells faintly
of must. His closet is empty. No picture books. No model cars,
no stray sock catching on the door.

Backtracking, to my parents' room next and then Baba
Rose's, and with each empty room I can feel my brain wanting
to break into pieces.

My room, the one I shared with Aunt Maja. Dark wood

panels; it had been my grandfather's study before he died. The bed frames are gone here, too. I scan the rest of the room. I'd pasted posters on my walls, travel advertisements from train companies. Someone tried to scrape them off, but I can make out half of the Eiffel Tower.

If Abek had been back to this house, my room is where he would have left me something—a letter or a memento. I'm sure of it. Something to say, *I was here. Wait for me.* So I pick up a mildewed towel crumpled along a baseboard and shake it out, and I run my fingertips along the windowsill in case a slip of paper is jammed in the pane.

Inside my closet, naked wooden hangers clatter together. On the shelf above, an upholstered valise I don't recognize. I pull it down and upturn it, but nothing falls out. It's empty, and the clasp is broken, a beaten-up piece of luggage the previous occupants couldn't even bother to take.

They left me trash. They left me nothing. They left us nothing. This apartment is both familiar and strange. *How can something feel like too much and not enough?*

On the floor of the closet sits a wooden box. It's flush with the corner as though it was placed there intentionally, not just left at random. My heart speeds as I drop to my knees.

When I slide it out, it's heavy; it scratches the floor. And then, from near the front door, I hear a familiar click and whir. Someone is here.

"Abek!"

I race back down the hallway and, in the foyer, skid to a stop. The figure at the door is a reed-thin woman, broom held aloft in self-defense. She startles when she sees me, looking over my shoulder to check whether I'm alone.

"Pani Wójcik?" I say, making sure to use the right honorific for my neighbor. Her face is lined in ways it wasn't when I last saw her; her hair has turned gray. "Pani Wójcik, it's Zofia. Zofia Lederman."

Her eyes flicker; she doesn't put down the broom, but she lowers it a fraction. "Zofia?"

I step closer. I knew Mrs. Wójcik the least well of the other three on our floor, but I am nearly moved to tears at the sight of her now. She's from Before. The only evidence I have yet that parts of my life from then can still exist now. "Yes. It's me. Who did you think it might be?"

"Squatters," she mumbles.

"Squatters? Is that who's been here?"

"A friendly German couple lived here for a while, but . . ."

"They're gone now," I infer.

"Just before everything ended. Since then, just vagrants. I've had to chase them off. They make the building unsafe." She looks at me as if she thinks I'll explain these vagrants and then sighs a little when I can't. "Anyway, you're back."

"I'm back," I say unnecessarily.

She lets the broom drop to her side and scans the rest of the apartment, the scattered furniture and broken chairs. "There's not a lot left in here, is there?"

"I guess the squatters must have taken things."

She shrugs. "Or burned them. It got cold."

"Oh," I say as we stare at each other. I don't know how to

talk to my neighbors anymore. *Are your poppies still growing well?*
*Are your dogs still alive?* The last clear memory I have of Mrs.
Wójcik, she was walking them on the street as a soldier had just
asked for my papers. He'd asked the man next to me, too, and
the man was hoisted away by the armpits. *Did you see many more*
*people taken away, Pani Wójcik? How was the rest of your war?*

Mrs. Wójcik doesn't know what else to say, either. After a
few minutes, she puts her hand on the doorknob and raises her
eyebrows, a sheepish goodbye.

"Wait," I say. When she turns back toward me, the movement is tired. "Pani Wójcik, am I the first person to be here?
The vagrants, I know, but am I the first person from my
family?"

I can't make myself say Abek's name, and I don't want to
explain why the rest of my family won't come looking.

She shakes her head, a definitive little jerk. "Just you. And I
barely even recognized you."

"You're certain? Not my brother?"

"I haven't seen anyone else from your family. Frankly, I
didn't think any of you would be back."

She pauses again, hand twisting the knob but still not
walking through the doorway, as if trying to think of what
else to say. "We don't have a trash collector anymore" is what
finally comes out. "If you have something to throw away, you
have to carry it down yourself and burn it in the street. If you
don't burn it, the animals get to it."

"Thank you."

I manage to find the manners to see Mrs. Wójcik out

the door, and I lock it once she's through so nobody else can barge in.

I need to reset myself again, stop my brain from circling. The walls are buzzing with the memories of vagrants, who came in and burned my family's things for firewood because it was cold, because they had no place to live, because they were vagrants. So they burned my family's things, and so the walls are buzzing.

*No. Stop it.*

I go back to my room, stand in the doorway. I was doing something before Mrs. Wójcik came. What was I doing? Mrs. Wójcik came in, and I was—*the box in the corner of the closet.*

It's a hope chest. Polished maple, a flower carved on the lid. Aunt Maja's? I have the faintest memory of something like this tucked under her bed, filled with linens and handkerchiefs, her initials already stitched onto all the fabric next to blanks meant for her future husband's. The latch is rusty and takes careful jostling. But eventually the lid comes off, and I gasp.

Inside is what remains of my life.

When my family was forced out of this apartment and into the ghetto, we were allowed to take only what we could carry. Only clothes that were practical, only enough dishes to eat out of. And photographs. Photographs were precious enough that we took them, slipped out of their frames and pressed between paper, so I already know there will be none left in this trunk.

But other things are here. Layer after layer, folded between tissue, is what we couldn't carry and couldn't stand to give away. Mama's wedding gown. The dress I wore to my thirteenth birthday. All of it kept by the "friendly German couple," who were most assuredly Nazis. Is this the kind of gesture that passes for kindness if you are a Nazi?

In the Chomicki & Lederman clothing factory, Baba Rose was most famous for her beautiful embroidery, but I could handle a needle and thread, too. I would have been better than her in a few years. Machines assembled most of the clothes, but we sewed the labels and embroidery by hand. It made the pieces feel custom-made, Baba Rose said; it made customers feel cared for: *Chomicki & Lederman*, in fine, stitched cursive.

When I made my own family's clothes, sometimes I sewed in something special. Something hidden, tucked beneath the label or in a seam. Maja's name, in royal-blue thread, along with a line from a romance novel she wasn't supposed to lend me. Baba and Zayde's wedding date, stitched into the tablecloth we gave them for an anniversary.

Now, when I unpack my old school uniform, I can run my fingers over the hem, where I know the names of all my friends have been embroidered on a secret piece of cloth. Now, in the lining of my mother's old winter coat, I know there are a few hidden lines from a poem about spring. Nobody could see it; that wasn't the point.

When we first moved into the ghetto, Abek got lost. He wandered off and was missing for hours; he didn't know the new address. My mother loved him, of course; she loved us both. But when Abek was born, she was sick in her room for a long time—*fragile*, my father and grandparents said. *It was hard on her body.* I took care of him when he was small. And on the day he got lost, when he was returned hours later by a helpful passerby who had wandered the streets until Abek recognized our building, it was me he ran to, crying. And it was me who promised him nobody would ever have trouble returning him home again.

I sewed his name into the label of all his shirts. His name and address, the real one and then the ghetto one, and our parents' names and mine.

And then I started to sew more. Whole stories in the tiniest handwriting on the thinnest pieces of muslin. I folded the cloth half a dozen times and sewed it inside the label.

There was a story in his jacket the day we all went to the soccer stadium. It was a birthday gift from me to him, my best work yet. The story of our family, told in the alphabet:

A *is for Abek.*

B *is for Baba Rose.*

C *is for Chomicki & Lederman, the factory we own, and* D *is for Dekerta, the street we attend synagogue on, even if only on the high holidays.*

H *is for our mother, Helena;* M *is for Aunt Maja;* Z *is for Zofia.*

Something like that. I can't remember all of it. All the way from *A* to *Z*, some of the letters given whole paragraphs, and some just a few words. At the last minute, when we were getting ready to go to the stadium to get our new identification photographs, I took that story, which had been hanging on the wall, and I sewed it into his jacket, and I made him put that jacket on.

I must have known.

I must have known what was going to happen to us.

That's the thought I came back to later. I thought it when I was starving in Birkenau, and when I was operating the loom in Neustadt—*this girl can sew, the guard said, plucking me from death, sending me to work*—and when the cold ate through my toes on the 140-kilometer winter march to Gross-Rosen because the SS evacuated the factory, and when I collapsed in the women's barracks because the Red Army had finally come to liberate the camp and the Nazis had already fled. I must have known we weren't just summoned to the soccer stadium to have new identification made. Otherwise, why would I have made Abek wear that jacket? It wasn't seasonal. It barely fit anymore. What kind of person sews a family history inside a coat?

Either I knew something bad was going to happen or I was already crazy.

I have to find my brother.

I have to find my brother because the war is over, but I still don't feel safe. I don't think he is, either.

*I didn't think any of you would be back.* That's what Mrs. Wójcik said. But she didn't say it with gratitude in her voice. She didn't mean it like, I am so relieved to see you. Her voice didn't sound happy. Her voice sounded disappointed. What she meant was, *I thought they killed you all.*

DIMA IS TRIUMPHANT WHEN HE KNOCKS ON THE DOOR A few minutes later. Through the crack made by the latched chain, he holds up a paper parcel. "Lunch," he says. "Sausages."

I unlock the door but am at a loss once he's inside. "I don't have any fuel for the stove, though."

"Cooked already!"

Now I can see oil leaking through the paper, and it makes my mouth water. "I don't have anything to put them on, either," I apologize. I meant, I don't have a table, but as soon as I say the words, I realize I don't even have dishes.

Dima reaches into his coat and pulls out a cloth wrapped around something bulky. "Plates. Picnic." Another bundle: "Potatoes."

Having emptied his pockets, he looks around the big parlor, curious but polite. "This is your home?"

"It looked different when I lived here. The furniture is gone."

"Today we sit on the floor. Tomorrow I find you some furniture."

He raises his eyebrows in the direction of the dining room, visible through French doors, and I nod that this is where we should eat. Once there, he confidently settles onto his knees, opens the parcel, and begins to slice the sausages with a pocketknife.

"My commander says he comes for dinner?" Dima says after I've sunk to my own knees and accepted the plate. "He would like to meet, learn more about the city."

"That's fine."

"I told him he can come tonight."

"Tonight?" I protest. "There's no food in the house. It's my first day back."

"I know the notice is short." Dima looks at me with saucer eyes, and I bite my tongue. It's my home, but I wouldn't be here yet if it weren't for Dima's help, I remind myself.

The nothing-girls were only half right. They thought it was lucky that Dima rescued me and then grew to like me. But really it was that Dima grew to care for me *because* he rescued me. Because I was helpless and he could help me. Because he was lonely and I needed him. This entire time, he's been nothing but a friend; he's asked for nothing in return for his kindness. And I haven't offered anything.

It can't stay that way, though. Sooner or later, my frailty

won't be appealing, my gratitude enough to make him happy. He'll want an actual partner.

"Your brother—" Dima pauses and looks down at his plate, keeps his eyes there while he finishes the question. "He is not here today?"

*Three potatoes in a row on damp newsprint.* Dima bought three potatoes, just in case.

I swallow my disappointment. "No."

"He was here before?"

"I don't think so."

He reached out to stroke my cheek. "We will find him, I'm sure."

"Yes," I say, setting my metal plate down on the bare wood floor. Smiling. *I'm trying, I'm trying so hard.*

Here I am, back in my family's home, but instead of china, I'm eating on camping tin, and instead of my family, I'm with a Russian soldier. And he wants me to talk about dinner parties. Eight months ago I slapped a girl across the face because she tried to take my holey shoes.

"Zofia?" He says my name kindly but not quite right; the *Z* is too firm. "Zofia, you're not talking. I upset you."

"I think we should have bread with lunch." Abruptly, I rise to my feet.

He's stricken. "It is not needed," he insists, nodding to where he's split Abek's potato between his and my plates.

"But, it's a celebration," I invent. "My first day back in this house."

"I will come, too." He sets the knife down, starts to rise awkwardly himself.

"No! No. I'll go to the bakery around the corner and be back in a few minutes."

Still, he's concerned; he thinks I shouldn't be wandering. "I can see if there are cakes to serve your commander tonight," I continue to improvise, waving him back to the floor. "And it will be good for my health. To do things on my own in a familiar place. The nurse said."

The nurse didn't say, but this is what convinces him, this mention of a cake and this appeal to my healing. He hands me some money and softly kisses my forehead.

Outside, the midday heat washes over my face. But once I've successfully left the building, I don't know where to go. I don't know if a bakery is still around the corner; the ones we visited when I was a child in this neighborhood had signs appear overnight, JUDEN VERBOTEN, in the early months after the occupation.

*The Skolmoskis.* The name flashes through my mind. The Skolmoskis were Catholic. Though they were forced to hang that "Jews forbidden" sign in their window like everyone else, I know Mr. Skolmoski felt bad about it. A few times before we were forced to the ghetto, he stopped by with leftovers. *Leftovers,* he claimed. But when was the last time any of us had leftovers of anything? I'll go to the Skolmoskis' old shop.

The street is busier than it was a few hours ago. It's noon, lunchtime, with people hurrying to or from their workplaces.

Two blocks down, when I arrive at the bakery, one of Skol- moskis' windows has been boarded up, but over the plywood someone has written, *Still open*. The words are in Polish and not German, which I take as a positive sign.

The bell rings when I push open the door. The man behind the counter isn't Mr. Skolmoski; he's younger and unfamiliar. I hesitate at the entry.

"Can I help you?" the clerk asks.

"Just bread," I mumble, edging toward the shelves lining the wall and reaching for the nearest loaf, dark seeded caraway, so I won't have to speak more. But the selection is meager, and as my hand closes around the loaf, so does an older man's, one of only two other customers in the store.

"I'm sorry," I say. "You were here first."

He snatches his hand away, gesturing that I should take the bread at the same time I'm telling *him* to take it, and now I'm not sure whether he's trying to be polite, as I am, or he doesn't want the bread because I've touched it. What must I look like—the threadbare dress, the uneven gait, my gaunt frame?

My face grows hot. Maybe I should just leave, find another bakery, or tell Dima they were all closed.

"Zofia?"

The hand on my arm makes me yelp in fright.

"It's okay." The voice is reassuring as I turn. The woman standing in front of me is a few years older than I am. She's paler than she used to be, and one of her eyes is bloodshot. But she still has the same throaty voice that I used to admire and traces of the same dimples on her cheeks even though there's no longer enough fat to properly crease.

"*Gosia?*"

Before I can say anything else, Aunt Maja's best friend drops the bag in her hands and throws her arms around me.

I throw my arms around her, and the laughter that comes out of my body is as much from relief as delight.

"I can't believe it's you," Gosia says at the same time I'm stroking her hair, wondering whether I can trust my own eyes.

"I can't believe it's really you, either!"

The clerk at the counter has taken a sudden interest in our movements. "Could you lower your voices? You're disrupting the store," he says.

"We're the only customers left," Gosia protests. She's right; the store is empty. The older man must have slipped out while I wasn't looking.

"This is a place of business, not a party."

Gosia sighs. "We'll go."

"I haven't bought my bread yet," I begin, but Gosia shakes her head and takes my arm. Outside, in front of the store, she pulls her own loaf from her yarn shopping bag, ripping it in two and handing me half.

"Start from the beginning," she instructs. "Why haven't I seen you before now? You're just back?"

"Just this morning."

"Where were you?"

"Birkenau first, Gross-Rosen in the end." She winces

when I say these names; she knows by now what they mean. "Where were *you*?"

Gosia's color darkens, and she looks down at her shoes. "I had a dispensation. Because I worked in the hospital, I was an essential employee. When the dispensations stopped, one of the doctors let me hide in his cellar. It was safe for all but the last few months. Then, Flossenbürg. But only for a few months." Her mouth twists uncomfortably; she's embarrassed by this good fortune.

"A few months is long enough. I'm glad for you," I reassure her. "I'm glad you stayed safe as long as you could."

"I'm living with my sister and her husband now. Their hiding place was never raided." She hesitates, finding the words. "Is Maja—"

"No."

My answer is complete in itself. *No, Maja isn't.* But I make myself continue because Gosia is a friend who deserves to know. "Just after the soccer stadium. All of them except Abek were killed."

"No." She closes her eyes, and I let her have her moment of grief. When she opens them again, she lowers her voice. "Almost none of us are left," she says quietly. "A few hundred at most. I just don't understand how so many of us can be gone."

"I'm looking for Abek now. We were separated at Birkenau. I guess this means you haven't seen him back here?"

"I wish I had. You've been to your apartment?"

"I just came from home—from Mariacka. It's been looted, but nobody else is living in it. Next I'm going to try Środula.

Maybe he forgot where we planned to meet. Maybe he thinks of the ghetto as home?"

Gosia is shaking her head. "Gone," she says. "Bombed. He couldn't have gone to the ghetto; it doesn't exist anymore."

"You're sure?"

"I went there myself first thing, when I got back in June. You should see it, Zofia, that part of the city—there's almost nothing left standing."

Nausea, a dropping in my stomach. Abek isn't at my family's house. He couldn't go to our old room in the ghetto. Gosia has been back in Sosnowiec since June, and she's known my family since she was a child; we have all the same friends. I don't see any way Abek could have come back without Gosia's hearing about it, especially not if there are as few of us as she says.

"Who else was with you?" she asks. "On the train to Birkenau—anyone we know?"

"You mean, that day?" I repeat slowly.

"Yes, on the transport. Who was on the transport to Birkenau?"

I knew that's what she meant. Of course it is. I was just buying time. Answering that question requires me to think back to that day, and that day is something I try to never think about.

"On my transport, there was only—" But before I can continue, I'm slipping back into the horrors of that day: yelling in my ears, the smell of decay in my nostrils, feeling so thirsty and so weak and barely able to breathe. "There was—"

"Zofia? Are you all right?"

I look down, and the bread in my hand is shaking. My hands are shaking. *We're not in a cattle car. We're on a street. We're not in a camp. We're in Sosnowiec. It's not that day. It's not that day.*

The train station at Birkenau is my black ice, a sleeping black monster guarding the door of my memory. Nudge it too hard and it will wake. If it wakes, it will consume me. I creep around the edges of that memory. Even the edges are hell.

"There was Pani Ruth," I finish. "With the long gray hair. She was with us. She—"

"Any men?" she interrupts, and now I understand what she's asking: Do we have any friends who would have been on the men's side of camp, who could have seen Abek after I last did?

The pharmacist. The pharmacist was praying in the mud, and—*No.* The pharmacist died in the soccer stadium, I remind myself. The pharmacist died before we got on the train. I need to think about what was after the train, on the platform, on that last day, on that day when—*No, no, no.*

"Pan Zwieg," I choke out. "Pan Zwieg, the librarian. He was with us. And the skinny boy from the butcher's shop. I think his first name was Salomon."

Gosia grabs my arm. "Salomon Prager."

"Yes. Salomon Prager." The name retrieved, I claw my way back out of that memory.

"He's back. He's alive. My brother-in-law saw him just last week."

"At the butcher's?"

"The butcher shop is closed; he's working as a farmhand now. After my shift this afternoon, I can find him and ask if he knows what happened to Abek."

"Can we go now? Let's go right now." I've already forgotten about bread, and lunch, and Dima, but Gosia is shaking her head apologetically.

"I only have an hour for lunch, and it's my brother-in-law who knows who Salomon is working for. I promise I'll find him after work."

"Come for dinner, then," I tell her reluctantly. "It will be me and—and maybe a Russian soldier, too. Dima helped me. He's stationed here now."

I feel my own face redden as I explain, but Gosia barely blinks. She must have heard of all kinds of arrangements.

"Oh, Zofia, it's good to see you again." Gosia puts her hands on my cheeks, and I put my hands on hers; we touch our foreheads together. "I'll come tonight. I promise."

She tells me the names of a few nearby stores that are open and friendly, where I might be able to pick up food to prepare for dinner. When I get home, I climb the stairs again, preparing to apologize to Dima for the length of the errand.

And at the top of the stairwell, I see it. Tucked in Mrs. Wójcik's flowerpot, where I'm sure there was nothing before, is a tiny flag, the kind children would wave at a parade, and on that flag is a swastika.

GOSIA COMES THAT NIGHT WITH GIFTS: A BLANKET. TWO extra pairs of underthings. A packet of laundry powder for my clothes and a bar of soap for myself, white and medicinal, not like the soft brown bars we used to buy from the shop. "The rationing isn't as bad as it was before," she explains. "But everywhere has been out of soap this week. I took this one from the clinic."

"Thank you." I'm grateful for what she's brought, but the overly eager way she hands me the bundle—I can immediately tell the items are an offering to make up for bad news.

"Salomon couldn't help."

Her eyes lower. "He didn't see him. He didn't remember seeing him at all there."

"I see."

She moves to take my hand, but since I'm still holding the bundle, she ends up taking my wrists instead. "Salomon asked

me to apologize. He said he would have looked out for Abek—
he wanted you to know that. If he'd known Abek was there, he
would have tried to look out for him."

I can hear Salomon's guilt spilling out of Gosia's mouth.
But I don't blame him. The camp was the size of a small city.
Salomon's not being able to remember seeing Abek didn't mean
anything.

It just means I need to look harder. It just means I need to
write more letters. Tomorrow I can go talk to Salomon myself.

Dima walks in from the dining room, broad smile on his
face, kissing Gosia's cheeks in a way I've learned is considered
merely friendly for Russians, not overly familiar. She startles in
surprise but rearranges her face by the time he pulls away.

"You are Zofia's friend? It's my pleasure to meet you."

"Gosia, this is Dima Sokolov, whom I told you about. He's
also invited his commander to join us for dinner. So it will be a
little party, if you don't mind."

"I am going to meet him now," Dima says to Gosia. "Zofia,
you have everything you need? For cooking?"

I nod, and when he leaves, Gosia raises her eyebrows. "He's
handsome."

"He's been nice to me." I gesture for her to follow me to the
kitchen, but she holds back, uncertainty on her face. "Gosia?" I
ask. "Was there something else?"

She looks back toward where Dima just exited the door.
"Salomon mentioned something—I don't know if it's useful.
But, he said the Red Army liberated Birkenau in January."

"I know that," I tell her. "Dima already found that out."

"But, listen. Before the liberation, Salomon said, they started to transport people away. The SS knew the Allies were coming, so they were trying to evacuate the camp before they arrived, by sending prisoners farther into Germany. Salomon didn't go; they left him in the infirmary, and the camp was liberated a few weeks later."

*Evacuated.* This is what happened at Neustadt, too. Roused from our beds, told to abandon the looms, told to walk for days in subzero temperatures until we reached Gross-Rosen on the fuzzy border of the Reich. Our evacuation didn't outrun the Allies for long: the Red Army liberated Gross-Rosen a few months later. But if the camp had been deeper in the Reich— the Allies didn't reach central Germany until late in the spring.

Now I see why Gosia didn't begin with this information. There are two ways to read it, a bad way and a good way. Either Abek was in Birkenau for liberation and he should be home, or...

"Abek went to Germany," I say.

"No, I mean, I don't know."

"But Salomon didn't see him in the infirmary? He didn't see him left behind?"

"No, but—"

"Gosia, at the time of liberation, was there anywhere else he would be?" I ask. "In the infirmary, as Salomon was, or on a transport west to another camp in Germany. Those were the choices?"

Gosia looks uncomfortable. "Unless—"

"Unless what?" I ask sharply.

"Zofia. I loved Abek. You know I did. But he was so young. He was young, and the work was so hard, and so many people—"

"—And that is why it is lucky he was strong," I interrupt. "Besides, I had organized something for him. A special position. He was *valuable*. I made sure he was *useful*."

She sees my face. She sees my face, and her next words are careful. "If Salomon is right, then when the camp closed, the infirmary or on the transport are the most likely places he would have been."

"We know he wasn't in the infirmary," I say. "So he was on that transport."

"So he was on that transport," she repeats slowly. "Of course he was."

Commander Kuznetsov is a tall, thin man with gaunt cheeks but friendly, intelligent eyes. He doesn't speak Polish, but he speaks fair German, which Gosia and I are fluent in but which Dima doesn't speak at all. Gosia also knows some Russian, and between the four of us, we manage to limp along, languages changing every few sentences, an imitation of a dinner party.

The commander has never been to Poland before, he explains as we sit with plates in our laps, again on the floor. Dima spread a tablecloth between us, and he brought flowers, which are on the windowsill. He also made sure there was a bottle of vodka. The rest of the apartment is as it was when I walked in, peeled and abandoned, which the commander says is the point. He asked for the invitation because he wanted to know something about the region he'd been assigned to, he says, how we're living and making do.

I made holishkes, with tinned tomatoes and the only meat available at the butcher: a graying, tough mutton. I tried to enjoy the cooking, with the army-issued pots Dima brought along. I tried to enjoy being in my family's kitchen again.

"Zofia?" Dima says gently. "Commander Kuznetsov asked you a question."

"Yes, it's a traditional dish," I say, pulling myself back into the conversation.

*If Abek was sent to Germany, will he know how to get back? Where in Germany—the country is huge. Will he have been given the same letter I was, to allow him to board a train?*

"We eat it at our harvest holiday sometimes," Gosia adds because I've gone silent. "We also have, oh, apple cake and potato kugel."

*We eat it because it's Abek's favorite meal*, I add to myself. We eat it on his birthday, and as I bought the ingredients, I hoped somehow I would be making it for him. That Salomon would have known where he was, and Gosia would have brought him home tonight.

"You have known Zofia's family for a long time?" the commander asks Gosia, the more talkative of his dinner companions. "And what are you doing for work now?"

"I'm a nurse at a medical clinic. And yes. Zofia's aunt and I went to the same primary school. I've known Zofia since she was born, which means—" She nudges my shoulder, tries to draw me into the discussion.

This isn't how I wanted my first night home to be. This isn't how I wanted anything to be.

"It means eighteen years, doesn't it, Zofia?"

Dima looks at me, worried. This isn't how he wanted the evening to go, either.

"I apologize, Commander," I say quietly. "I'm very tired. As Dima might have told you, I'm looking for my younger brother. I had hoped he would be waiting for me here, but he wasn't."

The commander nods at me, but it's Dima he speaks to next, in rapid-fire Russian I can see Gosia struggling to keep up with. By reading their faces, I think I make out the basics. He's asked Dima whether my brother was in a camp, like me, and Dima has said he was. The conversation continues to the point that I can't follow it, until Gosia at last cuts in.

"He says there are helpers. Organizations, I think he said," she tells me.

"I know. I've talked to them; I've written letters."

The men keep talking, and when Gosia cuts in the second time, her voice has an edge to it. "He says he wonders if Abek is in Munich."

Dima and Commander Kuznetsov stop midsentence and look at her. The commander seems humbled, and he switches to German. "I apologize for leaving you out of the conversation," he tells me.

"Why would he have gone to Munich?" I ask.

"As we understand it, the prisoners from Auschwitz-Birkenau, at the end of the war, went mostly to two camps: Bergen-Belsen and Dachau," the commander explains. "For Dachau, the city it's nearest is Munich."

"Why not Bergen-Belsen? Is that also near Munich?"

Commander Kuznetsov looks confused, but it's Dima he turns to, not me, asking him something in Russian. Dima answers him softly, lowering his voice to almost a whisper, his eyes darting periodically over to mine. There's something I don't like in the language of his body—something protective but also secret.

"What are you telling him?" I ask, my voice rising. Then, to Gosia, "What are they saying, Gosia?"

Gosia purses her lips, reticent to translate. "The commander said—he said that—he was made to think Abek was not in Bergen-Belsen."

I shake my head in confusion. "Why would he think that?"

Again, the three of them exchange glances I don't understand. I pick up my cup and bang it against the floor to get their attention. "Who would tell him that?"

After an eternity, Dima drags his face to meet mine. "I tell him that. I tell him Abek was not in Bergen-Belsen. Because when I write the camp, he is not in their records."

"When you wrote to—" I repeat the words slowly, trying to make sense of what he's saying. "When you *wrote to the camp?*"

"The helpers," he tries to explain. "The soldiers who are there now."

"But you knew there was a chance he could be in this place and you already wrote to them? Without telling me?"

Dima flushes a deep red. "He was not there," Dima continues. "So I did not want—so I did not want to *worry* you, Zofia. I am trying to help. You need to *rest*. I thought, if I could find him for you—"

Gosia and the commander are staring at their plates, trying to disappear themselves from this exchange. Dima is staring at me, pleading.

"Did you hear from Dachau, too?" I ask. "Or Birkenau? Damnit, Dima, is there anything else you're keeping from me?"

"Don't swear, Zofia. You are not a girl who swears."

"I'll swear if I want to," I insist, tears filling my eyes.

He shakes his head quickly. *No*, he's saying, no, those places didn't write back.

*Is this betrayal?* Is it betrayal if he was trying to help me? If he did it in secret, but the goal was to find my brother? *He meant well.* I tell myself that. He was trying to help. And, he *did* help, actually. He found a place where Abek was *not*.

Next to me, Gosia slides her hand across the floor until her fingers are splayed over mine. "The commander said Munich because a lot of the prisoners from Dachau, after the war, ended up going to another camp near Munich." She exchanges a few words with Commander Kuznetsov before continuing. "A different kind of camp," she clarifies.

And now she's speaking not in Russian or German or even Polish, but Yiddish. The language of our kitchens, of our private family time, the language acknowledging that the commander and Dima are not part of what happened to us. "A big refugee camp run by the United Nations. There are several. They're for Jews who can't get back to their homes or who haven't been able to find their families."

"And it's where Abek is likely to be if he was evacuated from Birkenau."

She takes her hand away. "That's what he said. It's called—" She switches back to German. "What is it called?"

"Foehrenwald," the commander says. He looks relieved to offer a piece of information that won't cause me to be upset. "It's impossible to know from here, though, whether your brother is in this camp. The staff is small and overworked. From what we've heard, it's barely organized—it's thousands of refugees, coming in and going out."

"Impossible to know from *here*," I repeat. Now I've switched to Polish, but Dima, to my right, is shaking his head before I even say a few words.

"Abek will come here," he says. "That was your plan."

Sosnowiec was the plan. Staying together was the plan. Finding him was the plan.

*But what if he forgot the plan?* He was only nine. What if he forgot our address? What if it's not a place he knows anymore? What if he's stuck, or hurt, or in a hospital as I was?

"Did you know about this place?" I ask Dima sharply. "Is this another place you were keeping from me?"

"No, I promise," he says. "I didn't know about this camp. We can write to it tomorrow."

"We can write," I repeat. "But what if he leaves in the meantime?"

"If he leaves, he will leave for here," Dima says simply.

"But what if he can't *get here*? Or the letter doesn't reach him?"

"Zofia, you must be patient, but—"

"What if he needs me? What if he's alone and needs me *right now*? Aunt Maja just said—"

"Who?" Dima interrupts politely.

"Aunt Maja. Just now."

"Zofia."

"*Aunt Maja.*" My voice, rising with every syllable, until it's almost a scream. "Aunt Maja *just now* said the prisoners from Birkenau went to Germany. Didn't you hear her?"

The silence in the room, the painful squeaking of a floorboard, is what makes me realize my mistake. My face reddens.

"I mean Gosia, obviously. I know that's Gosia, not Aunt Maja."

Quickly, I lower my head to my plate and saw off a piece of cabbage. But I can't seem to get it to my mouth. In that moment, I *did* mean it. I was sitting in this dining room, and the person sitting next to me was my beautiful aunt Maja, and I lost myself again.

Next to me, Gosia looks pitying and worried; her eyes flicker briefly to Dima's. I saw them talking earlier while I finished cooking dinner. I wonder what he told her, how they have diagnosed me.

They think I'm crazy already, so there's no point in explaining how I was only briefly confused, by being in this apartment.

There's also no point in explaining the sudden certainty in my heart, which began building at the mention of this place called Foehrenwald. I know that I protected Abek as best as I could. Through all the war, I could feel him with me. If I hadn't been able to feel his presence, I wouldn't have been able to survive. I survived, so he must be in Foehrenwald.

"I know it's Gosia." One more time I repeat it, more quietly this time. "Never mind."

Gosia leaves a few hours later when her brother-in-law comes to collect her. She hugs me and says I should come to the clinic tomorrow; they can always use volunteers. Over her shoulder, Dima nods at her. It must be something they planned, an excuse to keep me occupied. "Either way, I'll stop in tomorrow evening," she says. "I'll try to bring more clothing and a spare lantern."

Now there is only one lantern in the house, and stubby candles. The apartment is shadows; Dima and Commander Kuznetsov are outlines as they talk near the door.

Dima breaks away and comes over, taking my hands. "The commander says there is room for you if you come with us. You can stay there instead of by yourself."

"I'll be fine here. Gosia brought me some things."

"The floor is so hard," he presses on. "You at least need

a—" He searches for a word he doesn't know in Polish, before mimicking unrolling something on the floor.

"A bedroll? I don't." The alcohol is getting to my head; it feels light and spinning. I'm still annoyed with Dima. I've slept on so many worse things than a clean blanket on a wooden floor.

"No, I can bring one." He looks back to where the commander is adjusting his hat, politely trying to give us privacy. "I will walk him home and come back."

"You can't keep going back and forth. You've already been twice today."

But he insists, and finally it seems easiest to just agree. To let him bring back a bedroll, to cluck over me like I am a figurine.

I GATHER THE DINNER PLATES, BUT THERE'S NO RUNNING water to wash them with. Gosia and I ate our plates clean. Dima and Commander Kuznetsov left scraps on theirs: a crust of bread, a few leaves of cabbage. On the commander's plate, a piece of meat, mostly gristle, which he must have discreetly spit out.

It's blobby and chewed there on the plate, swimming in congealed tomato. I stare at it for a minute, nauseated.

But then I'm putting those desiccated morsels into my own mouth. Scraping my finger along the tin, not even bothering to use a fork. The gristle sticks in my throat; I force it down. I am revolted by myself but also starving, or remembering what it was to be starving.

*What is wrong with me? What has become of me?*

In the next room, a knock at the door. I shove the plates into the dry kitchen sink, trying to put myself together.

"I'm coming," I call to Dima as the knock gets louder. "I'm sorry, I was in the ki—"

I don't finish, because it's not Dima. Standing in the dim doorway are three men I don't know, two who look like brothers with flat noses and clefts in their chins, and a third, taller and thin with bags under his eyes.

"We heard there were Jews here," says the taller of the men with flat noses. "This neighborhood is Judenrein."

Judenrein. That was the German term. That's why we had to leave this apartment to begin with. *This neighborhood is Judenrein.*

But German words can't dictate what neighborhoods are free of Jews anymore, can they?

My mouth is dry as yarn. "Where did you hear that?"

I don't know why I think I can buy time. They'll learn the truth eventually. Everything about my appearance looks as though I was in a camp.

Faintly, coming off their clothes, I smell alcohol and sweat, and now my heart starts to pound. The speaker brushes past me into my own house, and the others follow, backing me farther inside. Their eyes roam the apartment, what they can make out of it in the dark.

"There's nothing to take," I manage. "You can see, the only furniture left is junk. And I'm the only one here."

*Stupid,* I chastise myself as soon as this sentence passes my lips. I'd meant, *maybe you can leave me be because I am obviously no harm to you.* But now the original man's face is leering in the lantern light at this discovery that I'm alone.

"If you're hungry, I can—I can get you some food, maybe," I improvise, trying to find a way to edge around closer to the door. "My friend is on his way back, right now."

"You said you were alone, Jewess."

"I'm alone now, but my friend will be here soon. He's a lieutenant. In the Red Army."

"Convenient, there's a boyfriend now," the dark-circled man mutters under his breath.

There's no place I can go to maneuver myself away from all three of them. Already, the second brother has positioned himself in front of the door. The other two are still wandering about my apartment.

"There is a boyfriend," I insist in a way that sounds so fake even I wouldn't believe me.

I don't see any weapons, though maybe they're hidden beneath their jackets. Please let them just steal my things and not beat me. Please let them just beat me and not rape me. Please let them just rape me and not kill me.

*Please kill me. Please just kill me. Why not; how else will this ever be over?*

"I can pay you," I offer, desperate. "For—for the trouble of having me use the apartment."

At this, two of the men look mildly interested, so I keep talking about the money. I'll give them everything left from what Dima provided for groceries and try to keep the large, unbroken bill from the hospital. "Just let me get it. While I'm doing that, there's vodka in the kitchen. Nearly a whole bottle; you can take it."

I don't want them drinking more. But the vodka is a distraction, and I don't want them following me into the bedroom, either. So as two of them go to the alcohol, I rush past the one guarding the door, into the bedroom, fumbling in my checked gingham cloth where I'd stuffed all the money.

From the hallway, I hear more noises, whispering. And then, one of the men calls out to the original speaker, whom I've begun to think of as the leader.

"Piotr."

I peek around the corner. The men cluster around Dima's cap resting on a chair, prominent sickle and hammer.

"I told you." I find my voice, stepping back into the room. "His name is Lieutenant Sokolov. He works at the—he works for Ivan Kuznetsov." I don't know whether this name will be familiar to them, but I say it as though I expect it will.

"Shut *up*, Jewess."

His voice is dismissive, but I think it mattered, what I said. The Russians are in control here now. That has to mean something.

"He'll be back soon." Now, I stalk toward the door as if I have more courage than I really do and hold out the leftover grocery money. "So I think you should take this and leave."

The one named Piotr menacingly snatches the bills from my hand. "Next week. We'll pay you a little visit next week."

When they leave, I relock the door and then sink down against it. My thudding heart aches in my chest. My heart hurts even when it's not beating. But that can't be right, because my heart hasn't stopped beating, my heart has continued beating even while the hearts of almost everyone else I ever met have stopped beating, and that is why my heart hurts.

A *is for Abek.*

Z *is for Zofia.*

I'm still on the floor twenty minutes later when Dima tries to open the door. He pushes once, twice. "Zofia?" His voice rises in panic.

"One minute, please," I manage, raking my fists across my eyes and dragging myself to my feet. I open the door. "Some men came. I locked the door when they left, for safety."

"What men?" He looks back into the hallway; his voice tenses and deepens. "They will come back?"

"I don't know."

Dima edges past me. Setting the bedroll down on the floor, he stalks around the apartment, checking to make sure the windows are locked.

"If they come back, it won't be tonight," I say. "They saw your cap, and it scared them."

He finishes his window inspection. He's still worried, but there's a small amount of pleasure in his eyes at this last thing I said about his cap protecting me.

"I have this." He points to the bedroll, army-issued, olive green.

"Thank you."

"You are sure you don't come with me?" He takes a few steps toward me, closing the space between us.

"I have to stay. I don't want anyone to think this apartment is empty."

"What if I stay tonight?" He's come all the way across the room now. He strokes his index finger along my cheek. "Not in your room," he adds hurriedly. "But, for protection."

"I don't know."

"You know, my parents did not speak same language, either," Dima says, shy-sounding. "He was a soldier, too. Already, I speak more Polish than my father. I think they are very happy now."

"I'm sure they are," I say quietly.

This is the first time he's spoken so plainly about his feelings, plainly enough that I can't pretend something has been lost in translation, or that I think his kindness is merely friendly.

I have no job. The money given to me at the hospital will run out. I am not safe here alone. Dima cares about me. He wants to protect me. All I have to do is be kind to him. All I have to do is accept this life.

Dima might care about me mostly because he rescued me. But I'm using him, too. The times I theatrically clapped my hands at the gift of lipstick. All the times I watched him swell with pride at the coos of the nothing-girls. The fact that I could leave the hospital because I was leaving with Dima.

Does that make it wrong, though? Relationships have been built on less.

"Do you want me to stay?" he asks.

"All right," I say, and then wet my lips and make myself start again. "That would be nice, but you don't have to sleep out here. I still have only one blanket. You would be cold."

In my childhood bedroom, where I have not slept since

before my family was murdered and my country was broken, I unroll the bed mat brought to me by a Russian soldier. I make it up with the faded blanket brought to me by the friend of my dead aunt, and then I lie down in the dress I'm wearing because I still don't have any nightclothes.

Dima lies behind me, respectful. His breathing isn't steady enough for him to be sleeping. He's awake, looking at me, at the outline of me in the dark. I feel his hand on my hair, stroking from the top of my scalp to where my hair stops. He does it three times, and just as I'm waiting to see if he'll do more, I can tell he's waiting on the same from me, to see if I turn over, or wriggle back so my rear nestles in the crease of his hips.

Baba Rose would stroke my hair in this room, intently and reassuringly, as if she had nothing else to do and nowhere else to be.

Aunt Maja would stroke my hair in this room, talking through her own problems.

Mama stroked my hair in this room, and though she always seemed tired and sometimes fell asleep with her hand heavy on my head, she also told me fairy tales and sang whatever songs she'd heard on the radio that day.

I hear a crack coming from the next room. I know it's the sound of an old building settling, but I have to stop myself from crying out: *Abek?*

Behind me, Dima's hand has stopped, resting on the mat behind me, accidentally pinning a few strands of my hair to the bedroll below. I lie there, pinned, not wanting any movement to be misinterpreted, and after a few minutes, I feel him shift behind me, turning over, facing the wall, lightly snoring.

The scene from dinner keeps creeping into my mind. Dima didn't apologize for keeping the Bergen-Belsen letter from me, not really. It obviously pained him to hurt me, but he said he'd done it only to protect me. *Do I want that kind of protection?*

Is this the best life I can build now? Security and kindness, and a man who will leave in the dark to bring me something soft to sleep on, but keep things from me if he thinks they could cause me hurt? His parents were happy, he told me. He wanted me to know that we could be happy, too. *Do I want to be happy this way?*

*Do I?*

I ease out of the makeshift bed, crawling across the floor on my hands and knees so as not to make a sound. In the closet, I feel for the upholstered valise with the broken clasp and fill it with the belongings I have: the undergarments and soap from Gosia, the kerchief from Nurse Urbaniak. My eyes pause on the hope chest, and I wonder if I should take some things from it. But I don't know how far I'll have to walk, and I don't want to be weighed down. *And this time I'm coming back*, I remind myself. Better to leave these possessions where they'll be safe.

Dima snores behind me. Near the doorway, I find his clothes, his jacket hanging on the back of a chair, his pants folded neatly on the seat. I slip my hand into the jacket pocket and feel a packet of bills. In the dark, I can't tell if they're zlotys, or deutsche marks, or whatever money they use in Russia, but, trying to ignore the pang of guilt, promising myself I'll make it right later, I take all the money.

I write Dima a note, an insufficient one scratched by moonlight, laying it on top of his pants:

> *I have to go find him. Stay in the apartment as long as*
> *you want. Give it to Gosia if you don't. I'm sorry. I'm*
> *so sorry. I have to find him.*

The valise is light in my hand. I clutch it to my chest as I ease out the door.

*THE LAST TIME I SAW ABEK, ANOTHER VERSION I DREAM SOME-times:*

*I had heard of Auschwitz. We all had by then. Rumors of torture, rumors of death.*

*Please don't send us to Auschwitz, I begged the soldier in charge of guarding us when my family had left the stadium, when we'd been sent to tenement apartments on the outskirts of the city to await the next leg. Please not Auschwitz; we can work hard. Especially my brother. Didn't I hear you say your commander needed a good errand boy? My brother would be a good errand boy. He's healthy; look at him. He already speaks three languages. Wouldn't this be useful?*

*This young soldier said he could manage something, but it would be a big favor, requiring payment. I put my hand down his pants; I was very pretty then. Three minutes later, he agreed. He wouldn't send us to Auschwitz. He would send us to Birkenau.*

*The train crawled along the earth. By the time we got to Birkenau, we'd been on it for so long. The distance was short, but we kept stopping, for hours, with no reason or warning, nobody paying attention to our pleas. The car was crowded, so crowded we didn't even stumble when the train lurched. During the first night, people began dying. Bodies sank to the floor while the rest of us tried not to step on them and begged for water. My father gave us his. That whole trip, my father didn't have any water at all.*

*I didn't realize, of course, that there could be more than one city of nightmares, and so close together. The soldier whose pants I had reached down had kept his promise in the cruelest of ways. In a way intended to mock us. I realized it almost immediately.*

*Like Auschwitz, Birkenau was also on the outskirts of the town called Oświęcim. It was constructed barely a kilometer away from the original camp, built because the original camp could not keep up with the volume of people it was designed to torture and kill. The soldier sent my family to Birkenau. He didn't tell me that it was also known as Auschwitz II.*

*We reached the gate, Abek and I. We were sorted to the right. He walked into the camp in his jacket with the alphabet sewn in the lining. And then he turned to me because suddenly this was dream Abek again, not real Abek. It was dream Abek, and he was walking away from me, saying goodbye, and I was trying so hard to stay there with him, but instead, I was waking up.*

# Part Two

## Allied-occupied Germany, September

I CAN TELL WHEN THE TRAIN CROSSES THE BORDER INTO Germany.

When the train is still in Silesia, this annexed land that was Poland once and maybe is again, the tracks are haphazard and the route is meandering. The ticket master at the Sosnowiec station warned me: The Red Army was dismantling tracks, digging up the metal ties to create routes that would lead to Russia, not to Germany. The Katowice-Munich line was once direct, but now the route is circuitous—we backtrack, we divert, we reach portions of the track where multiple locomotives must share a single line, and we spend entire days waiting for another train to pass. While in Poland, the tracks and the land look confused and forgotten; the train feels like a mouse trying to escape a maze.

But I can tell when the train crosses the border into Germany, because here, the same rolling hills become scorched and scarred. The green farmland is interrupted by angry black gashes cutting open the earth. Everything was bombed here, recently, by the Allies, who were trying to cut off the German Army supply lines.

We move even slower. We stop even more frequently. Train employees tell us the tracks ahead are being cleared of debris.

An old man took the seat next to me just before the departure. He had a full gray beard and a dark coat, and he reminded me of my grandfather Zayde Lazer. He didn't say anything at first; I wasn't even sure we spoke the same language. But as the rumble of the wheels began, sending vibrations up our legs, he pulled a small bottle of amber liquid from his coat and handed it to me for a taste.

Nalewka, spiced vodka, sweet and strong, the small sip burning my throat. I passed the bottle back, he took his own drink, and returned it to me again.

"I don't like trains anymore," he said to me.

"I don't, either."

Now this man has become my nameless friend. The seats fill with passengers, and then the aisles fill. The old man and I rise to use the bathroom only when we can no longer wait, saving each other's seats each time. And then the roof of the train is full, too: With nowhere left to sit, people climb up the ladders on the side of the train or pack together on the platforms linking the cars.

The trip is so long. So long and so hot, and at times I can't even tell whether I'm awake or dreaming. At times I think I see Abek next to me. My past and my present blend together, and I let them. The hours pass, and my bad foot aches as if all my toes are still there, as if I can still wiggle them. And the days pass, and then my whole body hurts and my whole body is numb, like I'm not sure any of it exists at all.

"For bad dreams," the old man says at one point, handing me another bottle of something that makes my head fuzzy and my mind quiet. He says this to me after I've just woken, gasping for breath. It's the rhythmic motion that makes my brain scream. As soon as I fall asleep, my body remembers the train to Birkenau. I can tell my brain not to think about it, but when I fall asleep and feel the rhythm of the train, my body remembers.

"For a noisy mind," the old man says. Another bottle.

This makes the trip bearable. It's not a cure for what's wrong with me, but it feels like a temporary solution. The bottles, and the fact that every time I look out the window—every time we stop and women reach up to the window with bread or boiled eggs for us to buy—I know I am getting closer to the place where Abek might be.

Finally one morning, just before dawn, the train lurches to a stop. There are no more tracks, not for a gaping fifty meters. Just remnants of twisted metal sticking up like claws from the charred soil. There are no other tracks we can divert to, the porter explains. No other way to backtrack and join up with a new line. All the tracks in this stretch of land have been demolished. So there is nothing to do but deboard, all of us, and walk ten kilometers to the next usable station.

We stumble off the train, onto a bedraggled barley field. I'm surprised to see clusters of people waiting for us. Mostly girls, my age or a few years younger, wearing farm dresses. Some hold baskets of food for sale—wrinkled plums, underripe apples—but others have no food. They stand by skinny horses hooked up to carts.

"Welcome committee?" jokes my older friend as we stand in puffs of steam and dust.

It soon becomes clear what the girls are really doing. For a fee, they'll take us in their carts to where the tracks pick up again. They approach the soldiers first, the men in uniform who they know must have spending money. They negotiate prices with flirting smiles, but those disappear as soon as the transaction is finalized and the coins are tucked into their apron pockets.

One of them, a wiry girl of sixteen or seventeen, avoids the competition over near the soldiers and comes to me instead.

"Ride?" she asks me in German.

"I can walk."

I'm worried about walking, though. Ten kilometers is a long distance with my bad foot, with the pain that still shoots up my calf. But I'm worried more about unnecessary expenses; this entire trip, I've been buying only the cheapest rolls.

The girl jerks her head toward the old man. "He probably can't walk. But my wagon has a cushion for him. And if you don't ride with me, you might not get to the next train in time to have a seat. He'll have to stand the whole way."

"I will pay," the old man offers chivalrously. "If you don't mind being my seatmate a little longer."

The cushion is lumpy, the wagon is high, and the girl doesn't bother to help either of us into it. She keeps her eyes straight ahead as I hoist myself into the back and pull the old man after me.

We've barely settled before she clucks the horse forward.

I've been to Germany only once before of my own free will. My father took me on business to Berlin. He said it was the capital of modern civilization: The clothes we saw women wear there would be what we would make for Polish women in five years. These girls now, though, the ones driving the wagons or selling fruit, don't look fashionable. They just look tired.

We pass a man painting a sign: We're still a long distance from Munich. But the notice is not only in German, it's also in Russian, French, and English.

"They divided up the country," the girl says when she notices me reading the sign. "Four Allies, four corners. All of them get a piece of Germany. Where are you going?"

"Munich."

"Americans are in charge of Munich," she says.

"Who's in control here?"

"Nobody," she says cryptically. "Nobody controls himself here. Everything is a mess. They're still finding bodies."

"Bodies?" I ask.

"From the Allied bombs. Buried under the rubble. As long as they still find bodies, no one will pay attention to the other things happening."

She turns back to her horse, and then she doesn't say anything until we're almost at the spot where the tracks pick back up. The new "station" isn't an official building. It's a rusted boxcar, nestled in the grass. Someone has painted a word on the side, the name of the closest town, I presume.

Clusters of soldiers already wait there. They're bawdier than when they got off the train an hour ago, enlivened by fresh air or girls.

Our driver sets her mouth in a firm line, her jaw working as if she's deciding whether to say something. Only when she's stopped the cart and I'm beginning to climb down does she reach out and clamp my wrist with her skinny fingers.

"British or Americans, but not Russians, okay?"

"What?" I ask.

She keeps her eyes straight ahead. "Soldiers can help get things, and that's useful. But ask British or American soldiers, not Russians. The Russians have ideas of what you owe them. And they'll take it if you don't give it willingly."

"What do you mean?"

"I don't care if you believe me, but I'm not the only German girl who will tell you that."

"A Russian soldier saved my life," I tell her.

"Good for you." Her voice is full of bitterness. She keeps her eyes ahead, bringing her hand to her throat and rubbing there. "That's really good for you."

My limbs ache; my skin is creased with sweat and dirt. No lice, though, I remind myself. No bedbugs. No empty stomach. No room left to complain. I have been through worse.

The old man whose name I never learned rode the train all the way to Munich. He said his daughter was meeting him there, and when we reached the station, he was met by a slim, red-haired woman who shared his nose and broad shoulders. They held each other and didn't let go, and I didn't stay to say goodbye. I didn't have a role in this family reunion.

Then, in the chaotic marketplace of the train station, I found a stand of drivers for hire. Trucks mostly—men calling out destinations and grouping passengers by the direction we're traveling in.

Now, several hours later, my driver has dropped off everyone else but me. He pulls to a stop off to the side of a gravel road and says I've reached Foehrenwald. But I don't see a sign or anything to orient me.

What I see instead are fields, flat and brown. Dozens of men and women in farm clothes till the soil. Several hundred meters behind them, I see the pitched-roof buildings of a town.

I look back toward the man who drove me here to see if he has any other guidance, but he's already pulled away, too far for me to catch him. So I pick through a neat row of dirt and pause at one of the working women. Spade in hand, she's depositing seeds into the ground.

"Pardon, but I'm looking for the camp?" I ask in German. "For displaced persons. Is it close by?"

Her face is blank; she hasn't understood my question. I switch to Yiddish and then Polish and still get no reply, but with the last language, the woman's face lights up, and she beckons over another women, gesturing that I should ask her instead. This new woman answers in Polish, friendly but with a heavy accent that I think might be Italian.

"Foehrenwald is here," she says. "You're already on the boundaries." She nods her head backward toward the structures on the horizon.

"Which buildings?"

She laughs. "All of them."

"I'm here," I whisper. *I've done it.*

The girl regards me curiously after this last statement, but for a minute, I can't say anything else. I'm rooted to the ground with quivering limbs because I've actually done this crazy thing. For better or for worse, I've spent more than half of the money I had on train tickets and food. There's no way to turn back now, no way to get home. My stomach clenches in brief fear, but I've done it; it's done.

"The administration building is probably what you are looking for," the girl continues, a bit carefully, noticing my silence. "It's in the middle of the camp—keep walking toward that road, there. Michigan Street. Once you get close, someone else will be able to help."

I force a smile to look bolder than I feel, and I try to repeat the street name she's just said. It doesn't sound Polish or German or even Italian. "Mi-chi-gan," she pronounces again. "It's an American province. All streets in the camp are named after American provinces."

"Thank you."

The dirt road she pointed me down leads me farther into Foehrenwald, which is less and less what I was expecting. I'd pictured rows of long barracks laid out on a grid, the architecture of war. I'd steeled myself for this war architecture, steeled it to make my mind unravel.

But I can now see that Foehrenwald looks more like a small town, organized like a wheel with spokes. I breathe a sigh of relief.

Michigan is a street on the perimeter; others, with names like Illinois and Indiana, lead toward a hub in the center of the camp. Whitewashed cottages with pitched roofs line all the spoke streets, while the larger buildings in the middle—the administration buildings, I presume—are blockier and more industrial, clustered around a central courtyard.

At the front doors of administration, a group of people stands outside, smoking and talking. After my exchange with the Italian woman in the field, I'm not surprised to hear different languages, but I am surprised by the variety: Hungarian. Czech. Slovenian and Dutch. Most of the people are my age or a little older; a smaller number are my parents' generation, and smaller still are the very old, the age of the man on the train. Nobody is younger. Nobody who could be Abek.

I clear my throat, gripping the handle of my valise. "Excuse me. Is there a person in charge?" I ask in German, the language I hear most.

A sandy-haired boy interrupts his conversation. "Of which division?"

Division. I hadn't expected something so formal. "Of—I'm looking for someone in the camp. Another prisoner—refugee, I mean."

He nods to a smaller, adjoining building. "Then you want to go there. Ask for Frau Yost."

I don't have to ask for her, though. Inside the building, modern and with linoleum floors, a small woman with wire-rimmed glasses approaches me almost as soon as I walk through the door. She's wearing a plaid shirtwaist dress, foreign-seeming in a way I can't place my finger on, and when she shakes my hand, it's businesslike.

"*Englisch?*" she asks. "*Deutsch?*"

"*Ja,*" I tell her, explaining that I am Polish but can speak German. "My name is Zofia Lederman. Frau Yost?"

She nods. "That's me. I'm so relieved you speak German." Her own is accented, American or Canadian. "To communicate with a Hungarian woman the other day, I had to go through someone who spoke French."

I expect that she'll ask me what I'm doing here, or invite me to sit down, but instead, Mrs. Yost takes a hat hanging from a hook on a wall and pins it on her head as she ushers me back toward the door I've just entered.

"I told them nobody had time to clear out that much

housing." She holds the door open. "But we did the best we could—a bed here, a bed there, but we're already doubled up and desperately short on blankets. You knew that, right? In terms of food, with all the extra people, we can manage for maybe a week without additional rations. The gardens help."

"Mrs. Yost—"

"And *your* official ration cards will be eventually transferred over, I believe, but because absolutely nothing is working yet in this country—"

"Mrs. Yost, I'm so sorry, but—"

Finally, she breaks off, noticing that I haven't followed her through the door. She steps back inside. "Feldafing?"

"Pardon me?"

"You're from Feldafing?"

I shake my head. "No, outside they told me to ask for you in here."

She closes her eyes and pinches the bridge of her nose. "I'm so sorry. We received a telegram saying that the camp in Feldafing was overcrowded and that some residents would arrive by the end of the week. A representative was supposed to be here now to see to the accommodations. It's not normally my job, but I'm the only one who could take the meeting."

She reaches for the door handle again. I sense that if she were wearing a watch, she would be checking the time. "But, anyway. You're not from Feldafing, because of course you're not. Whom do you represent?"

"I came here on my own. I'm looking for my brother."

"Do you know what cottage he's in?"

"My family is from Poland. Abek and I were separated in our first camp, but I heard prisoners from there were sent to Dachau, and then the prisoners from Dachau came here."

"So you don't know what cottage he's in. Do you know for certain that he's here at all?" She has a pointed, matter-of-fact way of talking that makes me feel automatically foolish.

"No. But I think he is. I heard the prisoners from Dachau came here."

"*Some* of them did."

"So *I* came here. My name is Zofia Lederman. My brother is Abek Lederman. He would be twelve, but we told him to say he was older. He could be saying he's as old as fifteen, and—"

"This is an adults-only camp," she interrupts. "I'm sorry, but we don't admit anyone under the age of seventeen unless they're accompanied by parents or guardians."

"Could I just—"

"Check the records? Yes," she says, anticipating how I was going to finish my sentence. "I can sit you down with a secretary. You're here alone?"

"Yes."

"And you're coming from?"

"Poland."

"So you said. Your family is from Poland. But I meant, where are you staying? Where have you come from now?"

The impulsiveness of what I've done has begun to sink in. I'm not staying with anyone. I have no place to stay.

Suddenly I feel so tired. So dirty. Hungry and thirsty, and

wanting to lie down and wondering why I am here. "Poland,"
I repeat. "I've been on a train from Poland."

"Today? By yourself?"

"I arrived today. I left—several weeks ago, I think. It took
a long time. And yes, alone."

Mrs. Yost's demeanor changes. Her eyes soften. A minute
passes as she lets this news sink in. "That's a long way to come
by yourself."

"Yes."

"Just how long did it take?"

"He's all I have left."

She thinks for a minute, glancing over my shoulder, where
I see there's a clock on the wall, then sighs. "Follow me."

We pass through the main reception area and into a smaller
private office with a handwritten sign on the door: *Missing Persons Liaison.* Inside are a few large desks, messy with papers. A
black telephone sits in the middle, half-buried.

"Sit, please." Mrs. Yost gestures for me to take the more
comfortable-looking of the two chairs in the room, taking a
straight-backed wooden one for herself and finding a composition book and fountain pen from amid the clutter. It's leather-
bound, with the words I.G. FARBEN embossed in gold on the front.
The words are familiar to me, but I can't place from where.

"Miss Lederman," she begins. "Why don't you start by
telling me what you've done so far to look for your brother?"

"I put his name on the list."

"All right. Which list?"

"The Red Cross list."

She makes a note in the composition book. "Which others?"

"I'm not sure."

"The United Nations Relief and Rehabilitation Association?" she offers. "The AJJDC? The Bureau for Missing Persons in Munich or any other jurisdictions?"

"In the hospital, whenever they asked me to put his name on a list, I did."

"Miss Lederman." Her pen was still poised above her book; now she caps it and sets it down. "It's a very confusing time. But there are many organizations trying to help."

She lists off more acronyms, but they all run together. I understand what she's telling me. There are many lists. I was supposed to put his name on many lists, more than I ever could have imagined, and I was supposed to keep track of all of them.

It's a patchwork, is what she's saying. It's the continent trying to sew itself together using a blend of every kind of stitch and knit available.

I grip the armrests of the chair, trying not to let Mrs. Yost go blurry in front of me. My mouth is dry, and my voice sounds like it's coming from far away. "But waiting to hear from all those places could take months," I say. And, I'm realizing in horror, even if I did unknowingly contact some of these organizations when I was at the hospital, they would have no way to get in touch with me now.

"It could take months," Mrs. Yost agrees. "My job is to try to help the refugees here, but it could take months. Are you feeling all right? Put your head between your knees if you're dizzy."

"I'm not—I'm not dizzy."

"You're dizzy." She stands and calls through her cracked door to the secretary outside. "Could you bring a glass of water?"

I don't know if I have months, is what I want to tell her. I am alive in part because I forced myself to be alive to find Abek. I have barely held myself together. I don't know how much longer I can do this. Sending letters that go unanswered isn't enough.

I hear the rustle of fabric in front of me and bring my eyes into focus. Mrs. Yost has returned with a glass of water. She raises her eyebrows, asking if I can take the glass, and then settles it in my hands.

"I hope you know I'm not saying any of this to dissuade you," she says, waiting as I force the water down my throat. "But one girl I've been working with here has been writing ten letters a day for sixty days straight. She knows *for a fact* that her sister was liberated from Auschwitz, and she still hasn't been able to find her. But your chances are still better writing letters than traveling all over Europe by yourself. You can't visit every place in person. And even if you could, people are still moving around. Even if you find the right place, there's no guarantee you would be there at the right time. So, if you still have a home, your best option might be to go back there."

"I don't have enough money left."

"You could consider applying to a travel fund, for—"

"No."

"Or I could set you up with a liaison closer to where your family—"

"*No*," I bark. *"Not without my brother."*

I'm picturing the spindly, broken chairs in my abandoned dining room, the carpet that wasn't ours, the bakery with unfamiliar faces. That place will not be home again until Abek and I make it into one.

Mrs. Yost opens her mouth again, but I interrupt before she can speak. "Can I look at the admission records now?"

She looks like she wants to say something else, but instead nods once, efficiently. "A secretary will pull them for you; you can look right after dinner."

*Dinner.* The mention of the evening meal makes me realize I have no other plans for the evening. Nowhere to stay, nowhere to go. Mrs. Yost has already mentioned that the camp is overcrowded.

"And then—and then after dinner could I stay here?" I ask. "Just while I figure out where to go next. If you don't have a bed for me, I'll sleep on the floor."

Mrs. Yost sighs. "I'm not going to put you on the floor. Follow me. I'll tell the person in charge of housing assignments, then find someone to get you settled."

I pick up my bag, and she picks up her composition book, the one with the gold-embossed I.G. FARBEN. Something about the name still nags at me.

"What's that?" I ask. "The name on your notebook?"

She glances down. "Before this site was a camp, it was a

pharmaceutical factory. I'm still using some of the office supplies they left until our own shipments arrive."

"I've heard of I.G. Farben, and I'm trying to figure
out why."

"Zyklon B," she says finally. "I.G. Farben made Zyklon B."

So that's where I heard the name. Sometimes, in Birkenau, before they found out I could sew, I would be assigned to
unload supply trucks. The yellow containers of Zyklon B had
small logos at the bottom identifying the maker, I.G. FARBEN.

Zyklon B was a pesticide. It came in pellets that dissolved
into gas. I heard it was originally designed to kill rodents. In
Birkenau, I unloaded these canisters, and then guards would
take them to the buildings they called the showers. There they
would pack hundreds of people inside and use the Zyklon B,
and it worked on people, too.

I'VE LOST ALL SENSE OF TIME AS MRS. YOST LEADS ME OUT OF HER office. It's hard for Foehrenwald to feel real, for any of this to feel real. I half expect that if I blink, I'll wake up back in my family's apartment, still sleeping next to Dima, or back in the hospital, still in the ward of broken girls. But I'm not; I'm hundreds of kilometers from home. The doctors said I wasn't well enough to even leave the hospital on my own, but I've managed to get all the way here by myself. My devastation over Abek's not being here is colored by a small bit of pride.

The sun is low in the sky as we step out the back door. It opens onto a dusty courtyard of sorts, between the administration buildings. A few wooden benches line the perimeter, and behind them are the green sprigs of an herb garden, the smell of dill and parsley. Behind those, through an open set of double doors, I can see round tables in a building that must be the

cafeteria. Michigan Street, the road I walked in on, is now filling with people, presumably coming from the fields I passed.
Not just the dozen or so I saw tilling the land, but many, carrying hoes and shovels, gathering around the courtyard while
talking and laughing. Other groups, not in farming clothes, are
approaching from different streets.

"Mrs. Yost?" As soon as we exit the building, a man in a
checked shirt appears, picking his way across the dusty courtyard and extending his hand. "I'm from Feldafing."

"Of course you are." Mrs. Yost turns to me. "Zofia. My
apologies. I'll find someone else to show you to your bungalow."

She scans the crowd. "Mr. Mueller," she calls, gesturing
toward a lone figure sitting on one of the benches.

The man who looks up is lean and angled. Suspenders hold
up pants that hang low on his hips; a cigarette dangles from
the corner of his mouth. He's working with something in his
hands, using a sharp metal tool to bore holes into a leather strap.
A horse's bridle, I think. He sets it down when Mrs. Yost beckons him. "Could you come and carry Miss Lederman's bag to
Breine and Esther's cottage?" she asks.

From a distance, I'd thought Mr. Mueller was much older,
but as he approaches, I can see he's actually just a few years
older than me: dark curly hair, gray eyes, a lean sinew to his
body. He takes one last drag on his cigarette before flicking it
to the side.

The way his full lips curl around the cigarette paper, the
way his hips swivel as he grinds the butt into the dust, the way

he rubs a crick out of his neck using one long-fingered hand—
I feel myself blush, followed immediately by the surprise of
realizing I still know how to blush. There's a quick, urgent pull
low in my stomach, and this, too, is a sensation I thought had
disappeared. There wasn't enough left of my body, I thought,
to manufacture the feeling.

Mr. Mueller raises his eyebrows in a brief greeting when
he reaches me. "Hello," I manage, and then I am immediately
certain that the blush is in my voice, too, and that everyone
around me can hear it.

He's just leaned over to take the handle of my valise when
I see his neck stiffen. "What did you say?" he asks quietly, in
German.

"I—I didn't—" I stammer.

But he's not talking to me; he's talking to another man
whom he passed in the courtyard, barrel-chested with nice
white teeth. "What did you say?" Mr. Mueller repeats, this
time turning to the man.

Mr. Mueller drops my valise and walks back toward the
larger, barrel-chested man. His messy curls stick to the back
of his neck; his collar is damp with perspiration. I can't hear
what the two men in the middle of the courtyard are saying,
only that the man with white teeth looks angry and dismissive,
while Mr. Mueller is unreadable. Around me, other people
have noticed the conversation, and a few yards away, Mrs. Yost,
who had started off with the representative from the other
camp, pauses, trying to decide whether to intervene.

The bigger man makes a rude gesture. Mr. Mueller returns

it but then begins to step away. It looks like the conversation is over, and I unclench fists I didn't know I'd tightened. But then, without warning—with something barely perceptible traveling across his face—Mr. Mueller whirls back again. It happens too fast for me to register the full motion; all I know is that I see a blur, and then blood pours out of the bigger man's nose.

The bigger man lunges forward with both arms outstretched and hits Mr. Mueller with his full body weight. Mr. Mueller stays upright, but barely. He ducks the first punch, but the other man's second one lands just below his eyebrow. He takes a third to the rib cage. He's not an intuitive fighter, even I can tell that, and the other man outmatches him by at least ten centimeters.

Around the perimeter of the courtyard, doors and windows open as people lean out to see the source of the commotion. Now they're on the ground, the big man on top of Mr. Mueller, straddling his chest and pinning his arms to his sides. The bigger man's hand grinds the side of Mr. Mueller's face into the ground, and Mr. Mueller's legs scramble helplessly, wildly scuffing in the dirt.

*Get up*, I think.

I don't know why he threw the first punch, I don't know why he started this fight, I don't know why he doesn't give up and beg for mercy.

"Gentlemen!" Mrs. Yost yells, and then to someone I can't see, "Go get a policeman." But it will be too late. By the time an officer gets back, Mr. Mueller will have run out of oxygen, will be dead.

I should help him, but I can't move. *Close your eyes,* I instruct myself, but my eyelids don't work. *Cover your eyes,* I try. *Pick up your hands and physically cover them. Do it now.*

I should help him, but I can't move, because if I could have moved, I would have helped him, and I didn't help him, so that must mean I couldn't move, and all I can do is stare and stare, like the fight is far away, like it's happening in the movies.

I'm fading, I'm falling into myself, I'm unable to get my brain to stop, and then, just when I think I'm going to witness something horrible, Mr. Mueller frees one of his arms. He draws it back and, his thumb and index finger making the shape of an L, slams his hand into the bigger man's windpipe.

The big man's hands fly to his neck; his face turns purple-red, and his breath comes in pig squeals as he tries to find air. Mr. Mueller scrambles out from under him. Chest heaving, he staggers to the bench, to the sharp, leather-boring tool he was using before. He doesn't pick it up but leaves his hands on the handle, a warning that he'll use it if he needs to.

Watching him, something pushes in on my brain. A thought, a memory, trying to break through my spiraling, to bring me back to myself. *Mr. Mueller. Sosnowiec in the summer. Heat, the hottest days, standing in lines. My father.*

*Do I know this man?* Surely I don't—I couldn't—but something I've just seen him do reminds me of—what? *Sosnowiec in summer, standing.* The images are too vague for me to grab onto; I'm not even sure if they're real.

I replay everything that just happened, every moment since I first saw Mr. Mueller get up to take my valise, to this moment, now, as he dabs his bloody eyebrow with the hem of his shirt while warily eyeing the courtyard. But it's lost. Whatever I thought seemed familiar about him has disappeared again, if it ever existed at all.

I bite back frustration. Just when I congratulated myself on making it all the way to this camp, just when I dared to think I was showing progress. Why is my brain so broken and battered? Why does it betray me?

Back in the middle of the courtyard, the bigger man is on his hands and knees. The two friends he'd been standing with rush over, grab him under the arms, and hoist him to his feet.

I look up. Mr. Mueller is back in front of me again, his hand outstretched. There's a scrape across his knuckles. His shirt is smeared with dust, two buttons have been ripped off, and his breast pocket hangs, half-ripped. He motions with his hand again.

"Your luggage."

He's taller than me by an inch. His eyes, which I'd thought just gray, I can now see have a pebbly mix with brown in them, too, a dark, flinty color that's hard to read. I should be disgusted by him now, after watching him start the fight. The pull in my stomach should have disappeared. It hasn't, though. I'm cautious around him, but I still can't stop staring.

"My luggage?" I repeat dumbly.

"Mrs. Yost asked me. To carry. Your luggage." He says it very slowly this time, with one eyebrow raised.

"Oh. But you don't have to," I start. "Not after—"

"I said I would," he says simply, taking the bag before I

can protest again. He doesn't wait for me to follow, and when I don't see Mrs. Yost around to provide instructions to the contrary, I quickly dart after him.

He weaves through rows of cottages, checking once to make sure I can keep up, but not again. I speed up my steps so I can walk next to him, panting a little from the effort.

"Did that man do something to you?" I ask, breathless.

*Not breaking stride.* "Didn't you just see the fight? I'd say he did something to me."

"Yes, what I meant was—"

"He bruised my chest. And he smells like piss, and he was all over me, so he probably made me smell like piss, too." He stresses the word *piss*. To shock me, I think, or repel me, to get me to stop asking questions.

As we hurry, I try to pay attention to the route and everything along it: A wooden structure where women carry out baskets of laundry. A larger building, with a sign reading VOCATIONAL TRAINING. Foehrenwald is more like a town than I even realized.

"What I *meant*—and I think you know it—was, did that man do something to you *before* the fight?" I clarify. "Was there a reason you hit him? Or do you try to beat up all *piss-smelling* things?"

His mouth twitches. "Piss-smelling things? What is a piss-smelling thing that I could beat up?"

"A—a goat. You could beat up a goat."

"A goat," he repeats flatly.

"Or a latrine itself," I say stubbornly. "A latrine would be a very piss-smelling thing for you to punch."

"How, exactly, would I punch a latrine?"

"Wetly," I say. I can't explain why his indifference is making me so bold, but I feel the need to show him that I'm not cowed or intimidated by his swearing or his fight. "If you punched a latrine, it would probably splash."

Mr. Mueller laughs, sharp and staccato, as though the sound and the act surprise him. It's a nice laugh, wry but rich, but then it stops almost immediately. He's arranged his mouth back into a serious expression before I even smile myself, as if he's hoping I won't notice the laugh at all.

"I'm sorry, but have I met you before?" I ask.

A glance from the side of his eyes. "I don't think so."

"You seemed familiar to me, but it was very fleeting. I thought for a second I might know you from home—I'm from Sosnowiec—but your German doesn't have a Polish accent."

"I'm not from Sosnowiec."

"I thought not. You're German? Do I know you from somewhere else? Were you in—"

"Was I in where?" He stops now, facing me, and something in his question is a dare.

I can't finish my sentence. What was I going to ask him? *Were you in Birkenau, one of the men forced to dig graves for the bunkmates who died around him every night? Did I see you working in the men's side of Gross-Rosen, shit streaming down your legs because typhus had made you lose control of your bowels?*

Not everybody wants to talk about what happened to them. In the hospital, the woman we called Bissel would talk only about "being away" from her home. As if she were at university or on an extended trip. She talked about wanting to find a present for her little daughter in hiding. She said her daughter was waiting for her in a little German farmhouse somewhere, under the care of a kind old couple. I never knew if the farmhouse or the daughter actually existed. Bissel said this while there were holes in her legs from the medical experiments the doctors performed on her at Ravensbrück; her mind was as cloudy as spun sugar from the torture she'd been subjected to. I never knew really what I could believe.

Mr. Mueller takes off again, and I start after him. He turns another corner. I'm trying to remember all the turns we've taken since leaving the main building. I find my words again, but careful ones. "It's just, something about you back there seemed very familiar. Maybe it was the way you moved, or something you did—"

"I'm not from Sosnowiec, and I don't think we've met before. I'm not Polish, and I wasn't anyplace I want to talk about." He's lost patience. I am making him uncomfortable. I must sound crazy.

"I apologize, then," I say. "My mind must have been playing tricks on me. I get confused sometimes. It got confused back there."

"Anything else?"

"Anything—" At first, I think he means, will I be asking him any more questions. But then I realize we've stopped in front of a square white cabin with a simple wooden door to the left and a window to the right.

"This is where Mrs. Yost wanted me to take you." He pushes the door inward and hands me my suitcase. I see he doesn't intend to follow me in as he nods his head in goodbye. "Miss Lederman."

"Wait," I say, not wanting him to leave yet and not having a good reason to ask him to stay. "My name is Zofia."

I extend my hand in case he wants to take it for a formal greeting.

"I'm Josef," he says shortly, and when he turns to leave, my hand is still dangling in the air.

AND THEN I'M ALONE AGAIN. ALONE AND FAR FROM HOME, and left with the weight and reality of my decision. My bad foot aches from running after Josef. It's a spidery pain, the kind that seems to still live in the toes that are no longer there. No amount of warm poultices or aspirin powder can ever fix pain when it comes from ghosts.

I survey the small cottage. Plain wooden floor. Burlap-curtained window facing the dirt path we walked up on. In the room I'm standing in, there's a sink but no stove or icebox. Instead, two single beds, each covered in faded, neatly tucked quilts, each with a plain nightstand on which are a few personal items: a photograph, a hairbrush, a stack of blank stationery, and a fountain pen. A writing desk lines the side wall. Along the back, a door leads to a second room—three more beds and nightstands, a writing desk, a table with a basin for water on

it. On one of the nightstands is a stack of magazines, old ones
with yellowed, curling edges; on another is a stack of books.

The third has nothing. I surmise that it must be the one
I'm supposed to use, so I empty my belongings into the nightstand's drawer and sit on the bed. The wall is a dingy white;
above the bed I can make out the vague outline of something
that used to hang here.

"It was an iron cross." A tall, auburn-haired woman comes
through the door, sits on the bed that goes with the magazines, and begins to unlace her shoes. They're heavy work
boots, awkward-looking on her delicate calves. Her dress is a
bleached, worn pink.

"Oh," I say. "Did you—"

"They were in all the cottages. The UN tried to remove
them for us before we got here, but they missed some of the
ones in the back bedrooms. I took that one off the wall myself,
and some boys threw a pile of them in a bonfire."

"Are you Breine or Esther?"

She looks up from her laces. "Breine. Yes, I'm sorry—
I didn't mean to be rude. And you'll also forgive me for not
shaking your hand." She lifts her own hands to show me her
palms, calloused and covered in dirt. She was one of the girls I
saw outside, planting the garden. Her face is red from sunburn,
the skin peeling on her nose.

I point to my own chest. "Zofia. I was assigned to stay in
this cottage. Mrs. Yost probably told you I was here."

"I haven't seen her since I got back, actually. But I passed

Josef on my way in; he said that we had a new roommate and that I was supposed to show you around. So, I'm Breine; Esther sleeps in this other bed, and the front room is two Dutch girls, Miriam and Judith. They're both nice; Judith speaks German better than Miriam."

The way she says Josef's name makes it sound as though they're friends, or at least that she knows something about him. I want to ask her more, but I don't want to be nosy or obvious.

"You're planting a garden?" I ask instead.

She nods, tugging off her boots and wincing as she takes one foot into her hands, kneading the arch and wiggling her toes. "Some of us. Our own little experiment. Cabbage, carrots, potatoes, onions. If it all grows. I've never done anything like this before, but some of the others have."

"That will be nice."

"Better to not have to rely on rationing. We don't have any fruit, or eggs, or butter, or anything fresh here, really. So we're planting. Maybe there will be beets by my wedding."

"You're engaged? Best wishes."

Breine's face turns a satisfied pink; she was hoping I would ask after that. "I'll show you my ring; I show everyone my ring. They're all sick of it now." Turning her attention from her aching feet, she unfastens the top button of her dress where a tiny satchel hangs around her neck, attached to a leather thong. She shakes the contents into her palm: a gold ring, wound with string several times the way one would to make a larger piece of jewelry fit on a smaller finger.

"It was Chaim's mother's," she explains. "He managed to save it."

She hands it to me, and I can see I'm meant to admire it. "It's beautiful," I say, turning it over in my hand. "I hope you have a beautiful wedding."

"You'll be there—the whole camp will come to the ceremony."

"It will be here?"

"Next month, I think. We were going to have it immediately, but last Thursday I heard from an uncle I didn't know had survived. He's the only family we have. We're waiting for him to travel here, and then we'll have the wedding." I hand back the ring, and Breine tucks it back into the purse.

"Should we have dinner?" She goes to the table in the corner of the room and begins to scrub her face and neck using water from the pitcher. "Esther and I usually go at five thirty—she should be back from her classes soon—and we meet Chaim and his roommates, except for Josef, who—oh, you already met Josef."

I pretend to straighten my belongings in my drawer, though I did that before Breine came in, and try to keep my voice nonchalant. "Why doesn't Josef eat with you?"

She shrugs, running a brush through her hair. "He prefers to eat alone. Chaim says he's a perfectly fine roommate. He just keeps to himself, mostly."

"He got in a fight. Just before he escorted me here."

I look for surprise in her face, but instead, she just sighs. "Josef does that."

"Josef gets in fights? Why?"

"I don't know. I don't think he's all—I don't know his whole story, and like I said, Chaim says he's a perfectly fine roommate. But some of us aren't all there. The war ended, and some of us are here, but not all *there*. Do you know?"

I know—of course I know—and I feel a moment of wonder that Breine doesn't immediately realize that I'm also in this category, of those who are here and not all there. But she doesn't wait for me to answer, turning away from me and relacing her boots.

"Let's go eat," she says when she's finished. "I'm famished; are you?"

I'm not. The bone-weariness I felt earlier has returned; I want to lie on this soft bed under this clean quilt. Breine's friendliness is kind but also overwhelming.

But I haven't eaten anything for most of the day, so I let Breine lead me back to the dining hall, where she introduces me to Esther, a small, spectacled woman reading a book as she waits in line. She's less chatty than Breine, but no less kind, smiling at me shyly and asking where I'm from.

"Sosnowiec?" Breine exclaims when I give the name of my hometown. "I had cousins in Sosnowiec. Distant ones. Did you know any Abramskis? Or maybe, never mind. I think the Abramskis lived in Sochaczew."

"Breine," Esther sighs. "You walked her all the way here. Didn't you ask her before this where she was from?"

"I did," she insists. "I thought I did." I shake my head. "I didn't?"

"Did you ask her *any* questions, or did you just talk?" Esther asks.

"I talked," Breine says. "I fully admit it; I just talked."

*"Breine."* Esther shakes her head, but there's love in the gesture: she as the sensible nanny and Breine as her flighty charge.

The cafeteria is the building I'd seen before, long and low. We line up for mushy meats and vegetables from cans: C rations, Breine explains, provided by the occupying American soldiers.

After our plates are filled, she and Esther lead us to a round table in the corner where Breine's fiancé is saving seats. Chaim, a thin, light-haired man with a stutter in his consonants and a Hungarian accent in his German, introduces me to his housemates, whose names I almost immediately forget.

There must be hundreds of people in here. Breine said she and Esther liked to go early to avoid the crowds, but a long line still snakes almost to the door. I wonder if everyone comes early; I wonder if all of us still fear the food running out.

I follow my eyes to the end of the line, where the last person waiting is Josef. Hair still wild. Trousers still skimming over his lean hip bones. Hand running over his jawline, where he must have been injured in the fight.

It's peculiar: I assume Josef is at the end of the line because he's just arrived, but as I stare at him longer, I see that he's not moving forward. Every time a new person walks through the door, Josef gestures them ahead so he's always the last one in line.

Eventually, when nobody else comes through the door, Josef gets his own plate and takes it, as Breine predicted, not to us but to an unoccupied table. He eats quickly, shoulders hunched over his plate, eyes down.

Whatever familiar thing I thought I saw in him has disappeared. He's just a boy now. But I'm trying to square the excessively polite boy keeping himself to the back of the line with the one I saw earlier, viciously punching another man's throat. I would wonder if I'd imagined it, but he's wearing the same shirt, rust-colored bloodstain on the hem.

Breine notices me watching all this and nudges Chaim. "Zofia says Josef got in a fight."

"He d-did. B-but it was with Rudolf."

The rest of the table groans; this information means something to them it doesn't to me.

"Who is Rudolf?" I ask.

Breine squeezes Chaim's arm. "Tell her," she encourages.

"Y-you can."

"I like your voice better."

Chaim shakes his head, but he's smiling. I see him reach for Breine's hand under the table. She waits another beat to be sure Chaim isn't going to speak. "All right. Nobody cares if Josef got in a fight with Rudolf, because he's a collaborator. He volunteered his house to the Gestapo. They kept him fat the whole war. He's only here now because his street was bombed when the Allies came. Honestly, that's the thing about Josef's fights. You know they're terrible. But then you find out whom they were with, and you wish you'd done it first."

I'm confused. "The Germans let Rudolf *stay* in his house? They didn't just take it over? Did he bribe them?"

In my town, even at the very beginning of the war, if the Gestapo wanted something a Jewish family owned, they didn't ask to share it with you. They just decided it was theirs.

Breine has taken a mouthful of cabbage, so she motions for Esther to answer instead. "Rudolf isn't Jewish," Esther says, cutting her food into small, neat bites.

"What do you mean?"

Breine coughs. "Several people here aren't. Technically, this isn't a facility for Jewish people, it's only a facility for displaced people. Technically, Rudolf has been displaced from his home. And so have other Germans whose homes were bombed in the Allied invasion."

"Do all of them—did all of them..."

"No," she says, sensing my question. "They didn't all work for the Nazis."

My mind's still reeling from this. Maybe they didn't all house the Gestapo, but some might have turned us in, revealed our hiding places in exchange for money or a favor. Or placed swastikas in their potted plants. Some might have been surprised we were back, because they thought they'd never have to see us again.

But they do. And now we're supposed to live with people who either wished for our deaths or looked the other way while it happened.

I sneak a glance at Josef, head still down, mechanically finishing the food on his plate.

"Let's talk about something else," Esther offers.

"Zofia is here looking for her brother," Breine tells the

table. "Abek. All of you ask your friends here if they know any boys named Abek."

"And you—are any of you still looking for people?" I ask, thinking of the binders and papers spread over Mrs. Yost's desk.

A hush falls over the table. Chaim and Breine look down at their plates; she already told me her uncle was the last family they had.

"I haven't seen my wife since they separated the women at Dachau," says one man who looks too young to have a wife. "Her brother and I are both staying here until I learn what happened to her."

"My father was going to send for my mother and me when he got to England," says a pretty woman who introduced herself to me as Judith, an occupant of the front room of our cottage. "I'm trying to send word that my mother is—that he can still send for me."

"You know that he got there, though?" I ask.

"The last round of visas," she says. "I haven't been able to talk to him yet, but I saw him get on the boat myself."

We go around the table. Esther's parents are dead. A boy named Nev is still trying to find his. A man named Ravid has stopped looking, and so has his fiancée, Rebekah, whom he protectively places his arm around.

"It happens sometimes, though," Breine says. "Zofia, the girl who stayed in your bed before you—Chaya. She found her mother and a brother. It happens, for some people."

A chair squeaks. It's Miriam, Judith's roommate from our cottage, a short, freckled girl about my age, abruptly rising from her chair. "I need to write my letters," she mumbles, hastily grabbing her tray. "Please excuse."

"Miriam," Judith starts, reaching out a hand and speaking quickly to her in Dutch.

"No, I must go," she insists, and though the rest of her sentence is in a different language, I can understand the guilt and panic on her face, the sense that she hasn't written enough letters.

She walks off quickly, heels clicking on the floor. The mood at the table—I've ruined it with my question. We all watch Miriam leave.

"I shouldn't have asked that," I say. "She didn't want to talk."

Judith clears her throat. "Her twin sister," she explains. "Doctors did experiments on both of them. Miriam was the control; her sister was the one they hurt."

My throat starts to close. *The one they hurt.*

"At liberation, her sister was taken to a hospital to get better," Judith continues. "But Miriam was given the wrong information about where, and she hasn't been able to find her since. And now she writes—"

"Ten letters a day," I finish.

*Ten letters a day.* Miriam must be the woman Mrs. Yost mentioned earlier. She saw her sister only months ago, but now it's as if she vanished.

"Let's talk about something else," Esther says again.

"I'm sorry," I say again. "I shouldn't have—"

"You didn't know." She puts her hand on my arm.

"Don't apologize," Breine reaffirms. "We all want to talk about it and not talk about it all the time. We hate talking about it, and we don't know how to talk about anything else."

Chaim puts his arm around her and smiles at his fiancée through watery eyes.

"For now, we'll just talk about something else, though, yes?" She looks around the table for approval, and everyone nods. "I could, for example, tell you about my *wedding*." The table groans; Breine's joke has the intended effect of lightening the mood. "Or, we could play the happier game: What are you going to do when you leave here?" She turns to me. "Zofia, you're newest. You start."

"When I leave here," I start slowly. "When I leave here, it will be with Abek, and we will go home to Sosnowiec."

"Where I may or may not have distant cousins," Breine supplies.

"Where will you all go?" I return the question. "Chaim and Breine, after your wedding, whose homeland will you return to?"

Breine glows as she looks at Chaim. "As soon as Britain loosens the immigration laws, we're going to Eretz Israel. Most of us are, actually—most of us at the table."

"Palestine?" I ask.

She fans her soil-filled fingernails in front of me. "That's why we're learning to farm. We want to be ready to farm our own land when we get there."

Chaim affectionately brushes his knuckles under Breine's chin. "She's b–bad at it."

"Excuse me. I had never even *been* on a farm until I came here."

"I'm w-worse than she is."

"That's why we're practicing now," says one of Chaim's roommates, the serious-looking man who introduced himself as Ravid. He clears his throat, quieting everyone down, and then turns to me, raising his glass. "I hope you find your brother soon. May we *all* find what we're looking for soon. *L'Chaim.*"

*L'Chaim.*

The phrase hits me with such a sharp, unexpected pang it nearly takes my breath away.

We used to toast this way at weddings and birthdays, at happy events. One night in Gross-Rosen, a night when I couldn't sleep from the gnawing in my stomach and the lice on my skin, one of my bunkmates, a woman I barely knew, threw her arms around me as I writhed in agony on the wooden pallet. "*L'Chaim,*" she whispered. "It's my twenty-fifth wedding anniversary today." Then she laughed bitterly.

"*L'Chaim,*" the table repeats now. Breine with her mouth full again, and Chaim with his shy blush, and Esther, serious and earnest.

We raise our glasses.

To life.

AFTER DINNER, INSTEAD OF WALKING BACK TO THE COTTAGE with Breine and Esther, I walk to the administration building to check the admission records Mrs. Yost has already told me will have no trace of Abek.

I try to expect nothing. I try to expect less than nothing, if it's possible to expect that. I remind myself that Miriam's twin sister was alive, and survived, and was still vanished without a trace, leaving Miriam alone to write endless letters.

The Missing Persons Liaison office, which I thought messy before, is now in complete disarray. Piles of papers teeter not only on Mrs. Yost's desk but also on the floor—some handwritten, some typed with notes scribbled in the margins. She's not alone, either. A man is sitting in the chair where I sat before. He's slender with caterpillar eyebrows, holding some kind of heavy book.

I knock lightly on the doorframe but stay just outside the threshold. "I can come back later."

"No, come in now," she says, rising from her own seat and gesturing me into it. "This is Mr. Ohrmann. Mr. Ohrmann, this is Miss Zofia Lederman."

"How do you do?"

"Mr. Ohrmann works with one of the organizations I mentioned earlier—the Missing Persons bureau in Munich," Mrs. Yost continues. "He comes here once a week to go over open cases, and I also introduce new ones. Today I told him about yours."

"Oh?"

"As you might expect, there are a lot of open cases," she says. "A lot of leads that seem promising but don't go anywhere at all."

Mrs. Yost, so direct and frank when I spoke with her this afternoon, now seems as though she's avoiding something. A nervous swell begins to grow in my stomach.

"Are you saying there is a lead?" I ask.

"Well," she begins, looking slightly pained. Mr. Ohrmann clears his throat, signaling that he'll take over.

"Frau Yost probably also told you there is no central system for locating missing persons; it's not a scientific process. And with your case, we've found something that complicates the situation even further. A piece of...ambiguous information."

My heart is already thudding. "I don't understand. How can the information be ambiguous? Have you found my brother or not?"

He sighs. "I suppose it's easiest to just walk you through it."

He motions me closer to the desk and, as Mrs. Yost sweeps

piles of paper out of the way, Mr. Ohrmann lays the book on top.

I can see now that it's copies of pages from a ledger, with rows and columns. On the page it's opened to, lacy penmanship travels two-thirds of the way down one page, and then strong, inky script replaces it for the final third. A different person's handwriting.

"These are arrival records to Dachau, the period of time that trains from Birkenau would have come," Mr. Ohrmann says.

My mouth is cotton, dry and thick. "Where is he?" I bend in so quickly that I jostle Mr. Ohrmann as I try to make out the names on this page of the ledger.

"Often, the Nazis kept very good records," he says, moving the book just slightly away, forcing me to look up at him for this next part. "But what we're learning is, not always—it varies from camp to camp, or from commander to commander. And sometimes it depends on the guard: How much education he's had. How familiar he was with the languages spoken by the prisoners arriving that day. If he's not familiar with the language, he's more likely to spell prisoners' names wrong."

He hesitates, looking to Mrs. Yost for confirmation before continuing. "I just want to explain all this. I'm not sure any of it is worth raising your hopes. We don't have a record for an Abek Lederman arriving to Dachau," he says.

Only now does he push the ledger back toward me again. His neatly manicured index finger travels down the page until the line before the spidery handwriting stops. Toward these last rows, the end of the guard's shift, the writing becomes messier; the dots of the *i*'s become smudged and uneven.

"Here," he says. "Alek Federman. Age fourteen."

The realization comes to me slowly. "You think the guard spelled the name wrong?"

Mr. Ohrmann doesn't say anything.

"A cursive *l* can look like a cursive *b*," I say.

"And Alek is a far more common name, at least in Germany," he breaks in, though his voice is reluctant, like he doesn't want to give false hope. "And Federman is an equally common last name. It *might* be possible for someone to misspell it that way."

*Is this my brother?* My brain doesn't leap to embrace the possibility as quickly as I thought it would. Part of me thinks this sounds too desperate: People shouldn't be able to find or not find their brothers based on whether they can know or not know Alek is the more common name in Germany.

But I want to believe it. At the very least, I know it's possible. If the arrivals at Dachau were anything like the arrivals at the camps I was sent to, of course there would be room in that hell for a mistake. It was all a mistake.

I run my own fingers over the dry, finicky handwriting. "What happened to him next? Where did Alek Federman go?"

Mr. Ohrmann lowers his head apologetically. "I don't know. So far I've found only the reference to his coming into the camp. He's not in the roster of prisoners present for the liberation."

"So he came in, but he didn't go out?"

"He's not included on lists of the dead," he adds quickly. "He's just not on other lists at all."

"So he could have gone anywhere. He could have gone to any other camp in Europe?"

"Not anywhere," Mr. Ohrmann carefully corrects. "By the time these arrivals happened, Russia had moved through eastern Poland, America had come through France. The Reich was shrinking. Alek Federman, if he was transferred to another camp before Dachau was liberated, he couldn't have gone to *any* of them."

"I see." In my mind, I picture a map of Europe with a circle lain over top. And then I try to picture that circle getting smaller. I only have to look inside the circle. I only have to figure out how much land is inside. "So where do *I* go next?"

Mrs. Yost now leans forward to rejoin the conversation. "Next, you should write letters. I'll give you a list of all the organizations we know of. The one for Mr. Ohrmann's organization, you can leave with him tomorrow, but then we can get you started on—"

"I'll do that tonight, but then where do I *go* next?"

"The letters are your best solution."

"Like Miriam?" I break in, more pointedly than I meant to. "Like Miriam writing all her letters about her sister? I'll write the letters. I'll write letters until my fingers are raw. I don't sleep much anyway. But then where do I *go*? This is a place for adults; is there a camp for children? A different displaced-persons camp I could go to?"

This is rude; I sense that at some level. And overly

demanding of a woman I barely know. But I can't go back and just write letters. I'll have too much time to think, and my brain will get stuck. I can't be left alone with my thoughts.

Mrs. Yost looks at Mr. Ohrmann, her face saying, *I told you about this one.* "There are a few camps for children," she says. "But they're just like here—children pass through them. They arrive, and then they're reclaimed or they're adopted or they move on."

"Still," I insist. "Where is the one that children from Dachau would have been sent?"

Her mouth sets in a thin line; it's Mr. Ohrmann who answers. "There are a few in the American zone. The closest is forty or fifty kilometers from here."

"Good." I find a blank sheet of paper on that mess of a desk, and a fountain pen, leaking and sticky with the ink that has spilled out around the nib. "Tell me the name of the closest, please. I'll find someone to take me tonight."

"You can just as easily write a letter to that place, too."

"I have to go in person."

"Zofia, I promise you, most people are writing letters."

"And if most people are just writing letters, doesn't that mean I should go in person?" I press. "Mr. Ohrmann here, learning about Alek Federman—would he have gone to that trouble for me if I was one of a hundred letters he'd received this afternoon?"

She knows I'm right. She's proved my point by inviting me in to see Mr. Ohrmann instead of adding me to the long list everyone else must be on.

"You won't find someone to take you tonight. We're down

to one working vehicle at the moment, and even if we had more, we're rationing gas for emergencies only." She raises one finger, silencing the protest she can tell I'm about to make. "But, if you still want to, you can go the day after tomorrow; that's when we send one of our wagons on a supply run. Sometimes we trade supplies with other camps. You can wait two days."

"I—"

"You can wait two days, Zofia," she says firmly. "And I promise you, it's your fastest option."

My heart hasn't stopped pounding since Mr. Ohrmann showed me the ledger. I know I should try to manage my expectations. But how can I not hope?

By the time we arrived at Birkenau, there were less of us still. We smelled of sweat and urine but also of death. When the train stopped, through spaces between the slats that passed for windows in the cattle car, I could see swarms of soldiers, all of them with guns. They unloaded the cars one by one; they came to the cars screaming, with dogs straining at their leads, biting anyone who didn't move quickly enough. The guards pulled women by their hair. They brought whips down on their backs and legs, and they shoved families apart to send them to separate lines. Lines. Just as we were sorted at the soccer stadium, we were going to be sorted again.

"We will be okay," I said to Abek. "The other guard promised. I made him promise to wire ahead and recommend you be an errand boy. You tell them that when we get to the front of the line. You tell them that you are twelve, not nine, and that the guard in Sosnowiec said you have come to be the commandant's errand boy."

While we waited, rumors traveled down the line: We would have to strip completely naked and give up our own clothes. We would have to go through showers and, when we came out, put on different clothes that didn't fit. A girl wondered why we had to do it that way. I assumed it was just to degrade us, because there was never a lost opportunity to degrade us. But then another woman whispered, no, it wasn't just that. The reason we couldn't keep our own clothes was because the Nazis were going to cut them apart at the seams in case we tried to sew valuables into the linings.

I didn't have any silver or jewelry sewn into my clothes, but the thought of their being ripped apart felt like another death. All the careful stitches sewn by Baba Rose and the other seamstresses. All the attention and work and long hours and sore fingers—and now someone would undo it in the hopes of finding a few pieces of silver. The dismantling of the Lederman name happened every time a person wearing our clothes walked into a camp.

Later I would view this slicing of clothing as a good job. The prisoners chosen to sort through the clothing piles got to spend most of the day indoors instead of performing manual labor. If a guard wasn't looking, they might be able to slip away a sweater or trade the shoes they'd been assigned for a better-fitting pair.

We have to take off our clothes, I told Abek. I was talking as fast as I could because I knew the showers were separated for women and men, and I wasn't sure which line young boys would be sent to.

It's not important, I told him. They're just going to give you new clothes.

I knew it was important. I knew it was important because when they took Abek's clothes, they would also take his jacket. They would also take the family alphabet story I had sewn inside it, the way he was meant to remember me and find me after the war. But I couldn't tell him that; I had to be strong.

I remember all this, and I am strong up until the moment I realize that this, too, is just another dream version of the last time I saw Abek. A dream version, not the real version, and as soon as I realize that, I open my eyes.

I WAKE TO THE SOUND OF SHUSHING, ESTHER AND BREINE tiptoeing around the cottage and warning each other not to wake me. My face aches, pressed against something hard. I'd fallen asleep at the desk, arm as a pillow, nostrils filled with the heady scent of ink.

When I returned to the cottage last night, Breine had moved the small rug beside her bed closer to me so neither of us would have to step on a cold floor in the morning. Esther gave me a mug of coffee to help me stay awake while I wrote my letters. They were both such specific, immediate kindnesses from these girls I barely know. I'd earlier passed Miriam in the front room, huddled over her own letters, with her own cup of coffee.

"Good luck," I told her, and she said it back to me, too, in her lovely Dutch accent.

I wondered if I should apologize for earlier at dinner, for

asking everyone about their families, but I didn't know if that would make things even more awkward. "You have enough paper?" I asked instead, nodding down to the sheaf in my hand, provided by Mrs. Yost.

Miriam nodded to her own pile, and we shared the most imperceptible of smiles.

Now, my finished letters sit nearby, and I blink them into focus.

"You're awake," Breine says when my wooden chair squeaks across the floorboards. "She's awake," she says unnecessarily to Esther, and then their voices rise to a normal volume.

Last night they allowed me to keep the lantern burning until the soft orange of the morning. It's burning still, and Esther reaches over my head to deftly turn it down. I'm sure kerosene is rationed; it was selfish of me to use so much of it. I stretch my arms and legs, cramped from my night of sitting sleep, as Breine and Esther's morning routine unfolds around me. Breine sweeps the floor while Esther makes both of their beds. They wash their faces in the bowl, then Esther brushes Breine's hair while Breine talks through plans for the day.

*Trade school.* Breine is asking me something, and I'm trying to wrap my foggy brain around her sentences. Do I want to learn a new trade? she repeats. There's job training here.

"It doesn't have to be farming. If you don't want to farm, they're adding courses," Breine explains. "Bookkeeping, sewing. Esther's doing a stenography course."

"Sewing?" I repeat. My voice is thick and scratchy. As soon as I fell asleep, I had nightmares about Abek.

"Do you want to learn to sew? The supplies are terrible now."

I shake my head. I haven't done anything with clothes since Neustadt. Nazi uniforms, coarse and brown. The work took something I loved and poisoned it. "No, thank you."

"It can be good to keep busy," Esther says gently. I see Breine encouraging her; I wonder if I was screaming in my sleep again and what they heard me say. "Breine and I have both been the new person here, sleeping in a new bed, trying to figure out what to do next. We all have. And we've all been helped by the people who came before us. It can be strange to be here, and it's good to have something to—"

"Oh, just come out with us," Breine breaks in. "If you don't want to get muddy with me, go to Esther's stenography class. One hundred and sixty words a minute!"

Esther gives her a look; the bluntness of Breine's invitation is not how Esther was trying to communicate. But then she turns back to me. "I could help you catch up on what you've missed."

"I already have something to keep busy," I say. "Thanks for your concern, but I already have something to do."

Breine looks as though she wants to say something else but doesn't.

They have so much energy, Breine and Esther, in constant motion in our small bedroom. It's early yet, not even fully light, but I hear the noises of a morning routine happening on the other side of the door, too, from Judith and Miriam, who must have been up like me, writing her letters.

I feel a hundred years older than all of them. The four of them are nothing like we nothing-girls, with the vacant, tired way we moved and sat and talked.

But then again, we were still in the hospital three months after the war ended. We, who had trouble keeping track of the days, who sometimes needed gentle reminders not to wander in the hallways with our blouses half-buttoned, who laughed and cried at inappropriate times.

Bissel, the woman with the gashed, angry holes in her legs, the one from Ravensbrück, swore she would one day go to her daughter living on a farm. She sat on the windowsill one morning and laughed and laughed, and then suddenly she hurled herself outside, and we heard screams from passersby when her body hit the pavement.

But last night at dinner, I learned Breine was at Ravensbrück, too. And Esther was made to disassemble batteries with her bare hands in a camp somewhere in Austria. How have some of us healed so much faster than others? How are some of us better?

Esther finishes brushing Breine's hair and separates it into three plaits. I worry I've offended them by declining to go along to any of their training programs.

"Have you taken the stenography class?" I ask Breine, trying to find my manners. "The one Esther's doing?"

She laughs. "I'm going to be a lovely, docile farmwife. I am going to grow onions and make cakes and ask Chaim to impregnate me immediately. I won't have use for stenography."

Esther smiles indulgently, twisting Breine's hair into a braid. "Does Chaim know these plans?"

"This is the benefit of marrying someone who's known you for only five weeks. I'll make Chaim docile and content, too, before he has a chance to know these plans."

"Five weeks?" I blurt out.

Breine cranes her head to face me, while Esther pivots around to finish the braid. "Five weeks tomorrow."

I try to keep the shock off my face. I'd assumed Breine and Chaim had met as teenagers, and then somehow found each other after the war. Or even that they met in a camp. There was love in the camps. It seems impossible, but I saw it; I saw love poems composed in lice-filled barracks.

Five weeks is nothing. Five weeks ago, I was still in the hospital.

"We met here," she continues. "Plowing a field. Isn't that romantic?"

"But—I don't mean to make judgments—but you barely know each other."

I'm afraid Breine will be angry with me for puncturing her happiness, but instead she leans forward in her chair, stretching out a hand until I take it. "Chaim and I have known each other for five weeks. I knew my last fiancé, Wolf, for two years. We didn't have a wedding because we wanted to wait until the war was over, and every day I think about how I'd change that if I could. So now I'll have a wedding, and it will be with Chaim and not with Wolf. And I'm certain a part of Chaim wishes his wedding would be with the girl he loved in Hungary before me, who died and whose picture he keeps that he thinks I don't know about."

I start to apologize, but she cuts me off with a shake of her head. "Today I am choosing to love the person in front of me. Do you understand? Because he's here, I'm here, and we're ready to not be lonely together. Chaim is a good man. I won't let another wedding pass me by."

When they leave, I make my own bed and wash my face, then I gather my pile of letters to see if Mrs. Yost can tell me how to mail them. In her office, the telephone receiver is crammed against her ear. She depresses the button on the cradle again and again, trying for an operator.

"Darnit. I just had—hello? Hello?—*Darnit.*"

On the desk in front of her, the Foehrenwald arrivals log is open to a fresh page, with *Feldafing* written at the top. She must be preparing for the new influx of residents. Mrs. Yost catches my eye, then registers the sheaf of papers in my hand.

"Put them here," she instructs, nodding to a wire mail bin on her desk, already overflowing with other people's problems. "Hello?" This greeting isn't to me but to the phone receiver. "Hello?" she tries one more time before cupping her hand over the receiver and acknowledging me again. "And don't forget to remind Josef about tomorrow."

"Josef?"

"He's the one going for supplies. We don't have the other car working yet; he's best with the horses."

"But," I start to say.

"But?"

But nothing, but what am I supposed to say? That I met this man once and insisted he looked familiar? That I got carried away by his laugh when I'm supposed to be doing nothing but looking for my brother? That I kept sneaking glances at him all through dinner, wondering why he was alone and whether I should join him?

Should I tell her I made Josef so uncomfortable he left without even shaking my hand?

Mrs. Yost frantically depresses the telephone button, and I hear the faint, faraway sound of someone on the other end of the line. Her eyes light up.

"I'll go," I mouth, shutting the door behind me.

I find him in the stables, a whitewashed building on the outskirts of camp. It smells like dust and the clean hay tamped down on the floor.

He's sitting on a low, three-legged stool, tending to one of the horses, a fawn-colored animal whose mane is nearly white. A second one, chestnut with an inky-black mane, swishes its tail in a stall. The one Josef is with—a palomino, I think it's called—stands with its hooves in shallow pans of water. As I step through the doorway, Josef lifts the horse's right leg, tucking the hoof between his own knees, and begins scraping the bottom with what looks like a long nail file. The horse flicks its tail but otherwise submits.

"Cleaning its feet?" I ask. Josef must have heard someone at the door, but he doesn't turn to acknowledge me, focusing instead on his precise work.

"Trimming back her hooves. They grow just like people's fingernails."

"Does it hurt her?"

"Not if you do it the right way." His voice is—not friendly, exactly, but not as brusque as it was yesterday. But then he looks up for the first time, and when he realizes it's me standing there, they darken. He lowers his eyes and continues with his work.

"The water is to prepare her hooves?" I stumble on, pretending I haven't noticed the change in his mood.

"To make them softer. Easier to sculpt. Why are you here, Zofia?"

I try to ignore the small thrill of hearing him say my name, but I can't ignore how much I like watching him. There's an ease to his movement, a gracefulness. I like that when he finishes the front hoof and moves on to the horse's hind leg, he trails his hand along her back and makes clicking sounds so she never loses track of where he is. I like the way he smoothly draws the stool back to his new position with one foot. I like the slight unevenness of his shoulders, the way one is just a bit higher than the other.

"Can I help?" I ask, instead of answering his question. As soon as I answer, my reason for being here will disappear.

Josef presses his lips together and nods back toward the

door. "Actually, yes. You can get an apple for Feather to have as a treat when I'm through—there's a sack of bruised ones outside."

On a bench a few meters away, I find a canvas bag and carry it in. Josef motions for me to hang it on a nail, but first I take an apple out to have something to do with my hands. It's soft and warm; I bring it to my nose and inhale the scent of cider. "Mrs. Yost said you would take me tomorrow when you go to pick up supplies," I say. "That's why I'm here. To tell you."

I expect him to ask why I need to go, but after a small hesitation, he shrugs. "If that's what she told you. I'll leave early, though." He's turned back to Feather's hoof, so the only sounds are a soft scraping and the occasional slaps of the horse's tail against her flanks as she swats flies.

*My father, swatting flies off Abek as my family waited to be separated in the stadium.*

*My bunkmates, swatting flies off me in the textile factory, when I was injured and too weak to work one day and I knew I'd be killed if I couldn't get better.*

"Josef. Your fight yesterday. What was it about?"

"Why is it important for you to know?"

*Because I keep thinking about you, and I don't know why.*

"Because I'm going to get in a wagon with you tomorrow, alone, and I would like to know whether I'm going on a trip with someone dangerous."

He opens, then closes, his mouth. "That's...I suppose that's reasonable."

"I think so."

"I'm not dangerous," he says.

"Then what was your fight about?

Feather stamps one of her feet in the pan of water. A gentle stomp, with a gentle splash. Josef stops his work to make sure she's okay. "It was about you."

The flush that spreads across my collarbone stems from confusion, but it's also pleasure. "Me? The fight was about me?"

"Yes. Something Rudolf said."

"What was it?"

"I want to make sure you understand—it was the third time I've heard him say something like that," he says. "The time before, the girl was only fourteen."

This, I think, is a way of saying, *I didn't do it for you*. Of saying, *don't be either flattered or alarmed, you were more of an excuse than a reason*. "What did he say, exactly?"

Josef's mouth twists. I think for a minute he'll refuse to tell me.

"Rudolf said, 'Put her in the right dress and she's still fuckable.' He said, 'In the war, all Jewesses would fuck for a scrap of bread.'"

"In the war, all dirty men were glad for our starvation," I spit back reflexively, overcome by anger at Rudolf's disgusting sentiment. "Since they could use it to try to get us to fuck them."

It's only after my initial rage dissipates that I feel myself blush, surprised I've said those words out loud, less than a day after I also said *piss*.

Josef laughs, the same sharp, surprised laugh I heard yesterday. Maybe I cursed this time because I wanted to hear that laugh again. And suddenly I am laughing, too. About something dark and terrible and not at all worth laughing at, but I'm laughing anyway.

"It's true, right?" I press. "A horrible man like Rudolf wouldn't be able to get it any other way."

"Something tells me that a horrible man like Rudolf has never gotten it under any circumstances," Josef says. "He's a true latrine-puncher."

"A piss-goat," I concur.

"I promise you, very few people here were sorry to see something happen to Rudolf."

"So you're, what—the avenger of the camp?"

"No." Josef is still smiling, but there's less mirth in his eyes now. "I'm not. I'm just the person who doesn't really care if Rudolf hits me back."

"What do you mean? Why not?"

"Nothing. It was a joke." He turns abruptly back to his work, coaxing Feather's final hoof out of the water. She nickers again, a noise that sounds almost like a laugh.

"Josef," I say softly. "Why didn't you tell me this yesterday, when I asked about the fight?"

He answers with his back to me again. "Because I didn't want you to think I thought I was a hero," he says. "And I didn't want us to owe each other anything."

"Oh."

I'd thought his explanation would have to do with the

vulgarity of it all, with his wanting to protect me from pro-
fane words. That's what Dima would have done. Protected me.
Gallantly, like a knight. Josef's explanation—transactional,
matter-of-fact—isn't one I was prepared for. It throws me off
balance.

Josef finishes Feather's last hoof, moving to the other horse
and telling me I can feed Feather the apple now.

I notice for the first time that he's wearing the same shirt
from the fight. It's been laundered; the bloodstains are barely
visible, and the two buttons have been sewn back on. Sewn
clumsily—I can tell that from here—but attached nonetheless.
The ripped pocket still hangs loose, though, a flap against his
chest.

"I could fix your pocket for you," I offer. "The one that got
torn in your fight."

"No, thank you. As I said, I don't want us to be beholden
to each other."

"This isn't you being beholden to me; it's me evening the
score. For Rudolf. Besides, it's just a pocket. And I'd do a pro-
fessional job. I've been sewing since I was six."

I see hesitation in his shoulders before they hunch protectively. "No."

The air around us has shifted a little; it's uncomfortable
now. But I try not to take it personally. In the camps, I would
not have handed my clothes over to a stranger, either. They
were as likely to be stolen as mended.

"So I'll see you tomorrow morning?" I try. "Bright and
early? Dark and early?"

This time, he doesn't even bother responding; he merely nods, shortly, as if I'm barely present.

Feather finishes the apple from my hand, and as soon as she's through, I wipe my hands on my dress and make for the door.

THE COTTAGE IS EMPTY WHEN I GET BACK TO IT, HOT AND quiet in the middle of the day. The pen still lies where I left it before, next to the few sheets of paper I didn't use for my letters to the relief organizations.

There are other kinds of letters I didn't write, which I know I should. The one weighing on me most heavily is to Dima. I should tell him I arrived safely in Foehrenwald. I should apologize to him properly for taking the money from his pockets and thank him properly for the help he gave me. But when I press the pen to the paper, words don't come. I know writing to him would be a kindness, but I wonder if it would also be unfair, that it would sound as if I was asking more from him or telling him to wait for me.

*Dear Dima.*

*Was* I telling him to wait for me? I want to make sure my apartment is safe for when I bring Abek back to it, but do I want Dima to be waiting in it? Right now, he feels far away. Right now, when I try to picture his face, I instead picture him telling me that he'd kept things from me because he thought I needed to be protected.

I cross out his name, using thick black lines, and start again.

*Dear Gosia.*

Before I can figure out what to say next, the door swings open, saving me from myself. Breine dashes in, sunny and pink from her work outside, out of breath as she scans the small room. "Esther isn't here?"

"I just got back and haven't seen her. Is everything all right?"

"We'll try to find her on the way." She dashes to the writing desk and glances at my feet to make sure I'm wearing shoes. "Quick!" she says, extending her hand.

I'd be worried by Breine's rush, but she's laughing—it's clear that whatever she wants us to hurry for isn't something bad. Slowly, too slowly for her liking, I cap my pen and slide my chair back.

"Breine, where are we—"

"Donation boxes! A big truck. Hurry, before all the good things are gone."

I let her drag me out of the cottage, through the camp, and to the dining hall.

A cluster of people has formed inside, with more streaming in every minute, flushed and excited like Breine. They're gathered around the central dining tables, which are piled with wooden crates. The lids are already removed, clothing and books spilling out.

"Grab some things quickly, even if you don't like them," Breine advises as we shoulder in at one of the tables. "That way, even if you don't find anything else, you'll have some things to trade later."

The two women we squeeze between hover possessively over the table, positioning their bodies so the crates in front of them are just out of our reach. But when one of them recognizes Breine, she immediately makes room and tells the others to do the same.

"Breine's getting married," she loudly admonishes. "She gets first choice of anything that could work as a wedding dress."

The other women step aside for Breine, who pulls me forward with her.

"What are you looking for?" I ask her. "If you could have any kind of wedding dress you liked?"

"White," she says. "Long sleeves. And a neck that goes like—" She traces a curly pattern along her collarbone.

"A sweetheart neckline," I offer.

"Yes, like that. Tell me if you find anything like that."

I move next to Breine and dip my hands into the box. Familiarity shoots through my fingers like an electric buzz.

Cotton. Wool. Gabardine. Twill. The coarse butcher linen used for homemakers' aprons, the nubby, textured Shetland used for winter suits. My hands get lost in the fabric. Deep inside the crates, I can identify them by touch. If I couldn't touch them, I could probably identify them by smell. The quiet musk of a flannel suit; the pungent blush of taffeta transformed into a woman's first party dress. The doll dresses I made as a child, dozens of them, out of the scraps of fabric my father brought home. The handkerchiefs, the coin purses.

Even more than walking into my family's abandoned apartment in Sosnowiec, the expectedness of these clothes feels comforting. It feels like home.

Around me, women pluck sweaters and skirts from the crates, holding them up to one another for size or slipping them on right there over the clothes they're wearing. The unwanted garments are left spread on the tables, a chaotic kaleidoscope of color.

"Oh, can I try that if it doesn't fit you?" one woman says, pointing to the skirt another is wriggling over her hips. "Robin's-egg blue is my favorite color."

"It's yours," the other woman promises, stepping out of the skirt again. "But help me find something in a floral pattern. I always wore flowers."

There's something so tender in the discerning, critical way these women pick through the clothes. Not just grabbing things because they're warm or because they fit, but looking for clothes that will help them reclaim the pieces of themselves they had to give away.

That's what my family's business did, at its best. Zayde Lazer was a businessman, and so was Papa when Zayde first hired him. But Baba Rose was the one who understood that clothing isn't always a practical business. Customers buy things that make them feel more like themselves.

A young woman jostles into me, trying to maneuver her way into a fitted woolen jacket. "I love this, but I can't raise my hands above my head," she complains to her friend, demonstrating the tight squeeze, the strained threads.

"You just need to insert some extra fabric under the arm," I say automatically.

She turns to me. "Is that difficult?"

"It shouldn't be. You don't even have to remove the whole sleeve. Just cut away the bottom, and sew in little ovals the size of eggs."

She looks skeptical. "Are you sure?"

"It fits you everywhere else. See? It's not straining at your shoulders. It's straining here, by your armpit." I pinch the fabric to show her.

The advice came from a part of my mind I haven't used in a while, a bear waking from hibernation. The girl's mouth drops open in gratitude, and she immediately begins to make plans for the jacket. She'll wear it to a job interview, she tells her friend. She heard that one of the camp administrators is looking for a typist; this jacket is exactly the kind of thing she was hoping to find.

As I'm basking in the long-dormant sense of feeling useful, Breine taps my shoulder.

"I've found it!" she squeals, holding up a wrinkled garment from the bottom of a box.

Yellow silk, butter not marigold, the bodice dotted in tiny

seed pearls. She holds the dress against her body, swaying back and forth so the fabric swishes at her calves. "Isn't it perfect?"

This dress isn't remotely close to the gown Breine described wanting, and it won't look right on her at all. It's cut for someone with a much bigger bust than Breine's, and wider shoulders. Someone older, too. The color of the fabric is youthful, but the style is for a matron. It's the kind of dress an older woman would order if she didn't want to admit her age.

"Feel the silk; it's so delicate," she says. "I think Chaim will love it."

Quickly, I scan the rainbow of fabrics on the table for something better to suggest. But most of the dresses are shirtwaists or practical housedresses, nothing a woman would want to get married in. The only other formal option I see is a dark-colored, strapless velvet, appropriate for an American cocktail party but not a wedding gown.

Besides, Breine's eyes are shining. She pulled it out of the crate and declared it perfect, but I know if the dress had been green or brown, or if it had lace instead of beads, she would have said that was perfect, too, because Breine wants to get married.

The other women see the same thing I do—the light in Breine's eyes—and they tell her it's perfect. The mood is gay and laughing, like the day each year when the women in my family would all go to the factory to preview the spring line. Or on special-occasion shopping trips, when my mother and Aunt Maja and I would go to Kraków and accept the glasses of champagne at the department store.

"Isn't it perfect?" she asks again.

"If that's the dress you want," I say, smiling, "then you'll be the most beautiful bride."

Breine continues to admire her gown, and I turn back to the piles of fabric on the table. Breine was right earlier. More would-be shoppers are continuing to appear, scooping up garments, and the table is quickly becoming bare. If I don't get something for myself now, there won't be anything left.

I grab a dress in plaid, another in plum, a sturdy sweater, socks, and a pair of gloves. The gloves are impractical—they're made of soft kid, the leather so supple it ripples like silk. My father bought my mother a pair like this once. She wore them to go shopping, but only when she didn't have to carry home meat or cheese or something that could leave an odor. Only when she was buying nice things.

"Zofia?" Breine is looking at me curiously. I've pressed the glove against my cheek. I'm holding it there like a memory, like a memory that needs to be tied down.

My mother was wearing those gloves when we went to the soccer stadium. I can see that now, clearly. And she was wearing them after we left the soccer stadium. She smoothed back my hair with them; she used them to mop Abek's brow. I know this happened. I know this is a true memory.

*What happened next?*

I push a little further. My hands start to shake. My head is pulsing. The monster at the door is stirring; I don't want to push anymore.

I LEAVE Breine and Esther the next morning while it's still dark. Breine's bedsheets are tangled and half falling off the bed frame while her nose whistles in a snore. A few feet away, Esther sleeps with her pillow over her head.

When I get to the stables, Josef is hitching up the horses to a wagon that looks at least twenty years old. The ends of his curls are still wet from his morning washing. A drop of water clings to the back of his neck and then slowly rolls forward, tracing the curve and sinew of his skin as he works on the wagon, until it finally disappears down the open collar of his shirt. I picture it rolling down his collarbone. Rolling down his chest, rolling over his stomach.

"Hi," he says, but there's an element of surprise to the greeting. Maybe he wasn't sure I'd actually show up. As early as I am, he was still almost ready to leave, and I can't help but think he wouldn't have waited long to find out if I was coming or not.

"Good morning," I say. "Thank you, again, for taking me."

"Technically, I'm not taking you," he says, loading a crate of what look like canned goods onto the back of the wagon, the same crates that yesterday held donated dresses. "You're just coming along on a preplanned route."

"I guess this means that if the wagon gets crowded, you'll leave me by the side of the road instead of the C rations."

"Well," he grunts as he shoves the box toward the back. "I can't eat you in an emergency."

When he's hooked up Feather and the other horse, Josef nods to the spring seat at the front of the wagon, and I climb on. At the last minute, I decided to pack everything I own in case I don't return. It's a few more things than what I arrived with on the train, but I can still carry it all in the valise under one arm.

Josef points to a pail of food on the floorboard and then falls silent. The sun is still rising, but I know our trip is several hours long. The horses seem unhurried and unbothered; Josef drives them with the reins in one hand, a slight curve to his spine, his lean body rhythmically giving in to the movement of the wagon. *Several hours of sitting next to Josef.*

"Mrs. Yost says you go on supply runs," I offer after a few kilometers of silence. "Foehrenwald trades with other camps?"

"Sometimes. Right now, the administration is worried about housing all the people from Feldafing when they arrive."

"How often do you go?"

"Every couple of weeks."

"I heard her say we needed blankets. And we're bringing food?"

He nods but doesn't elaborate out loud this time, and the line of conversation seems exhausted, anyhow. Scrambling for another subject, I look at the horses' reins, easy in Josef's hand. "What's the other horse's name?" I picture something that would go with Feather, something like Smoke or Coal.

Instead, Josef's mouth tugs at the corner. "Franklin Delano Roosevelt."

I laugh. "The American president?"

"The Americans donated the horse."

"Franklin Delano Roosevelt," I repeat.

And then suddenly, like a swift kick in the stomach, this name brings forth a memory: a dark movie house, a newsreel, grainy footage, an announcer's voice saying the Americans had reelected their president for another term.

K *is for the KinoTeatr, where I take you when Mama needs rest, where we sit in the balcony and count the hats of the men below, where we watched the inauguration of Franklin Delano Roosevelt, because Mama needs rest, so we go to the KinoTeatr, because it has a balcony, where we watched the Inauguration of Franklin Delano Roosevelt because Mama needed rest.*

"KinoTeatr?" Josef repeats.

I snap back.

*Damnit. Damnit. Shit and piss.* My face flushes a deep magenta as I realize with complete horror that I've said at least some of that out loud. I wonder how much.

"KinoTeatr?" he asks again.

"Sorry," I mumble.

"What were you reciting?"

"Nothing." But obviously, it wasn't nothing. "It's just an alphabet game my brother and I used to play. A name for every letter. I don't know why I said it out loud. Sometimes my brain gets stuck."

"You said that when I met you," he says. "It was one of the first things you said—that your mind must have been playing tricks on you."

I flush again, even deeper red if possible. "It's—it's hard to explain," I stammer. "Sometimes timelines get mixed up in my head. Or I'll think I remember something that didn't happen, or I'll forget something that did. I'm better, though. They wouldn't have discharged me from the hospital if I wasn't better, and I'm still getting better every day."

Even though I'm trying to put Josef at ease, I'm realizing, with fragile pride, that the sentiment is true. I *have* gotten better. I arrived in Foehrenwald two days ago, and before just now, my brain has gotten stuck only once: when I watched Josef get in that fight. I don't know whether it's because I'm in a new place that's not haunted by memories or because I'm on my own, but until now, I managed not to act crazy in front of Josef, or anyone else for that matter. I made him laugh. He saw me be quick-witted. He saw me be a person. "I'm getting better every day," I repeat.

"You don't owe me an explanation," he cuts me off indifferently.

I wince a little at his nonchalance. "I'm sorry. I apologize for boring you with my health."

"All I said was, you don't owe me an explanation."

"Well, I don't owe you anything, apparently." This, I meant to sound like a joke, but it comes out caustic, too. He looks at me quizzically. "What you said yesterday," I explain. "That you didn't want us to feel beholden to each other."

"That's true."

His answer doesn't sound as though he's trying to joke. His tone of voice is serious, which I find both reassuring and frustrating for reasons that are hard to articulate. I *shouldn't* want to feel beholden to him, after all. I should be *glad* he's specified that I don't owe him anything. But at the same time, I just did something strange in front of him—I recited something odd about an old movie house—and told him I'd been in a hospital. Shouldn't he *want* an explanation? Even if I didn't want to give one, shouldn't he be concerned or at least curious?

"The horses. How did you learn to work with them?" I ask now, trying to find a thread from before.

"I grew up working with horses," he says.

"Did you grow up on a farm?"

"No. I grew up in a city."

"A city in Germany?"

He hesitates a bit. "You ask a lot of questions."

"Where I'm from, the people who still drove wagons were mostly the farmers who came into the city on market days."

"It wasn't a farm." It's clear he means that to be the end of his answer, his eyes are back on the road, and I'm still trying to put my finger on what it is about Josef and this conversation that's throwing me so off-kilter.

"I'm sorry if I'm—I'm really not crazy," I tell him.

"So you said. I just prefer to keep to myself."

"Because I know I was odd the first day we met, and if you're afraid of me, then—"

"My family had stables," he interrupts. "All right? That's how I know horses. At our summer house, where we would go on holidays. I took riding lessons, and the groundskeeper used to let me drive the wagon when he did chores." He turns to me and raises an eyebrow. "Happy? I'm not afraid of you or worried about you. I don't think you're going to tear off your clothes and run screaming down the road or do something else insane. My family had stables, and I used to help the groundskeeper."

*This is the first interaction I can remember having in months where someone didn't ask if I was okay.* That's what was confusing to me. That's what made me feel strange and off-kilter. Josef is responding to my prying questions as though they're legitimately prying questions, not like they're symptoms that my brain isn't working.

*Josef is not acting like I'm something that needs to be worried about.*

Mentally, I fill in the blanks of what he's just said. The "house" where he went on holidays must be a grand estate. Only the wealthiest families would keep stables and employ groundskeepers. And his family had a house in the city, too.

"The summer house sounds nice," I say.

"It *was* nice. Summer was my favorite time of the year."

"Why don't you—" I start to ask.

"Why don't I what?"

*Why don't you go home*, is what I was about to say. Nazis didn't burn down estates. They occupied them and preserved them; they loved the art. Josef could have tried to go home. But there's such a defensiveness in his response that I back off without finishing my sentence. "Why don't you like to eat with other people in the dining hall?"

He shrugs. "I told you. I just prefer to keep to myself. Not all of us in Foehrenwald hope to make new friends. Some of us are trying to leave as soon as we can. Like you. You're going to get your brother, and then you'll probably want to go back home and try to run your family's factory."

I bite the inside of my lip to hide a smile. I didn't tell him about my family's factory; he must have asked Chaim or Mrs. Yost.

"*Look* for him," I correct.

"What?"

"You said we were going to *get* my brother. But I'm going with you to *look* for him."

"You don't know that he's at the Kloster Indersdorf?"

"I have reason to believe it's a logical place to start looking for him."

"Then I hope he's there," Josef says. "And that he wants to be found."

The last half of his sentence catches me off guard. "Why wouldn't he want to be found?"

Josef keeps his eyes on the road. "Lots of reasons. He could have painful memories of before the war. He could want to start completely over. He could decide that's easier to do if he's not around you."

The back of my neck bristles. I shift a little on the wooden bench. "Of course he wants to be found. He's a little boy."

Josef presses his lips together.

"Josef, of course he wants to be found," I repeat. "Why would you say something like that?"

"Have you at least thought about it?"

"Thought about whether my brother might not want to see me? No, I haven't, Josef. I don't think it's a thing most people would consider."

"Suit yourself."

"And I don't think I want to continue this conversation."

"Okay," he says again. "I just—"

"I said, I don't think I want to continue this conversation," I spit. "He was a *little boy*. He still is."

"Not all people want to be found."

I can't tell what is infuriating me more now—what Josef is saying or the even tone he's saying it in. The fact that he isn't even looking at me. The fact that he's just said horrible things to me but pauses now to click something softly to the horses.

"You're an ass, Josef." He winces but glances over only for the briefest second before returning to the road. "*Look* at me, Josef. You're an *ass*. You're such an expert on what people want? The day I met you, you were attacking a man."

Still, he doesn't respond, his mouth set in a firm line.

How could I have been so stupid before? Bathing in Josef's

curtness because it reminded me of being normal? Pressing on with a conversation because I like the color of his eyes, the sheen of sweat on his neck? Convincing myself he was mysterious when I should have realized he was just rude.

"Stop the wagon," I order. "I need a rest."

He hesitates and jerks his chin upward. "There's a little village in about a kilometer. I usually water the horses there."

"I'd like to stop now."

"It's just *a kilometer.*"

"Fine. Don't stop. I'll get out now by myself and walk." I'm already standing, wobbly on my bad foot. My knee bashes painfully against the seat as I eye the distance to the ground. "I don't want to ride with you another second longer than—"

But then he does stop, pulling swiftly on the reins—and I lurch forward, grabbing the side of the wagon to steady myself. Part furious, part embarrassed, and part throbbing from where I'd hit the seat, I straighten my dress and climb down onto the dirt road. Knee stiff and aching, I start down the path, desperate to put distance between me and Josef.

Out of the corner of my eye, I see him pause for a moment, deciding whether to come after me. He doesn't. He unhooks the horses and leads them for a drink, one bridle in each hand, toward the stream we've been following.

*Josef doesn't know my brother,* I tell myself as I hobble down the road. *Josef doesn't know me. Josef doesn't know how any of this works any better than I do. Josef is an ass.*

Josef is an ass. But if he's right, then I have no hope.

I stop in my tracks, doubling over with nausea by the

terrifying prospect of hopelessness. This wish, to find Abek, to find one person in millions of people—it hangs together by the finest of threads. All it takes is for Abek to not add his name to one list, to decide he doesn't want to be found.

This thinking isn't good for me; this thinking will burrow into my mind like a worm. It already has. My hands shake; I feel as if I can hear the bones rattling inside my skin. If Abek doesn't want to be found, then I won't be able to find him because he doesn't want to be found, and if I don't find him, then I won't find him because he didn't want to be found and I will never see him again, and I failed, I failed, I failed.

I fold my hands together to keep them from rattling and try to think of something concrete that I can do, something that will occupy my brain. Josef said there was food. *Walk back to the wagon and get the food*, I instruct myself. *One foot in front of the other.*

The tin pail is still on the floorboard, where Josef pointed to it earlier. The food is neatly wrapped, two of everything. I divide it, leaving Josef's portion on the driver's bench, where Josef should see it when he gets back, and then take my own portion to a stump by the side of the road, forcing myself to sit and put pieces of bread in my mouth.

In the distance, I can see him by the creek with the horses. He coaxes them down the steep bank, and while they drink, he wets a grooming brush, brushing the sweat from their backs. Josef is too thin. It's easier to think of his flaws when I'm as angry at him as I am. He's too thin, and his eyes are a little close together, and they're weary like an old man's, with dark circles and crinkled lines.

*Josef is broken like me.*

I have no evidence for this. It's not an excuse for anything. But it's what hits me, watching Josef intently pour himself into these small actions with the horses.

*Josef is broken like me.*

When he's finished, he ties the horses to a post and comes back to the wagon, where he silently picks up the food I've laid out and eats with his back toward me. After a few minutes, he walks over, arm extended, a ripe purple globe sitting in the palm of his hand.

"There was a plum," he says, holding out the fruit. "It rolled out onto the floorboard, but there was only one. Half of it belongs to you."

"I don't need it."

He's already pulling a small knife from his pocket and slicing the plum around the seam. "Well. Half of it's yours. You can eat it or not; I'm not going to take what belongs to you."

He sets my half on the stump next to me, making it rock back and forth on its lush, bruisy skin, and then moves to untie the horses. He pauses halfway, though, turning back toward me. He's shoved his hands into his pockets and looks uncomfortable.

"I shouldn't have said that. About your brother."

"No, you shouldn't have," I agree stiffly.

He raises his eyebrows at the stump next to me, asking if he can sit. I shrug that I can't stop him.

"Maybe you're right," he says once he's settled. "The

things I was saying were more about me than you. It's just, you
seemed—"

"Crazy," I complete his thought. "I seemed crazy."

"Hopeful." He meets my eyes, full on, for the first time.
"You seemed hopeful, and if we get to the Kloster Indersdorf
and your brother isn't there—you seemed hopeful, and I didn't
want it to break your heart."

His shirtsleeve brushes against mine; he smells like grass
and clean sweat. I take my half of the plum from the stump.
Hold it. I'm not hungry anymore but can't bear the idea of
wasting food.

"I told him I would find him," I explain. "The day I was
separated from my brother, I said, we will meet in Sosnowiec.
The very last day I saw him, I told him, if you're not there, I
will find you wherever you are."

"I understand."

"I don't think you do. I didn't say, *if it's convenient for me*,
and I didn't say, *until I get tired*, and I didn't say, *unless you don't
want to be found*. I said, *I will find you*."

"When *was* the last time you saw him?" Josef asks. "The
very last time."

A laugh, bitter and rough, rips from my chest.

"What's funny?"

"I thought I saw him a hundred times. Through a fence or
from a distance or if one of us was being marched somewhere.
I thought I saw him once when I was assigned to weed the
commandant's flower garden outside the fence. I'd arranged

for Abek to work for the commandant; I thought I saw him in the window. I left him a turnip; I buried it in the ground. But when I worked there a few days later, the ground hadn't been upturned, so he must not have been able to sneak away to dig it up."

"But *when* did you tell him that you would find him again?" Josef asks. "What is your memory of that last time?"

"*I don't know.*" The laugh that bubbles from my mouth this time is throaty and wild. I'm afraid to meet his eyes. This is the first time I've said any of this out loud. Not to nurses, not to the nothing-girls. I haven't told anyone that I spent the war vowing to find my brother, and I can't actually remember the last time we said goodbye.

"I don't know how to answer your question. Because I actually can't remember the last time I saw Abek. I've been trying. For months, I've been really trying. But it's like my brain won't let me. I remember goodbyes, but I don't think they're right. In my dreams, all the time, though, I keep seeing new goodbyes. I keep inventing them. There's a block. There's a big wall where that memory should be."

"Why do you think there's a block?" he asks. "In your memory, why do you think there's a block?"

I swallow. My hands start to shake. "When we got to the camp—the chimneys were right there. The death was right there. Do you understand? I saw a soldier rip a baby from its mother's arms and slam it against a truck because it wouldn't stop crying. It went limp and crumpled like a piece of lace.

I think—I can't remember saying goodbye to Abek because I can't stand to remember that day. I can't stand to remember any more minutes of that day."

I reach up and touch my face. It's wet. I've started crying. The memory I've spoken out loud has dislodged something, and now instead of feeling foggy, I feel like I'm leaking, snot in my nose, tears on my cheeks.

"But what if the clue to finding my brother is in something I'm forgetting from that day? What if we made a new plan, or a new meeting place, and now I've forgotten it? What if I can't find my brother because I can't remember those things? What if I'm a terrible, terrible sister?"

Silently, Josef pulls a handkerchief from his pocket and hands it to me. He turns away while I clean my face, and he's still facing away while he says the next part. "I don't think that anything you did during the war because you were trying to survive could make you bad."

His voice is throaty and full of emotion, more than I've heard the entire ride. His voice breaks on the last word. I see his hand dart up to his eye, swipe quickly. Stunned, I realize he's crying, too, or close to it. For once, I'm drawn out of my own grief and into someone else's.

"Josef. Do you have . . . experience with that?" I don't know how else to phrase it; I don't know exactly what I'm asking.

He draws in a breath, low and wavering. "I have experience with feeling guilty for the things I did to survive."

A beat, two. We sit next to each other on this stump, on this gravelly dirt road in the middle of Germany.

"We should go now," he says finally. "I'm sure you want to get to the Kloster Indersdorf."

Josef puts his hands on his knees, readying himself, and the dirt crunches under his feet as he stands. In front of me now, he looks smaller than he did a few hours ago, and when he offers me his hand to help me rise to my own feet, I feel like I'm smaller, too.

WITH THE SUN RESTING IN THE MIDDLE OF THE SKY AND sweat pooling at my collarbone, Josef says we're getting close. Houses pop up nearer one another; we're no longer the only wagon on the road. Josef told me the Kloster Indersdorf is in the boundaries of a town, but when we slow to a stop near a building on the central square, I'm still surprised at *how* in the center of town it is: this displaced-persons camp for children is one old building, three stories of white stone taking up a full city block. At the far end of the side facing us, two square spires rise several more stories into the sky.

The windows aren't clear glass but stained: At the top of a steeple, I can see a cross.

"This is the right place?" I ask doubtfully. "It looks like a church."

"It's a convent, actually. The nuns don't run the camp, but

they still live here. Why don't you go to the door? I'll tie the horses and then meet you."

I climb out of the wagon, straightening my dress and smoothing my hair. "Zofia?" Josef calls after me. I turn, and he gives me a faint smile. "I hope he's there. I really hope he's there."

I feel shy, somehow, going in the ornate main door, so I walk around the side until I find a smaller, plainer one marked OFFICE with a brass plaque. I knock twice, no answer, but as I'm raising my hand a third time, it swings open. I'm met by a woman in a black habit, a white veil covering her hair.

"Pardon me," I say to the nun. "I was looking for the director?"

"Unfortunately, you've missed her. I'm Sister Therese. Did you have an appointment?"

"No, but I can wait. Will she be back soon?"

She shakes her head, apologizing. "A family emergency. She'll be a few days at least."

There was a convent not far from my school growing up, and those nuns all seemed to be a hundred years old, wrinkled as raisins. But I can see a lock of curly brown hair escaping from the corner of Sister Therese's habit. Her cheeks are full, and on the shoes peeking out of the bottom of her habit, her shoelaces, impossibly, are untied.

"Maybe you can help me," I try. "I'm looking for—"

Before I can finish my sentence, though, I'm interrupted by a knock. I look around, confused as to how there can be a knock at the door when I'm still standing in the doorway myself. But then I realize there's another door behind Sister Therese in the back of the office, which must lead to the interior of the convent.

She beckons me inside and points to a chair. "Just a moment," she calls toward the other entrance. The handle is already turning; I hear muffled giggling on the other side. Sister Therese sighs as she undoes the latch. "They all know when I'm in charge, and that I'm a soft touch. All right, you noisemakers. What do you want?"

The door flies open. Two boys, gangly twelve- or thirteen-year-olds, burst inside, and suddenly I'm struck mute.

They're not Abek. They're so clearly not Abek. Neither one looks a bit like him; their colorings are wrong. *Not Abek*, I tell myself immediately. But they could so easily have been.

"Sister," the one in front says, the one with a dense moss of hair hanging low on his forehead. "Sorry, Sister, we didn't know you had company. Frau Fischer keeps a bottle opener in her desk, and we came to borrow it."

"Which drawer?"

"The top one."

Sister Therese opens the drawer, rustling through pen cartridges and paper clips before she produces a small metal opener. Only as she's handing it to the boy does she hesitate. "What's this for, Lemuel?"

The boys exchange a conspiratorial glance, and then the silent one produces a bottle from his pocket. It's curved glass and filled with a dark-colored liquid that appears to be fizzing.

"It's called a Coca-Cola," he explains. "One of the American soldiers gave it to us. You can drink one sip, and your thirst is quenched all day."

"Did he give it to you like the soldier gave you the comic books, or did he give it to you like the soldier gave you his watch?"

"Like the comic books," Lemuel says. "I promise, we weren't gambling."

"How much alcohol is in it?"

"There's no alcohol at all."

Sister Therese uses the bottle opener to pop off the metal lid and sniffs the contents. When she's convinced the boys aren't lying, she hands the bottle back. "Share with your bunkmates. If there is any left after all your thirsts are quenched, bring some to me."

"Thank you, Sister!" Lemuel calls over his shoulder. "You're our favorite."

"And if the kickball game is still going in the cloisters, each team gets *one more* at-bat," she yells. "Then, dinner."

The boys leave, a tumble of energy, and then Sister Therese turns back to me. "I'm sorry. As you were saying? You're looking for something?"

I can't find my words, though. I'm still staring after the two boys. Could one of their bunkmates be Abek? Is he waiting, just behind the door or just down the hall, to try a sip of the Coca-Cola? A stupid, stupid hope grows in my chest.

The door opens again, and this time it *is* the one I came through, this time it's Josef, cap in his hand, looking at me without even exchanging pleasantries.

"Is he here?"

"Is who here?" Sister Therese asks, looking between us.

"Her br—"

"No, he's not here," I interrupt quickly, hoping Sister Therese doesn't notice that my voice is unnaturally loud, but hoping Josef does. "And it's a 'she.' The director is a woman, but we've missed her; she's not here today." I turn back to Sister Therese and prattle on. "Josef and I are from Foehrenwald. He was hoping to talk to Frau Fischer about trading supplies."

Josef's eyes are on me, confused. I look away because I can't quite explain myself. I know what I'm doing doesn't make any sense.

All I know is that this place, with its kickball games in the cloisters and red-cheeked boys who run in to ask for help opening bottles of Coca-Cola, I *want* my brother to be here. But if he's not, I'd rather have twenty more minutes of hoping.

"I'm sorry you missed Frau Fischer," Sister Therese says worriedly. "She didn't tell me anyone was coming. I can put you in touch with the man who runs our storeroom; he should be able to tell you what we can spare."

"That's fine," Josef says slowly, still trying to figure out what I'm doing.

"And if you like, you can stay for dinner. I was just about to go help with preparations."

"Of course," I say. "We'd like to stay and—and see the whole camp. All the children."

Sister Therese leads us through the back door, and while

she's busying herself locking up the office, Josef pulls me to the side and raises both of his eyebrows.

"It just wasn't the right time to tell her yet," I whisper. "I just didn't want to—"

"Here, let's cut through the cloisters," Sister Therese says, finishing up with the lock, sliding the keys into a hidden pocket.

The hallway we're in is lined with low, arched doorways. She chooses one, heavy and oak, and before she even opens its door, I hear cheering on the other side; the tail end of the kickball game. And not just kickball. The whole cloisters are alive with children. Three girls with braids have scratched a chalk hopscotch game onto the pavement; two older boys toss a ball between them. My breath catches at the sight.

Abek isn't in this group, either. I scan them all as soon as we walk through the door; it's the first thing I do, without even thinking about it. None of the children look like him.

But when is the last time I have seen so many happy children? Was the last time five years ago, before we started whispering stories to one another about Auschwitz? Was it before the Nazis closed the schools to Jewish children, so we were forced to hold classes in our apartments, small groups sitting at a kitchen table, learning in secret? Was it before the war started at all?

"How many are there?" I whisper. "Where have they all come from?"

"About three hundred are here right now." Sister Therese

looks on approvingly over the group. "It changes every day, though. Parents come, or we receive telegrams. Or new children arrive. A nine-year-old, just yesterday. We don't see many in that age range. He'd been traveling with the British Army. They adopted him, I suppose you could say, as a sort of mascot, but eventually they realized that was no life for a child."

"Nine years old," I repeat. "So most of the children are—"

"Most of the children who come here from the camps are between twelve and seventeen," she says. "The younger ones..." she trails off, but I don't need her to finish the sentence. Anyone younger would have almost no chance of being left alive in a camp.

"Do you have many twelve-year-olds?" That's how old Abek is, right on the brink.

"At least twenty. The stories of how they survived are miraculous." Sister Therese closes her eyes and raises her rosary to her lips. I'm jarred by this act of public devotion, a reminder that some people went through the war able to believe God was still watching over the world.

Then Sister Therese opens her eyes and briskly claps her hands. The yard games don't stop, but most of the children at least look up at the sound. "This is *really* the final at-bat for kickball. Does everybody hear me? Supper is in fifteen minutes."

The dining hall is much smaller than Foehrenwald's, lined not with the round tables we have but with long rectangles, benches on either side, in a room where the windows are stained glass. As we walk in, a few children set the places with flatware, and adult women help them, most not in habits but in regular street clothes. From the kitchen, more volunteers appear, carrying vats of what smells like stew.

"Place of honor." Sister Therese shows Josef and me to seats at a table near the front of the hall. "But your plates will be just as chipped as everyone else's, I'm afraid."

I take the spot facing the door so I can watch everyone as they arrive. A girl with freckles. *Not him.* A boy with a limp. *Not him.* A boy on crutches, missing a leg. *Not him,* I think with relief, because I can't bear the thought of Abek suffering enough to lose a limb. But then I think, of course my brother missing a leg, a foot, an arm would be a welcome sight to come through the door, of course we could work through that suffering. The children come in a stream first and then scattered clumps and then one solitary figure at a time, rushing in, late, wedging themselves between friends.

*Not him. Not him. Not him.*

"How long did the trip take you?" Sister Therese, presiding over the head of the table, passes me a basket of rolls.

"Most of the day, but we stopped to eat," I say, distracted. *Not him.*

He's not here. I know that for sure when the doorway has stayed empty for a full minute and the tables are full, when my ears are ringing from the clatter of spoons. "This is everyone?"

"There are two girls in the infirmary. Their meals will be served there."

"Other than those two girls—nobody else is sick or traveling with Frau Fischer?"

"Just the two girls. Otherwise, yes, this is everyone."

I blink back the tears welling behind my eyes. Why did I let myself get hopeful? How could I imagine I could wake up this morning and pluck my brother out of a sea of orphans?

"You should eat your stew before it gets cold." Sister Therese's voice snaps me back to the dining hall. "It's tolerable when it's warm and not so much after that."

I pick up my spoon and dip it into the greasy brown liquid.

Across from me at the table sits one of the smaller boys. He can't be more than ten or eleven, with pointy ears and sharp features.

He's not bothering with a spoon. He's using his fingers to scoop bits of stew directly onto his bread. His elbows hunch around his plate, making a protective barrier to guard his food. Two bread rolls are piled next to his plate already, but when he thinks nobody else is looking, he reaches to the communal basket in the middle of the table and grabs another, tucking it up his sleeve. When he catches me looking, he stares me down.

His body is too small. It should be taller, or fatter. His eyes shouldn't have to be so old. He shouldn't have to be here. He shouldn't have to eat like an animal.

I have eaten like this. I have sat in a circle of half-starved people and known I would fight someone who tried to take what I had.

Sister Therese notices the boy across from me, too. I wonder if he'll be punished or told he must finish what's on his plate before taking more. Instead, she gently slides the basket closer. "Have another," she says. "But try the soup with a spoon? We have important guests!"

The small kindness does me in. As if it could possibly be enough. As if there are enough tender gestures in the world to make up for the brutalities these children have suffered.

A sound escapes from my throat, wet and feral and anguished. I shouldn't cry here at the table, but I don't know if I can hold it in, either. I force bread into my mouth, but I can't swallow it. It just builds stickily in the back of my throat.

A few meters down, I hear a clatter: Another boy has accidentally upended his bowl of soup. The spoon skitters onto the floor, and his face melts in apology and sadness.

"No matter," Sister Therese says cheerfully. "Happens at least once a meal." She turns to me. "Zofia, as you're our guest, could I give you the honored role of taking care of Simon?"

"Take care?" I mumble.

"Help him get cleaned up," she elaborates, mimicking a gesture of washing. "Be in charge of looking after him. The washroom is down the hall."

Simon slides off the bench and comes over, expectantly. He holds out his hand. And I freeze.

My hand won't move, and my legs won't, either. They're shaking. My underarms flood with sweat. "I can't," I whisper.

"Pardon?" Sister Therese says, distracted.

*Take his hand*, I instruct myself. *Take him to the washroom; this isn't difficult.*

"I can't look after him," I say louder, more desperately.

And I can't explain the violent dread rising in my belly at this request, only that I know I can't. I can't be in charge of taking this small boy to the washroom. I can't be in charge of this boy, I can't take him to the washroom, I can't help him get cleaned up, because I can't take him to the washroom because I can't be in charge of this boy.

"Let me." Josef, his hand steady on my knee under the table, understanding something's gone wrong. "Simon's *definitely* too grown-up to want help from a *girl*. Isn't that right?"

"Right," the boy named Simon says uncertainly, not sure why he's been passed off.

"Off we go. Let's rinse this sweater, and you can show me where there's something dry."

After dinner, I sit mutely while the plates are cleared away, and while an older man appears to say he's in charge of managing the supplies. "Good news," Josef says, including me in the conversation. "They'll give fifty blankets."

"That's wonderful," I manage.

"Ernst can help carry them to your wagon," Sister Therese offers.

"They were just asking if we needed anything else before we left," Josef interjects. "Do we need anything else?" His question is pointed and, I think, a little baffled. *This is your last chance*, he seems to be saying. *Why haven't you asked about your brother?*

"Some food," Sister Therese decides. "While Ernst and Josef pack up the blankets, let's go see if the kitchen can spare some leftovers for you to take with you."

"I don't want to take from you. The food should be for the children."

"I'm at least going to pack you a few apples and a thermos of water. Unless I can find Lemuel's bottle of Coca-Cola?" She winks mischievously. "I wanted to try some. Didn't you?"

Josef has gone now, following Ernst to where the blankets are kept. I know he was right. This is the last chance I'll have to ask about my brother. Sister Therese turns toward the kitchen. I run after her and grab the coarse sleeve of her habit. "Please."

"Yes?" She looks perplexed.

"I'm looking for my brother. I haven't seen him in more than three years."

"Oh, my dear." She reaches for my hand, and her fingers feel surprisingly strong. "I hope you're reunited with him soon. I'll add him to my prayers, if that's all right with you."

"No. I mean, yes, if you'd like. But what I was trying to say—he's twelve, the same age as some of the children here. I think he was in Dachau. The same as some of the children here."

Understanding washes over her face. "Oh. *Oh.* You didn't come all this way here looking for him, did you? Is that why you were asking whether any were missing tonight?"

"He wasn't at dinner. But I was thinking, maybe he could still come here later," I say. "It sounds like you still have arrivals?"

"We do. Every day. Some children who come here, this is the second or third stop for them."

"Or maybe one of the children coming from somewhere else has met him already," I suggest. "And they'll remember him."

"Do you want to give me his name and a physical description?" Sister Therese asks. "I can post a 'missing' report on our bulletin board. Someone who crossed paths with him might see it."

We change directions now, not to the kitchen but back to the office, where Sister Therese opens the same drawer that had the bottle opener. She smooths a sheet of creamy stationery onto the desk, dating it at the top. "Start with what he looks like. Close your eyes if it helps," she offers. "Sometimes it does."

When I close my eyes, I can see Abek's face better than my own, but in a way that's hard to put together in useful words. *Fat cheeks?* He had them before; he couldn't possibly now. *A loose tooth?* It would have fallen out long ago. His hair might have been cut; his bruises might have healed or multiplied. I could tell Sister Therese that he was as tall as the armoire on the wall where my parents used to measure our height, but he would have grown.

"He has—" I start uncertainly. "He has brown eyes. Hazel, actually, the irises have some green. His hair is wavy. One of his eyebrows might be split down the middle. Just before we were taken, he had a wooden sword fight with another boy; we wondered if it was going to leave a scar.

"He would only be looking for me, Zofia," I continue. "Our parents are dead, and he knows it; they were sent to the

gas chambers as soon as we arrived in Birkenau from Sosnowiec." I go on and on, but at some point Sister Therese stops
moving her pencil. It doesn't even look like she's listening; she
has an odd expression on her face, somewhere between trepidation and annoyance.

"What is it?"

"Is this a prank?" she asks. "Because if it is, it's not very
funny."

"WHAT DO YOU MEAN?" I ask Sister Therese. "A prank?"

"Did Lemuel or one of the other boys put you up to this?"

"Lemuel or—of course not."

"That would be cruel, waiting until Frau Fischer is gone and pulling a trick."

"Sister Therese," I say frantically. "I promise you, I have no idea what you're talking about, and this isn't a joke."

Now the expression on her face has turned from irritation to something different—concern and worry. "You said Sosnowiec? All the way in Poland?"

"Yes."

"We did have someone here."

"*Someone?* Was his name Abek?"

She presses her lips together. "I don't remember his name. I remember the town, and I remember a boy who had been in

Birkenau. At that point, most of the children here had come from Flossenbürg; the Red Cross brought a group. I noted every time someone came who wasn't from there."

"Didn't you make him sign in somewhere?"

"This was early. Months ago. We weren't making anyone sign in then; we were barely even an official camp. I'm not even sure if UNRRA had sent Frau Fischer yet."

"You didn't keep any records." I'm trying to keep my voice steady, but it's careening.

Sister Therese lifts up her hands, a gesture to calm me. "You have to understand. Children streamed in without shoes. We tried to give them shoes. They came in hungry, and we fed them. Some stayed, and some left. But I remember one boy—I remember his saying he was going to look for his sister. He didn't seem to think he had other family, but he said his sister might have survived Birkenau. That stuck out to me because, as I said, we hadn't seen many people who had been there. He said his family owned a factory in Lower Silesia. He stayed for only a few days."

"Was it a clothing factory? Was it named Chomicki and Lederman?"

"I don't think he said. I really don't remember. I just know that he wanted to find his sister, and he left when he found out we were taking in only children under seventeen, which made me think his sister was older than that."

"Was he healthy?" I ask desperately. "Did he look healthy?"

"He seemed so, yes," she says, and a deep sense of relief courses through me. "He was healthy. He was well."

"But you didn't—but you couldn't—"

"I couldn't force him to stay." Sister Therese's face is stricken. "Or to give me more information. Please believe me, Zofia, we were doing the best we could. There were just so many people passing through then."

"Then why do you remember him at all?" I press on, insistent. "If so many people passed through—you asked me if Lemuel was playing a joke on you because I asked about him. How can he be important enough that the boys would use him for a joke but *insignificant* enough that you don't even remember his name?"

She winces at my words. "None of the children are insignificant."

"But *this boy had a name.*"

"I remember him because . . . because we had an incident."

I lean back, startled. "What kind of incident?"

"It doesn't matter."

*"What incident?"*

She sighs. Her next words come out like she's dragging them. "He stole from me. All right?" Beneath her habit, she lowers her eyes.

"We were so short of beds then that I let him have my room," she says. "I kept the grocery money in my nightstand—the money we were using for all the children. When I went in the next morning to check on this boy, he was gone and so was the money. I remembered that boy because the rest of the children didn't have enough breakfast the next day, and everyone here knew why."

*He stole?* I feel a jolt of confusion and shame. Abek stole the grocery money from Sister Therese? "I see."

Sister Therese didn't want to have to tell me this part of the story. She reaches up to tuck a loose curl back under her habit, and she looks older than she has all afternoon. "I didn't blame him, of course. I knew what he must have been through, and he was only a child."

My heart is leaping and falling at the same time. I don't know what to make of her story. Was this starving boy Abek? This boy who came and left without a name and disappeared with only hungry mouths behind him? Did I lose my chance to find him because instead of looking when I should have been, I was lying in a hospital?

"We should still put up a notice," Sister Therese insists. "In case he comes back. Or someone else arrives who's met him."

"We should still put up a notice," I agree, but my voice is as hollow as a cave.

I start again with my descriptions, and Sister Therese dutifully writes them down. When I'm finished, the whole page is filled with her handwriting. She replaces the cap on the pen. "I really am sorry that I didn't—"

"It's fine. There's nothing to be done about it now."

She takes the paper, and we walk to the hallway where the bulletin board is. As Sister Therese promised, it's in a prominent location, just inside the main entrance, where almost every visitor would have to pass. But when I see it, my heart sinks even further. Not a square inch of the actual board is visible. It's all been papered over with flyers, layers and layers of them, with descriptions of other people's family members and other people's losses. Some of the pamphlets have pictures attached—how lucky for them to have pictures—and there are old, wrinkled grandparents, and smiling fiancés, and gap-toothed daughters.

Sister Therese tacks the description of Abek in a corner. It'll be papered over in a week.

"I can copy more," she offers. "And send them with the workers who visit different camps, to be pasted on bulletin boards there." She bites her lip. "I know you're frustrated, but this is good news, isn't it? If it was him, it means he was still healthy after the war. I saw him with my own two eyes."

I try to force a smile. "Can I see where he slept?"

"I promise you, he didn't leave anything. There won't be any clues."

"I'm not expecting any. It's just that"—*this sounds silly, but I don't care*—"it's just that in Birkenau, we slept in crowded bunks with no mattresses. I would like to think of him sleeping someplace warm."

"Of course."

She leads me up a narrow set of stairs, wooden and squeaking, to the wing where children are already asleep. At the second room, she lowers her voice to a whisper. "This was my room at the time; now we've given the space to the children."

She opens the door just wide enough for us to slip through, and I blink to adjust to the light. Four single beds line the walls. Plain, but the bedclothes look clean, and each has a spare blanket folded at the foot. It looks like a fine place to sleep. Warm and tidy. *Why wouldn't he stay and wait for me to find him? Or if he left, why wouldn't he come home, as I told him?*

In the dim shadows, I recognize the boy in the bed closest to the door. It's the little one from supper, the one who had been sneaking extra food. He sleeps with his knees tucked to his chin and his arms wrapped around them.

Quietly, so as not to disturb the sleeping boy, Sister Therese lifts up a corner of his quilt and shows me the mattress below. It's been sliced open, and inside, what at first look like rocks are actually lumps of bread.

"He's afraid there won't be more," she whispers. "They're always afraid there won't be more."

As Josef and I clear the town and drive down a dark road through its outskirts, the wooden bench seat digs into my bony buttocks in a vicious way that it didn't before; every rock sends a pain through my back and down my phantom toes.

"So do think it was him?" Josef says quietly after I've told him what happened. "The boy who came to the convent?"

"I don't know."

"It seems like good news, though."

When I don't respond, Josef turns to face me. "Good news, right? If it was him, you missed each other by only a few months. Or, do you *not* think it's him?" He cranes his head to try to look at me. "Zofia?"

"I don't want to talk about it," I say, unable to find the words to explain my complicated feelings.

*Do I think it was him?* He was a boy from Sosnowiec's region who had been through Birkenau and was looking for his sister. Could there have been many boys like that?

But...I can't picture Abek stealing money from people who needed it, people who had been kind to him.

*I stole Dima's money.* I stole money from someone who had been kind to me, because it was the only way I could think of to find my brother. It's the only circumstance in which I could imagine myself a thief. Was it the same for Abek? Is the theft actually the best sign that it *was* Abek?

I can't figure out how to articulate everything in my head. How my hope is eaten by guilt that I wasn't able to get there sooner. How hearing about someone who might have been Abek is not the same as finding Abek. How arriving a few months too late feels the same as never arriving at all.

The situation with my brother is not the kind of thing where there are compromises or half measures. Either it is Abek or it isn't. Either I've brought him home or I haven't.

"But if she saw someone who might be him a few months ago—you're being ridiculous," Josef insists, breaking my train of thought. "Do you have any idea how lucky some people would feel with that news?"

"I will feel *lucky*," I blurt out, "when the person riding next to me in the wagon is my brother and not you."

It was a rude thing to say, but I'm so exhausted and so confused. And most of all, I feel I'm owed a rude thing to say after the things Josef said earlier. When I see him wince at the insult, I almost apologize. But I don't want to open up the conversation again, and I would rather him be hurt if it makes him stay quiet.

Neither of us say another word. He drives, and I sit like a statue; the road is long and empty. The only sound is the two horses clopping over the dirt. When, after an hour, it becomes too dark to see the road in front of us, Josef pulls up to a house where a light still burns in the window.

"I think we should stop for the night," he says, and I don't protest. "I'm going to go in and see if they know of a place to sleep nearby."

Josef leaves me with the wagon. Feather whinnies softly in the dark until he returns a few minutes later. "We can stay here, in exchange for helping out with chores tomorrow," he says. "You'll sleep in with their daughter. I'm in the barn."

Josef takes my valise, still stuffed with all the belongings I packed this morning, when I hopefully thought I might not return to Foehrenwald at all. Before he carries it to the door, Josef turns back and opens his mouth like he wants to say something. He doesn't, though, and neither do I.

The couple waiting by the lamplight is older, the man white-bearded and the woman with a gentle slope in her back. We've caught them as they were heading to bed; the woman— Frau Wölflin, she introduces herself—is already wearing her nightgown, her graying hair trailing down her back in a loose braid. They don't seem to mind that we've shown up nearly in the middle of the night. Frau Wölflin says they leave the lamp on just for that reason. They need help with the farm, and they feed and bunk travelers in exchange for assistance. She hands a stack of blankets to Josef, and while her husband takes him out to the barn, she pours me a glass of milk. I hold it and try to respond to her polite questions about how far we've traveled and the conditions of the road.

"It has been a long day for you?" she says.

"It's been a long day, Baba R——" I start and then stop, humiliated. I almost called this woman my grandmother's name. It's not even as it was with Gosia. I have no excuse; I barely know this woman. I'm just so exhausted.

Frau Wölflin doesn't notice the slipup. Or if she does, at least she doesn't say anything. "I mean, it has been a long day," I correct myself. "Thank you for asking."

"You don't need to drink that." She nods at the untouched glass of milk on my lap. "If you're tired, you can go straight to bed."

"I don't mean to be rude, but perhaps I will. We were riding for a long while."

I don't know what I was expecting when Josef said I could sleep in their daughter's room. But by the age of the Wölflins, I think I believed the girl would be my age or older. Instead, when I follow Frau Wölflin up the narrow staircase and wait as she whispers in her daughter's ear—*Hannelore, we have a guest; Zofia is staying with you tonight*—the blond pigtailed head that stirs beneath the duvet belongs to a child, not more than eight or nine.

"Don't worry." Frau Wölflin smiles. "Lore is used to this being something of a boardinghouse. She won't be startled to see you in the morning."

When Frau Wölflin leaves, I slip off my shoes but realize too late that I left my overnight valise downstairs. Rather than fumble my way down in the dark, I loosen the tie in the back of my dress and then climb into bed fully clothed, easing part of the goose-feather duvet aside and slipping in as quietly as I can.

I'm tired for so many reasons that it's hard to untangle them. I'm exhausted by hope. I'm exhausted by the fact that I woke so early this morning. I'm exhausted by this country. I'm exhausted by my own body, sometimes, which feels like it might not ever be as strong or resilient as it once was.

I'm exhausted by my own mind. That might be the most exhausting thing. My own mind, thinking a farmwife is my grandmother, and not letting me know what I should believe. If I could stop being at war with my own mind. Tame the monster. Stop my dreams.

IN THE MORNING, HANNELORE HAS WOKEN BEFORE ME. Everyone must have. I hear noises in the kitchen downstairs and smell porridge. Peeking out the warped-glass window, I see two figures, Josef and Mr. Wölflin, mending a fence; the sun is far above the horizon.

Hurriedly, I stuff my feet into my shoes, kicked under the bed last night, and rush downstairs. Frau Wölflin is clearing the plates from everyone else's breakfast; her long braid from last night now neatly pinned in a crown around her head.

"I don't know how I slept so long," I apologize, reaching for the stack piled on the rough-hewn wooden table. "I know Josef promised we'd help with chores."

Frau Wölflin waves my hand away, nodding toward a bowl in the middle of the table, resting on a rag place mat. "I saved you a few boiled eggs. When you finish eating, grab an apron and go outside to help with the washing? Hannelore has been excited for you to come down."

As if on cue, the door swings open, and Hannelore walks in, her own hair braided to match her mother's, a smattering of freckles across her nose. "Are you finally awake?" she asks accusatorily. "I had to take my clothes and dress in the *kitchen* so I didn't wake you up."

"I'm so sorry." I try to keep a straight face while apologizing for this crime, but her tiny voice is so indignant it's hard to keep from laughing.

"It's all right. You're up now," she acquiesces. "I'm allowed to show you how the spigot works outside, and if there's time later before you have to leave, I'm allowed to show you my dolls."

"You have quite the plan for visitors."

"We get a lot of them," she sighs. "For a long time, we didn't get any, but now we always have them."

"Why didn't you get any visitors before?"

It's Frau Wölflin who answers, walking over to stroke her daughter's hair. "During the war," she explains. "We tried not to have visitors during the war."

I sense there's meaning in that sentence, but I'm not sure what. What were they afraid of during the war? Looters, or Jews looking for protection. It had to be one of the two.

"Are you coming?" Hannelore's tiny hands are on her hips.

I can see she plans to monitor my whole breakfast, so I decide to abandon it, finding an apron in the cupboard Frau

Wölflin pointed me to and tucking the boiled eggs into the pocket.

Outside in the light, the Wölflins' land is scraggly and wild-looking. A vegetable garden out front needs weeding; a shutter needs to be repaired. It's no wonder they're happy to have boarders; this property is too much for an older couple.

Hannelore shows me how we'll fill a wash pan with water from the outdoor spigot. How one pan will be for dishes and the other for clothes, and how we'll save the leftover water for watering the garden later.

"Your friend Josef said you're from a city," she explains. "I didn't know if you'd know how to use a water pump outdoors."

"I am from a city, originally," I tell her. "But for a long time I lived…somewhere else. We only had an outdoor pump there. Sometimes we didn't even have that."

"Did the water in the pump freeze over? That happens here in the winter."

"Something like that. Are you going to school today?" I ask, changing the subject.

"I learn at home. Stiefmutter didn't like me to be out by myself while soldiers were around. Maybe I'll get to go now." *Stiefmutter*—stepmother. That would explain how Frau Wölflin can look so old but have a child as young as Hannelore.

"That will be nice. I liked school when I was your age."

The kitchen door swings open, and Frau Wölflin comes out, heading to the edge of the property where Josef helps Herr Wölflin repair the fence. As I watch, Josef heaves his shoulder against a rotted post, leaning into the wood, digging his feet into the ground. The front of his shirt—his grayed, faintly bloodstained shirt with a still-ripped pocket—is now damp with perspiration; his dark curls stick to his forehead.

I should apologize for being short with him last night. I should also stop looking at him now. I can't bring myself to do either.

Frau Wölflin finishes checking on the fence progress and comes over to Hannelore and me, dropping an absentminded kiss on the top of Hannelore's head. "Take him water soon," she instructs, nodding back toward her husband. "He's not as young as he thinks he is."

This is a family. It's not what my family looked like. But it's a family nonetheless; no wonder I wanted to call Frau Wölflin Baba Rose. I realize, watching her worry over her family, that I'll never again have someone worrying over me. Even if I find Abek, I'll always be the one doing the looking after.

I look down, trying to focus on cleaning the plates in front of me. When we finish the washing, and after we wipe the dishes dry and pin the dresses on a clothesline, Hannelore grabs my hand.

"They're still doing the fence; there's enough time!" she exclaims. "I can still show you my dolls, and we can draw pictures."

Across the yard, Josef sees us heading back toward the house. He raises his eyebrows, asking if I'm okay, and I wave that I am. But then he points to his wrist, as if he were wearing a wristwatch, though he isn't, to say we shouldn't stay much longer. Everyone at Foehrenwald is waiting for supplies.

Back upstairs, in the bedroom with sawdust floors and wooden beams across the ceiling, I sit where Hannelore directs me and obediently take the doll she hands me. The scene she wants to enact is a schoolhouse, her playing teacher to the dolls' students. Some of the details she makes up are funny, but she gets a lot of it right. Frau Wölflin must have been trying to prepare her for school.

After she's made all the students sing a song and take an exam, and I've run a pretend spelling bee, Hannelore says it's time to put the dolls away and asks if I'd like to draw pictures.

"I don't think I have time," I tell her regretfully. "My friend said we needed to leave soon. But thank you for spending the morning with me."

She purses her lips. "I can still give you a picture. I drew one of you while you were sleeping."

I smile. "You little spy!"

"I wasn't drawing it while I was *watching* you. I drew it while we were eating breakfast. I couldn't get your face right because it was hidden by the pillow, but Josef said it's okay."

"Well, I would love to see it."

She fetches the sheet of paper from the top of her bureau and hands it to me, picking up a doll to change its clothes while I admire the drawing. It's a group of people, standing in front of what I recognize is the farmhouse we're staying in.

"It's a lovely picture. Tell me about it. This is you?" I point to the smallest figure. "And this is me and Josef, and these two on the other side must be your parents."

"Stiefmutter and Stiefvater," she says.

"Silly," I say. "They can't both be your stepparents."

"They are."

I shake my head, certain she's just misunderstood the term. "Is your mother married to your stepfather, or is your father married to your stepmother?"

She looks back down at her doll, rebuttoning a pinafore over the dress. "Mommy's not here. She said she would be back for me later."

"Where is your mommy now?"

Hannelore adjusts the pinafore again, longer than she needs to, and suddenly she looks much older than eight. "I don't know where she is. She hasn't come back yet. I couldn't talk about her before, but Stiefmutter says now I am allowed to because the Nazis lost."

I swallow hard. "Did your mother leave you because it was safer? Is that what she said?"

"Yes. She didn't want anyone to take me. And I have light hair, so I'd be easy to hide."

*Is this what we should have done with Abek?* Beg a childless couple to keep him safe? If we'd done that, would I have been able to knock on their door now and find him in a cozy attic bedroom decorated with his drawings?

"I have a photograph," Hannelore says. She's gone back to the bureau, opening up the bottom drawer and taking out a box. From it she removes a book, and she's now riffling through the pages, pulling out photographs hidden between them. "I don't remember her very well, but she was so pretty I think she could have been a film star. Don't you?"

She hands me the photograph. "She's very beautiful," I agree, looking at the young woman with big eyes.

"Her name is Inge. Isn't that a pretty name?"

My voice cracks. "Very pretty." I suddenly don't want to hold the photograph anymore, hastily handing it back to Hannelore, only vaguely aware that I might be scaring a little girl.

"Hannelore, it's been very nice playing with you, but I should probably go."

"Nobody said we had to stop."

"I know, but—my friend, he wanted to start early, and we have a long trip!"

I'm on my feet, moving quickly toward the door, down the stairs, grabbing my bag from the foot of the stairs, where I'd never retrieved it from last night. Outside, Frau and Herr Wölflin admire the fence, now completed and straight, and Josef is rinsing his face off in the spigot.

Hannelore's mother, Inge, was beautiful enough to be a film star. But when I looked at that photograph, I could think only of another woman named Inge, a nothing-girl from the hospital who wasn't beautiful. Who was covered in scabs, and whose teeth and hair had mostly fallen out.

*It's not the same person*, I tell myself. *You know it's not; the stories don't match up.*

But so much of it does match up; so many of our stories are the same. The Inge I knew talked about her daughter, living with a kind German couple. She sat on the windowsill of the hospital and sang songs into the night sky, and then one night, in a way that looked like a graceful lean, in a way that almost looked like an accident, she leaned farther out until she tipped through the windowsill.

Her real name was Inge, but we all called her Bissel. *Bissel.* "A little bit," in Yiddish. Because of the time one of the nurses had tried to tell us none of us were crazy, but then she looked at Bissel and said, "Her, maybe. A little bit. She is maybe a little bit crazy."

I'M READY TO GO," I TELL JOSEF. HE RISES FROM THE SPIGOT, using a faded cloth to dry his hair. When he looks at me, he can sense something is wrong.

"I'll just go get our bags," he says.

"I already have them." I point to where I've set them by the wagon.

"We can't leave without saying goodbye to the Wölflins."

"You do it. I'll wait here."

I spent the ride yesterday trying to convince Josef I wasn't crazy, and now I'm undoing it with every sentence, with my abruptness, and with the off-kilter way I climb onto the wagon without waiting for a hand.

Josef is polite enough for both of us. He goes back inside to offer our thanks to the Wölflin family, telling them—I don't know what he's telling them. That I feel sick, or we're late, or I'm unspeakably rude. They make gestures that I can see are offers: *Do you have to leave so soon? Can we send you away with anything?* And Josef refusing, *No, thank you. We'll be fine, but how kind of you to ask.*

Back in the wagon, the horses hooked up and plodding, I watch the little white farmhouse recede until it looks like a postcard. Josef lets it disappear from the horizon before he turns to me. "Did something happen?"

"Everything," I choke out.

"Everything?"

"Everything happened," I say again, because right now that seems the best way to describe it. Sister Therese, and a mystery boy stealing money from a convent, and Inge falling out the window, and another Inge leaving her daughter, and Hannelore showing me a photo, and the similarities of their stories, of everyone's stories. All of it is cumulative.

"Zofia, I already said yesterday that I don't think you're crazy. So do you want to explain more?"

I twist the handle of my valise. The clasp seems even more broken than when I picked it up. "That girl. Hannelore. She's not the Wölflins' real daughter. She was in hiding."

Josef looks surprised that's what's on my mind. "I know. Herr Wölflin told me. Her mother was the daughter of good friends of theirs, the couple who used to own the feedstore. They were taken."

"Inge," I say. "Inge is dead." Just then, the wagon goes over a rock, so the word comes out as a stab. *Dead.*

"Zofia." He jerks the horses to a stop. "What are you saying? Did you know that girl's mother?"

"No. I don't know. I don't think so. I knew an Inge, but we called her Bissel."

I tell Josef, in messy fits and starts. I tell him how I barely knew Bissel at all, that none of us really did, except that she slept in a bed next to me for two months and talked all the time about her daughter, whom she was going to find when the war was over. But she didn't. Instead, she sat on the windowsill and leaned backward.

"And her daughter is *waiting*," I say. "Bissel's daughter is waiting somewhere like Hannelore is, thinking she'll come home for her. But she'll never come home. She'll keep waiting, but Bissel will never come home, and I know that, and she doesn't."

"Hannelore's mother isn't coming home, either," Josef says. "Hannelore might still believe her mother is coming to find her, but the Wölflins know better. Herr Wölflin told me; they're writing letters, but they already assume she's dead."

"They assume, but they don't know," I say. "And that's the worst of all. The worst possible thing."

"The not knowing?"

My mind is spinning. "Suppose you could learn the answer to a mystery you wanted solved. But of all possible terrible answers you'd imagined, this one was even worse. Would you still want to know?"

"Zofia, I'm not following," Josef says, confused but not impatient. "Hannelore's mother, Inge, reminds you of another woman named Inge, and both of them left their daughters with families who don't know what happened to them? What are you asking?"

*What am I asking?*

I am asking: If my options were never being able to find my brother, or knowing for sure that something terrible had happened to him, which would I choose? What's the line between the amount of information that brings hope and the amount that brings despair?

Do you choose the comfort of fantasy? Or do you choose real pain?

No. That's not what I'm asking. That's not what I've ever been asking.

Since the moment I woke up in the hospital, since the moment the war ended and I began trying to piece my brain back together, I have really been asking only one question.

"Josef." My voice is barely above a whisper. "What if my brother is dead?"

I've said it. The thing I've never allowed myself to say or allowed anyone else to say, either. That is the question I want answered.

I saw hundreds of people die. Shot. Hanged. Starved. Beaten. Broken.

I came here today chasing hope and coincidences. *The boy in the records from Dachau whose name looked like Alek Federman. The boy who came to Sister Therese.* What if none of the coincidences go anywhere because my brother is dead?

The reins twitch in Josef's hand. I wait for him to assure me Abek is not dead. I wait for him to tell me again that I've received a promising lead from Sister Therese and that I should hold on to it.

Indulgent optimism is the gift that every person I've met has given me. Gosia. Dima. The nurses. They all told me that it could take a long time, but I shouldn't give up hope. Or they patted my arm and found a way to avert their eyes. Or they wrote to Bergen-Belsen and didn't tell me when they received a response. They all found any number of ways to deal with me. With my frailty, with my pain, with my stubborn hope.

Josef stares at me. His pebbly eyes have never looked so deep or so clear. "What if he *is* dead?" He drops the reins now and leans forward heavily, elbows on knees.

"What if he is, Zofia? Do you think you could find a way to live the rest of your life?"

I wait to be angry at him for saying this. I want rage to unfurl in my chest and form a protective shell around my heart.

Do I think I could live the rest of my life if Abek were dead?

But instead of hot anger, I feel a chilling sort of calm.

*What if?* What if that's true? What if the thing I've been guarding against actually happened? And what if, instead of using all my soul worrying about it, I had to devote my soul to living with it?

Could I do that? Is there any way I could do that?

Lost in thought, I'm only vaguely aware that Josef isn't looking at me anymore. He's staring off toward the horizon, lost in something of his own.

"I have a sister who died," Josef says quietly. "Before the war. A long time ago. She was ten, and she was sick first."

He deflates a little when he says this. He deflates like a

balloon, and the sentence comes out raw like he's unpracticed at delivering it. "I know it's not the same; it's not the same kind of thing," he continues. "But it means I know what grief can look like when it has a chance to get old. My family had a long time to figure out what life would look like without her. How to do it."

"How did you do it?"

"Badly," he says, grimacing. "It wrecked my parents. It turned them into different people. Klara held the family together in ways we didn't realize at the time."

"What was your sister like? Klara?"

He draws his breath in sharply. "She was funny. Stubborn. Like, one day when she was about eight, she was mad at me for not letting her play with my friends, so she filed down the heel of my shoe. Only the left one. A little every day, for a week. I thought I was going crazy. Or maybe that I had some wasting illness because one of my legs was shorter than the other. I don't think many eight-year-olds have that kind of patience or that kind of, I don't know, *deviousness*."

"You were close?"

He shakes his head. "We weren't, really. I thought she was immature. But I guess I also assumed we'd become better friends when we were both older. Instead, she got sick."

"Oh, Josef. I'm sorry."

Without thinking, I rest my hand on his forearm. He looks down, and he doesn't pull it away. He leans into it. Almost imperceptibly, but he does. I can feel the tendons and muscles of his forearm ripple beneath his sleeve as he starts the horses up again. Slowly, he transfers both of the reins into his left hand, resting his right one open on his lap, palm up. Slowly, I slide my own hand down his arm and lace my fingers between his. This exchange takes forever, whole minutes. Only when he lets out a little breath am I sure that this is what he was hoping I'd do, and only when he gratefully curls his fingers around mine, like they're starving, like I am safety, do I realize he was afraid I wouldn't. His fingers are cooler than mine, and they feel solid and real.

"Josef," I say quietly. "What if my brother is dead—but *what if he's not*? I'm not ready to give up yet. Do you think that's stupid?"

He sighs. "I don't know. I'm not the right person to ask about stupid things. I start fights with people bigger than me, remember?"

"I get on trains and cross countries," I say.

"That's not stupid. That's brave."

The word choice surprises me; it's not one I'd choose to describe myself. The things I've done I haven't done out of braveness. I've done them out of necessity.

"I think I'm just doing what anyone would do to find their family," I say. "Wouldn't you, if your sister were alive? Or your parents. If they were."

His hand twitches in mine, and he shifts awkwardly. "I think they *are* still alive."

I gape at him. "Really?"

"As far as I know. I think so. But we can talk about something else."

He sets his face in a mask, the same kind of evasiveness from when I offered to repair his shirt. A closed-offness.

This revelation about his parents is unfathomable to me. How could you have living family and not be doing what I'm doing or what Miriam is doing, dedicating as many waking hours as possible to finding them?

"You're looking for them, though, right?" I ask. "You're still looking for them? Josef?"

Instead of answering, Josef coughs and abruptly releases my hand to cover his mouth. It sounds forced, though, high in his chest. When he finishes, he takes the reins in both hands again and shifts away. There's a gap of cool air now against my thigh.

"I didn't mean to pry," I try. "I just wondered about your parents."

"That's not it," he insists. "It's just that it's late. We were at the Wölflins' longer than I think we meant to be. I think I should focus on the horses."

"Oh. All right."

Nothing he says is rude or even impolite, but it's distant, a voice that could be measured in kilometers. I don't know what I've said or done, but I've become a stranger to him again.

It's late evening when we get back to Foehrenwald; most of the cottages are already dark. We pass a few vehicles, khaki-colored, official-looking ones, parked in a cluster by the camp entrance. They weren't there when we left; they must be the broken ones, now repaired, that Mrs. Yost mentioned earlier.

Leaving Josef at the stables, I walk back to my cottage. When I get close enough, I see it's one of the few that's still bright, with the glow of a lantern coming from the curtains of my bedroom. I hesitate, debating whether to wait outside until the lights have gone out. I'd rather not talk to anyone right now; I'd rather just fall into my bed, curl my knees to my chest, and sleep.

I tiptoe through the front room where Judith and Miriam are sleeping, hoping that the light in our room is on by accident. Or maybe Breine and Esther just left it on so I wouldn't have to fumble when I returned. But when I put my hand on the knob, I hear the scrape of wood and then a shriek of laughter—my roommates are unmistakably awake inside.

Opening the door, I blink a few times at the sight before me: Breine in her wedding dress, standing on a chair so she's tall enough to see her full length in the one mirror on the wall. Esther, standing behind her on Breine's bed, holding up a handkerchief meant to mimic a headpiece. Both are laughing hysterically.

"It's—it's so hideous," Breine chokes out, wiping a tear from her eye.

"Shhhhhh."

"It's so hideous," Breine whispers this time, and she grabs the handkerchief-veil to toss playfully at Esther's head.

The dress fits Breine about as well as I'd thought it would, which is to say, not at all. The darting in the bodice that should define her breasts stops not at her nipples, but halfway down her midsection, sticking out obscenely around her waist. The neckline is too high, the waist is too low, and the hemline cuts at the most unflattering part of her calves.

"It's not that bad," Esther says loyally, grabbing a fistful of fabric from the back, pulling it to one side, then another, unsuccessfully trying to find a more flattering cut. "You're beautiful."

"It's—why did I ever think I could get married in this?"

"You still can," Esther starts optimistically but falters when Breine gives her a look. "Oh, Breine. Why didn't you try the dress on when you first found it?"

"I didn't think it mattered. I kept telling myself anything that didn't smell like manure would be fine."

As I close the door behind me, Breine and Esther notice my presence.

"Oh, Zofia, come and witness the horror of this," Breine encourages. But as she beckons me in, a string of beading comes loose, flies off the sleeve, and drapes itself over the lantern. Esther's and Breine's eyes lock in the mirror. Esther maintains a dignified expression for approximately two seconds, then the sound of beads clanking against the lantern glass makes them helpless again with laughter.

"Come on, step down." Esther extends her hand. "Let's get this dress off before it murders someone."

"Let's get this dress off me and murder *it*," Breine agrees.

"Wait!" They both look up at me and freeze in an awkward tableau, Breine halfway off the chair. "Do you mind if I take a look?" I ask quietly.

"At the dress? I don't mind if you take it and burn it."

"Could you step back on the chair, please?"

Breine exchanges a look with Esther. They think my request is odd, but Breine obediently steps back onto the chair.

I walk around her first, taking note of where the dress is too baggy and where it's too tight; where the stitching is uneven, and how much of it could be taken apart without having to remake the whole garment. They see a dress that is hopeless. I see a dress that needs help. The kind of help I know how to give...or once did, at least.

Once I've made a complete circle, I step closer and feel the material between my thumb and forefinger, examining the thinness of the silk, wondering what size needle I would need for how delicate the fabric is. Pleating the silk between my fingers, I try to see what it would look like if it were taken in or gathered differently—the same way Esther had, but with better results since I'm practiced at this sort of thing and she isn't.

Dresses are different from soldiers' uniforms. It's been a long time since I've sewn anything beautiful.

Breine and Esther have stopped laughing. I see them look at each other and then back at me with expressions somewhere between surprise and awe. I realize, in the short time they've known me, they haven't seen me do anything I'm good at. Or anything, really, that was part of what made me myself.

Adding a sash might help the baggy waistline. The previous owner of this dress was obviously much thicker around the middle than Breine. Taking it in enough that it fits Breine's waist would require ripping out almost all the stitches, and I don't think the fabric could withstand that. But if I made a sash, I could gather the middle without much additional sewing.

Next, I move to the bottom of the dress, flipping over the hem to see if there's any extra material that I could use to make a matching sash. There is. And, there would be even more extra fabric if the hemline were raised a few centimeters, which would also make the garment look more youthful and appropriate for a twenty-two-year-old woman like Breine. I wish I had a sewing machine. But maybe this work would be better by hand. I wish, at least, I had Baba Rose's good set of needles and a spool of yellow silk thread.

Still, my fingers feel tingly and alive again, the way they did riffling through the donation box. I feel purposeful. A problem needs to be solved, and for once, I know how to solve it.

"I could fix this," I say.

"Really?" Breine asks.

"The material is too fragile for me to completely remake it, but I could raise the hemline and do something to fix the waist. Maybe rework the neckline, and rearrange some of the beads so it looks a little more modern."

"You know how to do all that?"

"I do. We owned a clothing factory."

"You never said it was clothes," Breine says. "My mother taught me to fix a button, and that's all I've ever managed. She said maids would do the rest."

"I can't even do that," Esther offers. "My father wanted me to come work with him at his newspaper. He told me editors don't need home economics."

"For private clients, we'd do fancier work, sometimes by hand," I say. "I haven't made anything like this in a while."

"But you have before?" Breine asks.

I nod. "If you trust me, I can try to fix this. I can at least make it better."

"Oh, Zofia, honestly. If you can even make it look like I have two breasts instead of four, I'll love you forever."

Esther hands me a pencil so I can make some markings for alterations, and then she and I slide the dress over Breine's head, while Breine stands with her arms straight up and tries to remain motionless. But the fabric is old and fussy. She giggles every time a bead hits the floor and then apologizes, but then Esther starts giggling, and then I do, too.

"You know what, it doesn't even matter," I say. "We'll remove most of them anyway."

"Really? Remove the beads?"

"Really, truly. They're not doing you or the dress any favors."

"Be free, beads!" Breine yells, shimmying her shoulders until a dozen come off at once, and then we're laughing again.

When we finally blow out the lamp, it must be two or three in the morning. I sink into my bed, and my pillow has never felt softer.

Then I'm thinking of everything. Of Hannelore and Inge. Of Josef and his sister. Of the conversation we had on the way home, about hope and happy endings and sad endings. And of Abek, always Abek, and all the last times I've dreamed I saw him.

I would like them to be better stories. Happier stories about last times. The problem is, my last times are inherently sad: The last time I saw my brother. The last time my family was together. The last time my city was Sosnowiec and not Sosnowitz.

I suppose there are stories about the last times of *bad* things. The last German uniform I had to help make. The last night I had to sleep, frozen in the barracks, before the Red Army liberated us. The last time I ate a raw potato with my bare hands, so starved I almost swallowed it whole. Do those count as happy last times? I don't know. The absence of pain is not the same as the presence of happiness.

And what if the times I think are last aren't really over? Some last times are open-ended. When I find Abek again, then our separation will no longer be "the last time I saw Abek," it will only be "the last time I saw him before the war."

I think of all this as Breine and Esther stop giggling in the dark and eventually fall asleep.

But I also think about a dress. A dress, and measuring tape, and tangy pins that leave indentations on my index finger, and the methodical work of putting something right again. It feels like a balm, a cool balm for my brain, to fall asleep thinking about a dress.

HIS BLURRY FACE APPEARS IN FRONT OF ME AGAIN. HIS VOICE IS so sad. And this time we're not in a memory, not one I can identify. We're sitting together in a dark space that could be my bedroom, or it could be my father's office, or it could just be a dark space. And this time, somehow, I'm aware from the beginning that it's a dream. Even while I'm in it, I'm aware it's a dream.

"Is it time yet?" he asks. "Is it time to think about the last time you saw me?"

"I'm trying," I tell him. "I'm trying."

"You're getting closer," he says. "You're getting closer, so please make a promise to me, Zofia. Make one guarantee: that this is the last time you lie about the last time you saw me."

"How can it be a lie if I don't know what the truth is?" I ask. "The absence of the truth is not the presence of a lie. I'm trying. I'm trying. I'm trying."

TWO WEEKS LATER, THE PEOPLE FROM FELDAFING HAVE arrived. That's why the extra cars were near the camp entrance when Josef and I returned—they carried the first round of Feldafing transfers. Over the next few days, the cars and a few trucks shuttled back and forth, bringing hundreds of new displaced persons to the camp.

In our cottage, the front room was rearranged to fit a third bed next to the sink. A young Austrian woman now occupies it. She slips off her shoes whenever she enters the front door. She walks on the balls of her feet more quietly than anyone I've ever seen. Later, someone told me she spent the war hiding in a crawl space under a neighbor's floorboards. She didn't see sunlight or stand up straight for three years. Now her spine crooks forward like an old woman's, and her voice is an unpracticed whisper. I left a pair of socks for her on her pillow because I thought of how Breine made sure to share the rug with me my first night here, because she said we all stumbled through this together. I'm not the new person anymore.

Josef left again. Two days after we got back from the Kloster Indersdorf, I saw him drive out of camp, in a car this time, with a male camp employee. At dinner that night, Chaim mentioned vaguely that Josef had volunteered to help with something near the border of British-occupied Germany. But Chaim didn't offer details, and I was too stung that Josef left without bothering to tell me to ask for more information.

The camp is becoming more organized. Mrs. Yost announced at dinner one night that they were transforming an unused room into a library, a central place to store all the books we receive as donations. The next time, she told us the telephone lines are back. Spottily, she said—but theoretically back.

For a few hours a day, we can now stand in a line that weaves out of her office and down the hallway, waiting to call a loved one or a relief organization or to inquire after an apartment. We talk fast and try not to waste too much time with pleasantries, hoping to finish our business before the line goes dead again.

"Miss Lederman?" says the fuzzy voice on the other end of the telephone line.

"Yes!" I shout into the receiver at the clerk from the American Jewish Joint Distribution Committee I've got on the line. "I'm still here! Can you hear me?"

"Hold one moment; what I said is, I was just about to check the files." He disappears, and while he's gone, the phone starts crackling again, which is usually a sign that it's about to break down again. *Come back, come back*, I silently beg.

There's a clattering as the aid worker picks up the receiver again. "Miss Lederman? I have your letter here. Unfortunately, we don't have any matching records for an Abek Lederman."

I close my eyes, trying to drown out the chatter coming from the queue outside the door. "What about Alek Federman? Did you check that, too?"

"There's nothing on that name, either. I'm sorry."

"I was calling to add something, too," I hurry before he hangs up. "It's possible he might have gone to the Kloster Indersdorf. Just for a few days after liberation. Could you add that?"

"We can add that to the file."

I hear the faint sound of a pen scratch, so I know he's doing it. "We encourage you to try back in a few weeks," he says when he's done. "We do hear from more people every day."

As I'm preparing to say goodbye, there's a knock on the door behind me, the next person waiting in line to use the telephone. I cover the receiver with my hand. *I'll be out soon*, I mouth. But then I realize it's not just anyone, it's Miriam. Her face is white as a sheet.

"Miriam?"

"My sister," she whispers, a mixture of stunned and elated. "I think I have found the right hospital."

"You found...oh, Miriam, that's wonderful!"

"Can I, when you are finished?" She reaches her hand out toward the telephone. "Outside, they say I could skip the line."

"Yes, yes, of course!" I exclaim. "I'm hanging up right

now!" I grab her outstretched hand, and she takes mine and jostles it in excitement.

"My sister!" she says again, now holding my hand with both of hers as we jump up and down.

"*Miss Lederman?*" The tinny, distant voice of the clerk in Berlin reminds me that I still have the phone pressed to my ear. "Miss Lederman, are you still there?"

"I'm still here, I'm still here," I assure him. "I'll try calling back next week, just as you said. Thank you."

When I hang up, I pass the telephone to Miriam. She takes a deep breath before picking up the receiver, calming herself, smoothing down her red hair. Her index finger shakes as she starts to dial. I think about staying, but then remember how when I'd returned to Sosnowiec, I'd wanted my reunion with Abek to be private. Miriam gives me one last terrified, joyful look as someone picks up on the other end.

"Good luck," I whisper, slipping out the door.

When I leave Mrs. Yost's office, I don't leave the building. Instead, I walk down the hall to the empty room that is going to become the library. What I'd really love is a fashion magazine, a thick one, with advertisements from ladies' clothing stores to give me ideas for Breine's dress or at least confirm that my own ideas aren't hopelessly out of date. I haven't worn a new dress in five years. I haven't set foot in a decent shop in longer, not since the Germans took over our factory. I would like to sit down the way I once did with my father, turning pages slowly, learning how to anticipate trends, what kinds of fabrics we might need to order more of.

But the library isn't finished yet: There's a drop cloth on the floor, the acrid odor of fresh paint clinging to the walls. Boxes, of books I assume, are piled in the middle of the room, but I don't feel I should open them.

I step outside and hear the clicking of footsteps: Breine rushing toward me. "There you are!" She grabs my hands. Hers are still dirty under the nails; she hasn't been to the room yet to wash them. "I have good news. My uncle's train hasn't had as many delays as we expected. I just got a telegram; he should be here tomorrow!"

"Tomorrow?"

"Isn't that amazing? In a few days, I'll be married!"

"Breine, your dress." I panic. "I'm not very far on it yet. I was just going to look for a magazine to get ideas, but I have hours' worth of work left."

"I know you've been busy."

And I *have* been busy, but that's not the only reason I'm behind. The few times I've sat down with the material, my hands have been wooden. I think part of me doesn't want to. Sewing a dress is moving forward with my life. Sewing a dress would be healing, which is why the nurses tried to get me to pick up a needle and thread when I was sitting in my hospital bed. Sewing a dress would be a betrayal. *Wouldn't it? Should I be allowed to move forward before I've found my brother?*

"I'll go start it again right now," I tell her.

"You don't have to go right this very second. Come eat first."

"No, I don't want to put it off any longer, and I also wanted to ask around for a better needle."

"We'll ask the other girls at dinner," she insists, pulling me toward the door. "However good you are, I bet I'll thank myself later for not letting you sew on an empty stomach."

In the dining hall, our regular corner doesn't look as it usually does: Instead of one small table, several have been pushed together, with twelve or fourteen people sitting elbow to elbow.

"Meeting night," Breine apologizes. "I forgot; I'm sorry. You'll just have to sit through our talking for a few minutes at the beginning."

I recognize a few of the new occupants, vaguely, as the ruddy, healthy-looking people Breine and Chaim work with in the fields every day. Chaim's front-room housemate Ravid, strong and sunburned, stands at the head and taps his water glass on the table to get everyone's attention.

"I don't want to impose," I whisper to Breine as we approach. The table is full; Chaim has saved a place for Breine, but there's no place for me to sit without making others move.

"Really, nobody will mind."

Breine settles into the spot Chaim has saved for her and then playfully elbows the man on her other side until he slides farther down to make room for me. Ravid raises one eyebrow at Breine's disruption—the squeaking chair, the clattering of silverware as she passes fork and spoon to the man she's just displaced. "Do you think I'm allowed to continue?" Ravid asks dryly. Breine makes a face at him.

"As I was starting to say," Ravid continues. "We're almost ready to move into the next phase of Aliyah Bet."

Around the table, nobody else seems as confused as I am about the phrase Ravid has just used. *Aliyah* means immigrating to Eretz Israel. I know that; it's meant that for centuries. But I've never heard of *Aliyah Bet*.

"Breine," I whisper. "What is Aliyah Bet?"

Ravid breaks off again, and this time he looks straight at me. "Is there a question?"

My face turns red, but his tone wasn't angry, just firm. "I don't know that phrase," I admit.

"Do you know about Britain's immigration quotas to Palestine?" he asks before launching an explanation. "The few people who can go there legally, they are part of Aliyah Aleph. Plan A," Ravid continues. "Aliyah Bet, however, isn't permitted under the laws. Plan B."

"Entering illegally?" I ask.

"Plan *B*," Breine corrects me. I marvel that Breine is going to be a part of this. She didn't farm before the war. She told me her father was the president of an insurance company. She told me she spent her days learning how to manage a household, hire good servants, and set a nice table. A different dress for every day of the week. A different hat and gloves for every dress.

"What happens if you're stopped?" I ask. "It's illegal; what happens if you're caught?"

"We've heard that if the ships are stopped, then the passengers will be taken to a refugee camp," Ravid says. "But we're in a refugee camp now anyway."

"Do you want to come with us, Zofia?" Breine teases.

"Come with you? I'm going home."

"We're all going home," she says. "Just a new home."

"I'm going to my home in Poland," I say firmly. "That was Abek's and my home, and after I find him, it will be again." I wriggle my way out of my seat. "And now I'm going to go work on your dress."

AFTER A FRUITLESS HOUR OF TRYING TO WORK ON BREINE'S dress in our cottage, I finally decide there's just not a large enough flat surface for the project, and I end up carrying the heap of unflattering yellow back to the dining hall. By then, the tables are mostly empty, aside from the volunteers for cleanup duty. I fan the dress out on a table that's been wiped down. Smoothing the silk with the flat of my palm, I sit and again assess what I have to work with.

In front of me: A makeshift sewing kit, as much as I could assemble after asking around camp. Thread wasn't a problem to locate, but finding the right color was—the two best candidates are either more orange than the dress fabric or too white. I also have a frayed measuring tape, a collection of needles in need of sharpening, handfuls of loose buttons, and some pins gathered in a butter dish. Nothing looks new, which means everything in front of me was secreted away in camps, or scavenged immediately after. Hidden in pockets, tucked in straw mattresses. Small acts of defiance—to own a useless button that the Nazis didn't know about, to hold a spool of thread in the middle of a frozen night. But now the women gave them to me willingly.

Normally, I might layer a piece of muslin behind the silk to make the silk behave better with the scissors. I don't have any of that, though, so instead, I've gathered a pile of newspapers. I remember my mother using this trick a few times when she was trying an experimental design and didn't want to waste expensive supplies, but I've never done it myself. I worry about the ink of the newsprint rubbing off on the pale, delicate material.

My hands are rough and chapped, as they have been for years, but now, as I sit with the dress, I'm surprised to realize they're not callused. Not in the places they used to be.

Baba Rose never let me use thimbles. She said that they dulled precision and that detailed embroidery couldn't be accomplished with a thimble. Under her supervision, I let my index finger get raw and bloody and then get strong enough that I barely felt the throb of pushing a needle through even the thickest wools. But now I no longer have a seamstress's hands; my index finger is no more or less battered than any other part of me.

"Breine said you needed a pair of scissors?"

I look up. Josef, standing a few feet away.

Shirt open at the throat, the hollow in his neck drawing my attention in a way I wish it wouldn't. Now that he's standing in front of me, I realize I wouldn't have known what to say to him, anyway, even if he had been around these past few weeks. I don't know why he keeps pulling away, but I know it exhausts me and makes me feel embarrassed.

"Scissors?" he says again, and now I see he's holding a pair in his hand.

"You're back," I say.

"Just this morning."

"I hope you had a nice trip," I say stiffly, not allowing myself to say anything else, especially anything that would reveal how much I'd noticed his absence. "And I already have regular scissors. I was looking for pinking shears."

"What are those?"

"They have a serrated edge that keeps the silk from fraying."

"Ah," he says. "She didn't specify that." Now I look closer at the ones he's holding: silver-colored with narrow, tapered blades. "These are for the horses' manes when they get burrs or tangles. I washed them," he adds. "But it doesn't sound like they're what you're looking for."

"Let me see." I take the scissors from him, run my finger along the blade, test the weight in my hand. "These are actually sharper than the ones I have. I'll use them if you don't mind."

"Of course. I brought them for you."

But then he doesn't leave. He sits down at the table. A respectful distance but the seat next to me, just the same, which I try to ignore as I begin my work. First, I use a small, borrowed paring knife to pick loose the stitching on the bottom hem. It's a tedious, delicate motion that I'm terrified to mess up, so I do it slowly, my nose only a few centimeters from the material. Out of the corner of my eye, I see Josef get up but return a few minutes later. He's fetched a lamp to give me more light.

And then I can feel him looking at me. Not at my face, but at my hands, which somehow feels more personal.

The grooming shears he's lent me are unwieldy at first. The blades don't have an angle to them, so I can't cut the fabric directly along the table as I normally would, which makes it harder to create a straight line. If I'd realized Josef was going to watch me, I would have used a ruler and penciled in where I planned to cut. But I make it around the circumference of the dress anyway, cutting to where I'd earlier marked the dress against Breine's legs, scavenging fabric for me to fashion the sash I'd envisioned and to patch over any parts of the dress that are stained or threadbare. Now that I've shortened the garment, it's time to rehem it. Before I can look for a pin, Josef has handed me one. And then he hands me another, and another after that. My hands are sure on the silk, and I'm remembering what it feels like to touch something expensive, what it feels like to do something I am skilled at and have done a hundred times.

As I work, the other tables in the dining hall start to fill again—card games and letter writers and other people just trying to get away from their cramped quarters for a little while. The dead-quiet background rises into a low, friendly hum.

The next pin he hands me, our hands brush together. I secret a glance to see if he's done it on purpose, because I'm doing it on

purpose: I reached too wide, so that instead of my fingers closing around the pin, they close around his angular knuckles. But
as soon as I do that, Josef jerks his hand away. And then, while I
flush in embarrassment, he slides the butter dish over to within
my reach so he won't have to hand me anything anymore.

"Did you hear about Miriam?" he asks quietly.

My face still burning from his subtle rejection, I nod. "I
saw her in Mrs. Yost's office. She found the hospital? It's wonderful news."

But Josef is shaking his head, his expression dark. *No*, he's
saying. No, that's not what happened.

"Josef, what about Miriam? She didn't find her sister?"

He swallows. "She found her sister. But it was too late."

The fabric falters in my hand. "What do you mean, it was
too late? Her sister is . . . *dead*?"

"She heard this afternoon."

"But this afternoon is when I *saw* her. She was about to
make a call." I cut myself off, realizing. When I saw her, she
was about to call the right hospital. She was minutes away from
receiving the worst news of her life.

Yellow silk swims in front of my eyes, blurry and nonsensical. Miriam and her letters. Her hundreds and hundreds of
letters. Miriam and the hope on her face when she peered into
Mrs. Yost's office a few hours ago. Should I have offered to stay
with her when she made the call? Instead, she had to receive
the news alone.

"But her sister was alive," I protest. "She was alive *after* the
war. She was taken to a hospital."

"She was too sick," Josef says. "It happened just a few weeks after liberation. She couldn't get better."

"But still, Miriam could have had a few *weeks*. A few extra weeks with a person is a lifetime."

"I know."

"And the only reason she didn't get it was because of some, some clerical error that told her the wrong hospital."

"I *know*," Josef repeats.

I'm filled with fury and anguish. She survived the war. Miriam's sister survived torture, she was alive, she was rescued, and she died anyway. Meanwhile, Miriam sat in our cottage and wrote hundreds of letters.

"Anyway, I didn't know if anyone had told you," Josef says. "And I thought you'd want to know. She won't be back in your cottage for a few days; she asked administrators if she could have a private room in the infirmary so she could grieve alone."

I nod, unable to find the right words. Instead, I focus on making the pins and then the needle go through the fabric, one stitch at a time. One thing that I know how to fix, one broken thing I can repair. Tiny, even, incremental. I focus on my work and hold my brain in place, something I've gotten better at doing these past few weeks, something that sewing helps me do. It's easier to stay in reality when I'm anchored by the tangibleness of fabric.

"You're very good at your work," Josef whispers finally, rising from the table.

"You don't have to go."

"I don't want to disturb you."

"But I just invited you to stay," I protest.

"I know you have only until tomorrow to finish Breine's dress."

"Josef, that's bullshit." Now I lay down my work and glare up at him, fueled by my anger over what happened to Miriam's sister and the injustices we're all still feeling every day. "If you want to leave, you should leave. Fine. But you can't tell me that *I* need you to leave when I just told you to stay. You can't hold my hand in the wagon and tell me about your family and then ignore me. It's not fair. I can't tell whether you like me at all, or don't like me, or want to be my friend, or want to be something—I can't tell how you feel at all."

He's standing very still. "It's not that simple."

"It's not that complicated, either." The back of my neck is sore from bending over the table. I forgot that Baba Rose made everyone stand up and stretch every fifteen minutes. I rub it, irritated.

"Zofia," he says, pleading.

"Josef."

My voice has an edge to it, but I can't even tell what I'm asking, what I want from him. If he said right now that he did like me, would I want that? And what would it mean? Would I want something like what Breine had—a marriage proposal from a person I barely know?

I wouldn't; I know that. I wouldn't want a wedding dress, I wouldn't want to arrive back in Sosnowiec with another strange man the way I did with Dima. But then, touching Dima's hand always felt more like gratefulness than desire. I never wanted to raise my face to Dima, to linger a little too long in the hopes he would lean down, slowly.

"What's not simple, Josef?" I demand. "If you don't like me, you need to just say it."

Josef opens his mouth, a struggle on his face. "It would be easier if I didn't—but I do, and..."

"What are you *talking* about?" I start to say, but then I'm interrupted.

Behind Josef, a clatter—the heavy door to the dining hall has opened, and the person responsible for it has dropped something. A satchel or a half-filled pillowcase, it looks like; I can only see in silhouette. A few people look up briefly, then return to their card games, but Josef looks over in elaborate concern. *An act.* He just wants an excuse to leave the conversation.

The newcomer has scooped their belongings back into the bag but still lingers near the door, scanning the room. A Feldafing straggler, probably, one who missed the last car.

A male volunteer finds his way over and asks if he can be of help. Now that the new arrival is obviously cared for, I think Josef will have to turn back to me, but he continues to pretend to be deeply interested in the exchange by the door. Frustrated, I try to focus on Breine's dress. I try to tell myself that his lack of an answer is an answer in itself.

"I'm so sorry, but we only have places for adults and families," the volunteer is saying to the new arrival. A boy—I can tell it's a boy now from the straight-hipped way he hoists the bag over his shoulder. "Of course you can stay for the night, but tomorrow we'll have to find the camp director and figure out the best way to get you resettled at one of the homes for people your own age. The nearest one is less than a day's drive, and we have—"

"I've just come from there," the boy interrupts.

"Did they say they're full?" the volunteer interrupts sharply. "They know they're not supposed to do that."

The boy shakes his head. He fishes into his satchel and pulls out a folded piece of paper. "There was a letter left for me there." He traces his finger to the bottom and points to where the signature must be. "I'm here to find *her*."

I'm standing without even realizing it. I'm dropping the pins without even realizing it. Breine's dress is clinging to my skirt with static; I'm pulling it off the table along with the scissors and tape measure.

I feel like I'm in a dream because it turns out nothing that's happened in my waking life has prepared me for how this feels right now.

The scissors have clattered to the ground, and the boy finds my eyes.

"Zofia, is that you?" he says.

"Abek?" I say, and my world falls into place.

# Part Three

**Foehrenwald, October**

MY BROTHER IS ALIVE. HE IS ALIVE, AND HE HAS RECOGNIZED me. He's spoken my name out loud.

*Other people heard him, too.* This is the second thought to come to mind, and it's such an odd thought to have in this moment that I first can't figure out why.

*Because it means you're not imagining things,* I answer my own question. If other people in this room have also spoken to Abek, it means I'm not crazy and I'm not seeing ghosts. Ghosts are spirits, and my brother is flesh, and he is alive.

Abek is faster than I am; he's run across the room while I've barely moved from the table, and now he throws his arms around my waist. The way he used to, I think, when he was too short to reach any other part of me. Now he's grown. I'm still taller than him, but not by much; the downy-soft of his head hits at my nose instead of my rib cage.

My own arms are still at my sides, which I don't even realize until Abek whispers something.

"What?" I ask, my voice sounding hollow to me and like it's coming from far away.

"*A* to *Z*," he repeats. "Abek and Zofia, *A* to *Z*."

And then I throw my arms around him and start to sob.

Standing in the middle of the dining hall, we're surrounded by an audience. Someone has run for Mrs. Yost, and she's here, crying. I see Esther and Ravid and the others I normally eat with. And then people I haven't even met come over to touch my hair, or Abek's hair, as if good news can be absorbed through proximity.

We are possible, their touches say. All things are possible. Someone shoves a cup of tea in my hand. Someone else appears with a tin of meat for Abek, an extra from dinner. My brother holds it awkwardly under his arm because he still has his satchel in one hand and I won't let go of the other.

*Josef.* He was just standing here. I scan the room, sure he must still be in the crowd, but by the time I catch him, it's in profile. He's already turning to slip out the door.

"Sit down. Are you hungry? Sit down," I babble to Abek, too emotional to think about Josef. "Or stand, if you've been sitting in a wagon all afternoon. Or maybe we should go somewhere?" I ask. "Mrs. Yost, can he come to my—"

"Of course, don't be silly."

I offer to take his satchel. He doesn't let me, holding it close to his chest as he follows me past the happy, envious residents.

In the cottage, I realize how incomplete my imagination has been. The part that I pictured a thousand times is the part that's already over: the first minutes of our finding each other, the first joyful tears.

I also pictured the parts that come much later. I envisioned a future life, one where we live in Sosnowiec, find our old friends, and piece together our lives.

But it's these intermediate minutes I didn't plan for. The ones where we are blood-related strangers who haven't spoken to each other in years. The ones where I'm waiting for my brain to catch up with itself, to realize that I'm going to be okay now.

My brother stands in the doorway to my room, cautious, while I ramble on for the sheer purpose of filling the silence. I tell him nonpertinent information about the squeaky desk chair and cold floors; I tell him about how one of my roommates snores. I think about asking to take his satchel again but see the way he's clinging to it, the only familiar object in a world of strange ones.

*And me. I am familiar now.*

"Are you hungry?" I ask again, as if I hadn't just asked ten minutes before. He nods toward the tin in his hands, still unopened, indicating that he could eat that if he was hungry.

"I could get you a fork," I offer. He shakes his head. He's not hungry.

I'm making him nervous. I'm making myself nervous. I force my hands to stop fluttering. Finally, I gesture for him to sit on my bed, while I lower myself onto Breine's across from him.

*His face.* I feel like I'm doing with it what I did with the buildings in Sosnowiec: trying to make sense of the way it looks now and reconcile it with what I remember of then, layering Abek's appearance over the top of the one that exists in my memory. The hazel eyes I've thought of so often. The brown hair, a bit darker than it was when I saw him last, the way mine got darker, too, as I got older. And there's some on his face, I'm stunned to realize—a smattering of fuzz above his upper lip.

The biggest difference, of course, is that he's almost a man now. I've missed all the connective moments of the transition between the Abek I remember and the new one before me. It's as if I've been given the first page of a book and the last, and I have to use only those to make up the plot in between.

What was his story? What have I missed? What did he have to live through alone?

As I prattle on, Abek takes in the room the way I did when I first arrived. His eyes sweep over the beds, the desk, the basin. But when his eyes reach mine, his glance is wary, and he almost immediately looks away. He's shy with me. I can't blame him for it. It's got to be unnerving, the voracious way I'm staring.

Finally, after what feels like a long time, I run out of things to tell him, and I fall silent. It's only when I allow this quiet

that I realize why I was trying so hard to fill it. And it's only
when I let there be stillness that I realize why I couldn't stop
fluttering around earlier: There are things I've needed to say
for the past three years. The monsters I've kept trapped, the
thoughts I haven't wanted to examine. The apologies I've hated
myself for not being able to make.

"Abek," I begin uncertainly, because all my practiced
speeches have flown out of my head.

"I want you to know, I didn't want to leave you," I continue. "I swear I didn't. One day they came looking for girls
who could sew. I thought it was just a work detail and I'd be
back by the end of the day. I thought there might be better
food or that it might be closer to the men's side of camp." I
slide off Breine's bed and kneel in front of him. The apology
spills from my lips inelegant and raw. Each sentence feels like
the opening of a wound, a reminder of all the small and large
ways I've failed. "I didn't know they would send us away. If
I'd known all that would happen, I wouldn't have—I left you
alone. I did the one thing I promised I wouldn't do, and I left
you alone. I abandoned you. I'm sorry, I'm sorry, I'm so sorry."
Tears squeeze out of my eyes, and my voice shakes heavily.

When I reach the end, the horrible end, I force myself
to confront the next possibility: that Abek won't forgive me.
What if he never realized I'd *volunteered* for the assignment that
took me away? What if he's angry that I didn't find a way to
take him, too?

He looks down at his hands now, clearing his throat before
speaking.

"It's okay, Zofia."

"It's *not*. You must have been looking for me in the camp. You must have wondered why I wasn't trying to sneak you food, or—" My voice breaks. "You must have thought I was dead."

"It is okay," he insists. "I didn't even know you never came back to Birkenau. I wasn't there very much longer, either."

"Where *were* you?"

He swallows. "Five places. I kept moving, but I ended up in Buchenwald. It's here in Germany. The Americans liberated the camp in April."

"You've been here in Germany?" I repeat, trying to process this.

*He wasn't there. All those times I hated myself for leaving for Neustadt or wondered if I should try to go back. He wouldn't have been there anyway. He'd already left. He didn't know I never came back.*

"But what about the job I'd gotten for you? The commandant?"

Abek looks down. "It didn't work out. He was transferred to a new camp, and I guess he thought he'd find someone he liked better."

The phrasing—someone he liked better—it's such a little-boy phrasing, it breaks my heart. Still kneeling in front of him, I take his hand, almost unable to believe his hand is actually here for me to take.

"Abek. Why didn't you go *home*? After it was over? I was in the hospital for months, but I went back to Sosnowiec as soon as I could after. If Buchenwald was liberated in April, did you try to get on a train? Where have you *been*?"

He shrinks back a little at my questions; I've been shooting them rapid fire without giving him time to answer. I can't help it; I'm so hungry to learn everything I've missed.

"There was an old widow," he begins, deciding to answer my last question first. "Outside of Buchenwald. She said she would give us room and board to help through planting season. I worked for Ladna, and on weekends I would try to travel to different camps looking for you."

"Ladna!" I exclaim.

He looks at me, curiously. "Yes. The old woman, her name was Ladna."

"I know, but—Ladna, like in *The Whirlwind*," I explain, waiting for him to catch on, to remember our favorite fairy tale. The daughter of the king and queen who was so beautiful that many princes came to woo her. "Like in *The Whirlwind*," I repeat. "Where the lovely Princess Ladna is kidnapped by a dwarf on her wedding day."

He laughs, just for a moment, and my heart fills with impossible joy at the sound. "I don't think *this* Ladna would have had a wedding day. She was very…particular. She was like Mrs. Schulman."

"I can't believe you remember Mrs. Schulman!" My parents hired Mrs. Schulman to teach Abek and me when we weren't allowed to attend school anymore. She was harsh, making us repeat assignments over again until they met her exacting definitions of perfection. We hated her, but Mama encouraged us to be kind: She had no one else.

"Poor Mrs. Schulman," I say.

"Poor *us*," Abek corrects. "Our poor knuckles. How could our handwriting be perfect if our knuckles were always bruised?"

"Still. Maybe, like Ladna in *The Whirlwind*, she just needed her own prince in a suit of golden armor to woo her. What was the prince's name in the story?"

"Oh, I can't remember," Abek says.

"He crawled into the giant's ear, and he came out the other end, and—what was it, Abek? We heard that fairy tale a hundred times. The prince's name, it started with a *D*? I'm sure you remember."

"I really *don't*." My brother shifts uncomfortably on the bed. His face has turned red. I can tell I've embarrassed him, that he feels badly for not being able to remember. And he shouldn't: *I* don't even remember. I just want more of this conversation, where we're laughing together. But in trying to achieve that, I've turned the conversation into an interrogation.

Abek's eyes flit briefly toward the door, and I'm worried, irrationally, that I've made him uncomfortable enough that he regrets coming here and might decide to leave.

Instinctively, I stretch out my legs, creating a barrier in his path to the door. *What am I doing?* It's such a bizarre, desperate gesture, but that's how I feel. Bizarre and desperate.

"You're so big," I say after a few minutes. "It's been such a long time. I'm going to have to get used to the fact that you're not the same little brother I remember."

A few feet away, Abek plucks at a loose thread on the quilt covering my bed, and I do the same on Breine's.

I let another moment of silence hang in the air before speaking again. "This is strange, isn't it? It's wonderful, of course, but it's also strange."

Abek nods before I even finish the sentence, relieved I've said it first. "Yes. I didn't really know what it would be like. But it's a little strange."

"We don't have to figure it all out now."

"I know."

"You must be exhausted," I say, noticing the dark circles rimming his eyes. "I'll sleep on the floor, and we'll borrow some extra—"

"I don't want you to sleep on the floor," he interrupts, flustered. "I'm sure there are men's cottages."

"No," I protest. "It's late; we'd have to disturb the staff and wake people up to get you an assignment. The floor is fine, or I could squeeze in with Breine, or Breine could with Esther. Those are my roommates; I'm sitting on Breine's bed. They're probably waiting somewhere to give us privacy."

I'm babbling again, the way I was when we first came into the room. But now it's not nerves, now it's me not wanting to let my brother out of my sight. Tonight I want to fall asleep knowing where my family is, and my family is the two of us.

"Abek," I say, suddenly thinking of something. "How did you end up in Munich to begin with? I came here because I thought all the prisoners from Birkenau were sent to Dachau.

But Buchenwald—I know that city. It's hundreds of kilometers from here. How did you end up here?"

"Because I also heard the prisoners from Birkenau were sent to Dachau." He sees that it still hasn't registered for me and continues to explain. "I didn't know you never came back to Birkenau, so I thought *you* must have come to Munich."

"Were you the boy Sister Therese told me about?" I ask. "The boy who stole the food money from her room?"

He flushes a deep red and nods. "I know it was wrong," he begins.

"It wasn't wrong; it's what helped me find you! I mean, it was *wrong*, but..."

"But I did it anyway," he finishes. "Because you said we would find each other. You said we would find each other no matter what."

I sleep that night with my hand dangling off the bed, onto the mats and blankets we've set up for Abek. I want to be sure of— I don't know what. That he won't be taken again, I suppose. That he won't vanish into thin air.

It still feels like a fairy tale, almost. Like the dust of a fairy godmother sprinkled over a town to lull it to sleep. Something too good to be true, something that could dissolve any moment. But it doesn't dissolve. And for once, I don't go to sleep fearing my own nightmares. For once, I know they won't come. The last time I saw Abek doesn't matter now that I have a first time: the first time we were reunited.

I wake in the middle of the night, once because my arm is cold, untucked from the covers; once because it has fallen asleep; and once more because Abek turns over and his hair tickles my fingers. But he is there; that's the point. Every time I wake up, he's still there.

The third time, I see he's awake, too, his eyes glinting in the dark, looking up toward my bed.

"Can you not sleep?" I whisper. "Are you thirsty?"

He shakes his head.

"Should I tell you a story? Should I tell you our story?"

I begin the alphabet story, quietly in the dark. I begin with the letter *A*, with his name, with the great-uncle Abek who died a few days before his birth. I move on to Baba Rose, and to Chomicki & Lederman and the busy hum of the sewing machines, and I whisper and whisper until my throat is sandy.

"*O* is for—" I begin, and then I cut off, because I can't remember what *O* is for. I haven't had to go this far into the alphabet in a long time. I'm out of practice and full of holes. Below, I see Abek shift in his blankets. "*O* is—" I start again.

"*O* is for Lake Morskie Oko," Abek whispers. "Where there was the cabin."

"Oko," I repeat in wonder. "That's right! We had the cabin. The water there was so deep and green."

That's where we used to go every summer, where we were on holiday before the Germans came. The clear, frigid water; Papa walking about in his undershirt; Mama reading novels on the porch, a half-eaten apple resting on her stomach as she let the dinner hour pass without putting anything on the stove. I'd forgotten completely. Abek has given me such a gift, to remind me of it. The gift of memory, the gift of our past. The gift of something I hadn't been able to complete on my own.

I continue on, but only get through a few more letters before hearing Abek's breathing even out, realizing he's fallen asleep.

"Good night," I whisper.

W E WAKE THE NEXT MORNING TO A KNOCK ON THE cottage door, the outer door first, where Judith answers, and then on our bedroom door. Esther stumbles into her dressing gown to answer this knock while the rest of us blink our eyes open. Me, with my arm still dangling off the side of the bed, and Abek, with puffy eyes and a look of confusion as he remembers where he is.

It's Breine's uncle, a tiny man named Świętopełk, who looks like Breine in the jaw. He has an old-fashioned, courtly manner—an elegant way of removing his hat—that seems both out of place in this camp and appropriate to his name, which is an old one I've only ever seen in history books.

Breine hurdles out of her bed, and then she and her uncle cling to each other. She told me that before the war, she'd seen him only twice in her life; he lived far away and wasn't close to his brother. Now they are each other's only family, and the old rifts don't matter.

"Our wedding," she announces, wiping away happy tears. "We can have our wedding tonight."

I'm apprehensive, at first, that Abek's first day here will be so busy. He deserves time to rest, not to be thrown into chaotic wedding planning. We both deserve time to settle in. I watch his reaction to Breine's announcement, worried that he'll be too overwhelmed. But, unless I'm imagining it, what I see on his face is mostly relief.

"Don't worry about the dress; I'll wear a potato sack," Breine tells me, but keeping Abek's expression in the corner of my eye, I shake my head.

"Of course I'll finish. Nobody in my family would ever let a bride look anything less than beautiful. Isn't that right, Abek? Can you imagine how angry Baba Rose would be?"

He smiles and shakes his head. I decide it will be good to have this distraction. Busyness can be a relieving antidote to a lot of things: grief, awkwardness, confusion. A wedding will be welcome.

Word spreads quickly that Breine's uncle has arrived, and all through the day it seems as if the whole camp is helping to prepare for the wedding. Men gather wood and fashion a chuppah, and women in the kitchen try to turn rationed food into a celebratory feast. A friend of Breine's, whose ancestors are from Spain, produces a small bag of walnuts, which she says she kept with her in hiding all through the occupation, determinedly saving them for a special occasion. This seems miraculous to me, that on the brink of death and starvation, she could keep walnuts. But she did, and now she grinds them to make wedding cookies.

And, while dining tables are moved and rearranged around me, and mismatched tablecloths are produced and smoothed over them, I spread Breine's half-finished garment on the same table I worked at before. The same pins by my side, the same thread, only now instead of Josef, I have Abek beside me.

"Come and help," I instruct him, nodding to the seat beside me.

We're formal, at first. Being around my brother—*my brother*—in the daylight hours is different, even, from knowing he's sleeping on a mat near my bed in the dark. So we're behaving around each other in the polite, distant way we used to behave if company was coming. When I ask him to pass me scraps of material or buttons or thread, I make sure to add a careful *please* and then a careful *thank you* at the end. And he makes sure to say, "You're welcome," just as effusively. After fifteen or twenty of these exchanges, it starts to feel absurd. Before we were separated, I would have just nodded toward something and grunted; he would have passed it to me while barely looking up from his toy cars.

"Are you bored?" I ask him, finally. "They may be done with the new library. You could go see if it's open yet and if there's anything interesting to bring back and read." I've chosen this phrasing carefully; I don't want to suggest something that would take him away for very long. "Have you had a chance to read much? Do you even like to read?"

"I don't mind staying," Abek says, and hands me another pin. "I like to read some. In one of my camps, there was a book. Someone had smuggled it in. A translation of Charles Dickens. I was trying to read it. But I don't need to get any books right now."

Charles Dickens. It's nearly impossible for me to square this idea, of my brother being old enough to read complicated novels by himself. He went through so much without me. There's so much of him now that is *without me*.

I finish the stitching around Breine's collar and turn my attention to the hemline, pointing to a wrinkle in the silk. Abek grabs the fabric where I'm pointing, pulling it flat against the table.

"Now that I know where you've actually been," I say, only a little shyly, "I'll have to revise my imagination. I never pictured you on a farm, for example. And I'm realizing how many times my mind must have played tricks on me, putting you in places where you couldn't have been."

"What do you mean? What kinds of places?" He obligingly holds the fabric where I point next. I take my time answering his question because I want to do it in a way that doesn't scare him or make him worry.

"I—I wasn't well. For a lot of the war. My mind wasn't working. I kept getting more confused. There are a lot of holes I filled in or other things I was afraid I made up. But I thought I saw you all these times." I force a small laugh. Now that Abek is safely in front of me, it seems simpler to act like I had merely been confused, occasionally vague like a dotty aunt, and not like I'd been very ill.

"One time, I thought I saw you through the window in Neustadt," I tell him. "Another time, I thought I saw you in line for soup in Gross-Rosen and then again walking into the men's barracks. In Birkenau, I thought I saw you while I was working in a garden. I buried a turnip for you, but when you didn't get it, I realized that either you couldn't get to it or I hadn't seen you. I was so disappointed. It was really hard for me to organize a whole turnip."

Abek has been watching me closely as I tell this story. I worry he'll be afraid of me or worried about me, but he seems reassured, actually, to know how much he was on my mind.

And now, when I get to the part about the turnip, he starts to shake his head. "No. No, I did find it," he says. "The turnip."

"You did?"

"Remember?" he says excitedly. "You buried the turnip in the ground, and you stood a stick in the ground so I would know where to dig for it."

"I did?" I don't remember the stick, but it sounds like a reasonable detail. How else would I have expected him to find what I'd buried?

"I didn't have anything to leave in return, so I used the stick to draw my initial so you'd know I found it."

I close my eyes, trying to sort through my confusion. I understand the story he's telling, but it's hard for me to remember it myself. It's like Abek's version is a loose scrap of cloth, but if I can sew it into a quilt, then it will stop being a story and start being one of my memories.

*The last time I saw Abek,* I practice telling myself. *The last time I saw Abek, he was eating a turnip that I managed to get for him. He was leaving me a drawing he'd made in the dirt.*

"Was it raining that day?" I ask him.

"I think so."

*The last time I saw Abek, it was raining. I didn't speak to him, but I came back to the spot where I had buried a turnip. On the ground there was an A. I looked at the dirt drawing until the rain rinsed it away.*

Sitting here at the table in Foehrenwald, a cautious little voice inside me is asking, *Is that really how it happened?*

I'm so used to that voice, so used to mistrusting myself. It will take me a while to figure out what I can believe now.

"I'm almost finished," I tell him, nodding at Breine's dress. "You can go and wash up."

"You don't need my help to finish? I don't have to wash up."

"We're going to a wedding tonight. You actually *do* need to. And stop by the donation boxes, and see if you can find a clean new shirt." I will myself to be okay with the fact that he's going to leave now and that I won't see him for an hour. "But come right back to the cottage when you're done, all right? Right back, and wait outside for me. We can keep talking later. We have plenty of time now."

After I finish my work, I take the dress to the communal laundry building and spread it out over the ironing board. In my family's factory, the irons were electric. They plugged in; their temperatures could be controlled by tuning a dial. Here, they're a heavy, cast metal, and heated over hot coals. I've barely ever used this kind before; it would be easy to heat them too high and leave scorch marks on the dress. I wonder, at first, whether it's better to leave Breine's dress unironed.

But it's her wedding. It's her wedding and my handiwork, and I can't let her get married in wrinkles. I pluck a still-damp bath towel off the laundry line stretched across the room and lay it across the dress to make a barrier between the hot iron and the fragile silk.

PRESSING THE DRESS WITH THE OLD-FASHIONED IRON TAKES longer than I expected, but when I race back across the camp, out of breath and worried Breine will be upset with my lateness, I find that I've beaten her home. She rushes in a few minutes later, skin still pink from a bath, fingers still pruned, laughing and apologetic.

The wedding is scheduled to start at dusk because Breine and Chaim wanted to work a full day before the ceremony. Esther had told her that was crazy, that there was no need for Breine to weed plots of land on her wedding day, but Breine insisted. Her relationship with Chaim was about building new things, she said. What better way to build something new than to tend to tender sprigs?

Esther arrives shortly after Breine, hands spilling with silver-colored tubes and compacts. Makeup—she must have gone around the camp and borrowed everything she could.

"I don't need all that!" Breine protests. "Chaim wouldn't even recognize me. He might not even recognize me as is, without dirt under my fingernails."

"Breine," Esther protests.

"*Esther.*"

While they debate the rouge and lipstick, I unwrap the dress from the bath towel and lay it on Breine's bed, holding my breath. There hasn't been time for Breine to see my work, much less time for her to try the dress on. Now, she breaks off in the middle of a sentence. She looks over to me, and her mouth drops.

"Oh, Zofia."

"Do you like it?"

"Do I—I can hardly believe it's the same dress. I *can't* believe it. It's marvelous. It's completely, completely—" She turns back to Esther. "Maybe a little lipstick."

"That's right," Esther says.

"But only a little, and only so my face isn't completely outshone by my dress."

Esther points toward the desk chair until Breine obediently sits, and then she holds up a series of lipsticks to Breine's face, looking for the most flattering color. "This one, I think," she decides, choosing a creamy pink. "Open your mouth a little. No—more natural, like this."

After Esther applies the borrowed lipstick to Breine's mouth, she dabs a little on her own fingertip to use as rouge for Breine's cheeks. "I'll just do a tiny amount," she promises in response to Breine's grimace. "You'll still look exactly like yourself; it will just be a bit of color in case you get nervous and pale standing up there in front of us all and knowing we're watching you."

"Well, you've made me nervous *now*." Breine laughs.

Watching the whole exchange, I'm overcome by a memory. "Use three dots," I suggest to Esther.

She hovers her fingertip just over Breine's cheek. "Three dots?"

"My aunt Maja always told me: one dot of rouge lined up below the pupil, one about two centimeters lower, in line with the tip of the nose, and a third high on the cheekbone. You make a triangle with three dots, and then blend in between for the most flattering appearance." I laugh. "I can't believe I suddenly remembered that."

"We'll do three!"

Esther finishes Breine's makeup and moves to her hair, beginning with a braid, as Breine always wears it, but then pinning it up at the base of Breine's neck. When she's finished, she holds up a hand mirror, and we all examine the work.

Breine raises her fingers, lightly touching her face and elegant hair.

"It's not too much, is it?" Esther says. "I told you it wouldn't be. Breine? Tell me you don't hate it."

"It's not too much," Breine says quietly. "This is how I used to look all the time. My mother said a woman should never leave the house without wearing lipstick, and she always made sure I'd tidied my hair." Now she smiles ruefully, and her eyes grow a little distant. "She would have wanted such a different wedding for me. She would have wanted such a different life."

Esther and I look at each other. Breine is usually so optimistic; I'm not sure how to respond. Esther puts a hand on her shoulder. "I hope she would be happy for you anyway. Chaim is a wonderful man."

Breine sucks in a deep breath and then reaches up to return Esther's touch with a brisk pat on the hand. "Let's get me dressed," she says.

We give her a towel to hold over her face to keep her makeup from smudging. And then Esther keeps Breine's hair in place while I slide the dress over her head and button the back.

When I'm finished doing up the back, Breine splays her palms upward, eyes quizzical. "Well?"

Esther brings her hands to her heart. "Oh, Breine, you're perfect."

Breine's face lights up, and she motions for Esther to bring her the chair so she can get a full-length glimpse of herself in the wall mirror.

I don't say anything yet, instead busily walking around her in a full circle, straightening hems, critically eyeing my own handiwork.

The new sash at the waistline gives Breine more of an hourglass shape, and a new sweetheart neckline draws attention to her pretty neck and collarbone. All those dozens of tiny beads, those infernal tiny beads, I reattached around the scalloped edges. Clustered together this way, instead of scattered over the whole dress, they catch the light and sparkle as if Breine is carrying around her own sun.

I've done a fine job. Maybe not completely up to Chomicki & Lederman standards, but a very fine job, especially given my limited resources and time frame. I wouldn't be ashamed for my father or Baba Rose to see this dress.

And earlier this afternoon, just before I took the dress to iron, I made one last adjustment because the garment didn't feel complete. Along the neckline, at the lowest part just near Breine's heart, I ripped out a few stitches of the seam, and before I repaired it, I tucked in a small square of silk:

*Choose to love*, I wrote. It's what Breine said to me when she first told me about Chaim: She was choosing to love the person in front of her.

*Choose to love.*

WE GIVE BREINE A HANDKERCHIEF TO TUCK UP HER SLEEVE, and when she's as ready as we can make her, Esther and I throw on our own donation-box dresses—hers, pink and frilled, and mine, the color of a ripe plum, a bit short in the hemline but otherwise a perfect fit. Both of them smell faintly of mothballs until Breine douses us all in perfume.

No sooner have we finished than Breine's uncle knocks at the door in a borrowed suit, hair impeccably combed, and Esther and I leave to give the small family private time before the ceremony.

Abek is waiting for me just outside the cottage, hair still damp and looking freshly scrubbed. He's found a new shirt, buttoned with a little gap between the collar and his neck. "This is all right?" he asks.

"I suppose I should ask if you washed behind your ears?"

I tease, pretending to inspect him. "It's all right. I'm so glad you're here."

On the way to the courtyard, I spot Josef in front of us. He is also in a new donation-box shirt. His is a soft hazelnut color, a shade lighter than his eyes. I've only ever seen him in the gray shirt he was wearing when we first met. This one fits better. This one skims more closely along his chest and stomach. This one is a bit too short at the sleeves, but short in a way that shows off his wrists. He has nice wrists.

"Hi," I say softly.

"Hi," he says back, and I'm glad I went with the dress that brings out the warmth in my skin.

"I didn't get to introduce you to my brother," I say, and watch proudly as Abek extends his hand to Josef in a grown-up handshake. "My brother, Abek. And this is Josef Mueller."

Josef returns the greeting, but his eyes stay on me. A lot passes behind them. An apology? Regret? Something sharp and rough, making my chest pang. I'm still trying to parse the expression when we're separated by laughing wedding guests, come to celebrate, carrying us along with the crowd.

The whole camp has been saving kerosene rations for this wedding. The courtyard is lit by lanterns, and as Abek and I approach, Ravid and his fiancée, Rebekah, pass out candles.

The courtyard itself is still ugly, mostly dust and dirt. Any flowers once here have been ripped up to make way for the herb garden planted to feed the camp. But that's not so visible in the twilight.

In the middle stands the chuppah, a plain white sheet

attached to rough-hewn wood. Chaim stands under it, waiting in a suit that's too big and a haircut that's a little too raw.

Behind me, the chatter quiets, and I realize it's because Breine is approaching. Her auburn hair glows with the setting sun.

It's beautiful, it's so beautiful, this wedding between bold Breine and shy Chaim. In a different world, the sheet might be a fine, embroidered cloth, just as in a perfect world, Breine would be escorted by her parents. But she no longer has parents, so when she comes down the path, it is between her uncle, whose face is shining, and an old woman I've heard referred to as Mrs. Van Houten.

"In pictures, it will look white, as she wanted," says Mrs. Yost, who has appeared next to me, as she nods toward Breine's dress.

"I don't think it would matter if the dress was the color of dishwater," I whisper back. "Look at her face."

And it's true. As Breine comes closer, I can look at her not as I did in the cottage, as the mannequin for a sewing project, but rather as a bride. She is radiant; she's so much lovelier than any dress even the best seamstress could have made.

"But in the picture, it will look white," Mrs. Yost insists. "If they show a photograph of this day to their grandchildren in fifty years, nobody needs to know it was taken in a camp."

Breine's uncle and Mrs. Van Houten walk Breine to the chuppah and in a circle around Chaim, who lets his eyes follow her while he faces the crowd.

A Hungarian man is marrying a Polish and Czech woman, who is escorted by a Dutch woman standing in for her mother and an estranged uncle standing in for her father, and they all know what to do right now because their faith is the same language.

I haven't been to a wedding in years, not since I was a child. Not since before the Germans invaded. But when the rabbi reaches the Seven Blessings, I find myself nodding along to the Hebrew words I didn't know I remembered.

*Blessed are you, Lord, who gladdens the groom and bride.*

Tears pool in my eyes and run, salty, down my face. Mrs. Yost, normally exasperated and impatient, pulls a handkerchief from her sleeve. Esther's glasses have slipped almost entirely off her nose because she's been too distracted by the ceremony to periodically push them up.

I see Josef where the men are standing, angular in the candlelight, his hair still unruly but his face smooth, recently shaved in a way that makes it look naked. As I watch, his eyes move away from the couple and, under the cover of the shadows, he meets my eyes instead. He must have felt me staring.

I should feel embarrassed, but I don't look away. I don't know if it's the joy of the moment, or my new dress, or the happiness of the past few days that emboldens me, but I want to be seen by him. On this day, when my lips are plumped with lipstick and my hair is freshly washed, I want to be looked at like I'm pretty.

I decide I'll hold his gaze until he's the one to look away. But then he doesn't. We're staring at each other between the poles of the makeshift chuppah, while wax runs down my fingertips and the ceremony carries on in the background. Our locked eyes are only broken by the sound of smashing glass, followed by a cheer.

Startled, I break away from Josef's gaze. Under Chaim's foot is a loose bundle of cloth, which now must contain broken shards. The breaking of the glass is the final part of the ceremony. It's supposed to symbolize a lot of things; my father once said it reminded him of the fragility of life. Now we know firsthand that life is fragile, and we don't need that reminder. But Breine wanted a real wedding, so I clap with everyone else until my palms hurt.

AFTER THE CEREMONY, WE MOVE BACK TO THE DINING HALL, where a few men have gathered instruments, playing lively music to accompany the dinner. Tables have been pushed to the periphery and piled with plates—dishes from Breine's and Chaim's home countries and all the other countries represented in the camp.

I make Abek go ahead of me in the food line, telling him to take double the portions of his favorites, and then lead him to our usual table, where Esther already sits with friends. It's everyone from our regular dinner group, except the spot where Miriam usually sits has been taken by Breine's uncle. I'm grateful, at least, that the infirmary is far away from the dining hall, out of earshot. Miriam always seemed to enjoy hearing Breine plan her wedding, but making her listen to boisterous wedding festivities just the day after she learned about her sister seems unbelievably cruel.

I feel a stab of guilt, watching Abek settle in with his plate: This wedding celebration came at the most horrible time for her and the most wonderful time for me.

"Did you have a good time?" I ask Abek, once I've introduced him to the people he hasn't met.

"Yes," he says. But as he responds, his cheeks tint with a salmon shade of pink.

"*Did* you?" I pry. "Are you sure?"

"It was nice," he insists. "It's just—"

"What? What are you blushing about?"

"Uncle Świętopełk," he finally murmurs, barely above a whisper, eyes darting to where Breine's fastidious uncle is cutting his food into tidy parcels, dabbing his mouth with a napkin in between each bite.

"Uncle Świętopełk?" I repeat, confused. "What about him?"

"I was standing behind him during the ceremony," Abek whispers. "And he was . . ." He bursts into giggles before he can finish the sentence.

"Was what? What was he doing?"

"He was *farting*." Abek barely gets the word out before he starts to fall apart in laughter. "The whole ceremony. It smelled *so bad*. The *whole time*."

"No."

"A-a-nd sometimes they were quiet, but . . ."

"*No.*"

"But there was one part where it was like, like . . ."

"Like a bugle?" I suggest.

"Like a piccolo! It was like, *teet, teet, teet! Teetle-teetle.*"

Abek buries his face in his napkin, trying to disguise his laughter from everyone else at the table, and I sneak a glance at Uncle Świętopełk, lifting another morsel of food to his mouth.

"Abek. *Abek.*" I jab my brother in the side, and he lowers the napkin just enough to reveal one teary eye. "Look at his plate. He's only eating *cabbage*. His whole plate is just piles and piles of cabbage."

I'm building this joke because it's funny, because the mood is so light that everything seems a little funnier tonight. But also because it seems like the kind of joke that Abek and I have had before. Because when he was eight years old, nothing made him laugh more than when I put the heels of my hand over my mouth and blew out what sounded like a very rude noise.

"Cabbage," Abek repeats in mock horror. "Oh no. Where is he sleeping tonight? Someone needs to warn—"

"Everyone?" I fill in.

"Someone needs to warn everyone in the camp, immediately." He cups his hands around his mouth, as if forming a megaphone. "Attention. We have an important announcement regarding Uncle Tootle."

"*Shhhhhhh.* He'll hear you."

"Uncle Tootle will be providing the music tonight."

I kick him under the table, such a familiar gesture it nearly makes me gasp, and Abek starts chewing the inside of his cheek as he tries to quell his laughter.

"*Abek.*"

"I'm trying," he wheezes.

"Why don't you go walk around?" I suggest. "Get some more food, and see if there's another bottle of wine for the table, and we'll both pull ourselves together in the meantime."

He obediently backs out his chair, and I watch him retreat toward the food table, shoulders still occasionally shaking.

Esther is watching me, her eyes wise and appraising. "You laugh the same," she says.

"Do we?" I smile with pride.

"You must be so, so happy," she says, and I reach across the table to squeeze her hand.

By the time Abek returns, I think it's safe: Uncle Świętopełk has left our table to go join some of the older folks having a quiet conversation in the corner.

Abek didn't bring another plate of food with him, but instead slides an open bottle of wine onto the table. He pours me a glass and then, despite my raised eyebrow, pours himself one, too.

"You know who I'm thinking of?" I tell him. "Papa. Watching that wedding made me think of him."

"About his and Mama's wedding?"

"No, not exactly. Though I guess I was thinking of them like that, too. But mostly, I was thinking about how Papa was a good man. When he married Mama, he might have wanted to move into his own house, not to move in with his wife's parents and little sister. But he did anyway—he really almost raised Aunt Maja, too, didn't he?

"He was always trying to do the right thing," I continue. "Even that day in the stadium, trying to defend the old pharmacist when he knew it would—" I break off. "Anyway, when Breine's uncle walked her to Chaim, it made me think of Papa."

"Because Papa walked Aunt Maja to the chuppah?"

"Because—no, Abek, Aunt Maja never married. Don't you remember?"

"Mmm-hmm. Do you want another glass?" he asks, lifting the bottle.

I wave my hand to show him I don't. "You remember what she always said about what a man would have to have in order for her to marry?"

"*Yes*. I said yes."

I realize now that my brother looks a little red in the face and glassy in the eyes and that his wineglass is already empty when mine is still nearly full. Remembering that the bottle was open when he brought it to the table, I have a sneaking suspicion that this glass isn't his first. So when he reaches for the bottle again, I move my hand first for the pitcher of water sitting in the middle of the table and fill Abek's glass with that instead.

"It's a wedding, Zofia," he protests. "A special occasion!"

"And it looks like you celebrated enough already. You're twelve."

"You told me to get more wine!"

"I didn't tell you to *drink* it," I say, laughing.

"You don't need to lecture me like that," he snaps.

Across the table, a few seatmates have noticed our conversation and are unsuccessfully trying not to stare. Abek leans back in his chair, arms folded across his chest. I can tell he feels embarrassed at being singled out as so young. Everyone else at the table has been drinking; I've had a few glasses myself. I'm wondering, suddenly, if there would have been any harm in pouring him just one more swallow so that he could save face rather than feel embarrassed in front of a group of new people he's just met.

"Maybe if you watered it down," I suggest, trying to compromise.

"Water it *down*?"

"Or in another few hours, you could—"

"That's not the point."

But I don't know what the point is. I can't believe he'd really get so upset over a glass of wine, but I can't think of what else would have made him suddenly so sullen and defensive.

Esther raises a sympathetic eyebrow; she's witnessed the whole exchange. Deciding something, she drops her napkin onto the table and circles over to us.

"Abek, I was wondering if you would like to dance with me? I'm not very good," she apologizes. "But if you don't mind a clumsy partner, we can have a go together."

I look up at her in gratitude as she extends her hand and Abek takes it. The two of them weave onto the floor, bobbing awkwardly to the music.

Lots of other people have also partnered up, and now I'm the only one left at our table, which is littered with mismatched cups and crumpled napkins. I down the contents of my glass while watching the dance floor.

There were bottles of good wine, and now they're empty; there were bottles of bad liquor, and now they're almost empty, too. By now I've drunk enough this evening that sitting still makes me woozy, so I busy myself by gathering all the dirty dishes into a pile and carrying them into the kitchen.

Josef stands at the big white sink, arms submerged to the elbows.

"You're not out there dancing?" I set the dishes on the counter.

He gestures to the soapy water. "We'd run out of plates." As if to further illustrate his point, he takes a dirty one off the stack I've just brought in and begins to wash it.

But on the other side of the sink is a different stack, nearly as tall, of clean plates.

"Don't you think that should be enough for now?" I ask. "Most people have already eaten. Why don't you come back to the party, and we'll just bring out the ones you've washed so far."

He shakes his head and grabs another plate. "I'm not much of a dancer anyway."

"Neither is Esther, but you should see her trying to teach Abek out there."

"I might as well finish. Someone is going to have to eventually."

It's clear he won't be persuaded, so I roll up my own sleeves and grab a clean towel.

"You don't have to," he protests as I tie a makeshift apron over my dress. "Especially not with your brother here."

"I'm trying not to hover over him. I think I've already embarrassed him once tonight. Here, you wash, I'll dry. This will be faster with two of us."

We move through the stack swiftly, but I can tell from his occasional intakes of breath that there's something he wants to say. The next time he pulls a dish out of the water, he doesn't let go when I move to grab it. Suspended between our two hands, it dribbles water onto the floor.

"I never congratulated you for finding him," he says. "Or apologized for saying you wouldn't."

"You were only being rational," I say magnanimously. It's easy to be magnanimous, of course, since my brother is right now less than fifty meters away. "Most people would have agreed I was foolish."

His grip on the plate only tightens. "But what if you'd actually listened to me? If you'd listened to me and you hadn't put up all those letters, or—"

"Josef, we're at a wedding," I sigh. "I'm in the nicest dress I've worn in years, and I'm wearing it to wash dishes in the kitchen. Now hurry up and let's finish so I can take this apron off and you can tell me I look beautiful in my dress." The words coming out of my mouth are fueled a bit by alcohol, no doubt, but not so much that I couldn't control them if I really wanted to.

"And *that*, by the way, is what a person in a new dress wants to hear when she walks in a room," I continue. " 'You look beautiful.' Not, 'We're out of dishes.' "

I've shocked Josef into letting go of the wet plate. It reels back against the front of the dress I've just finished bragging about. My grip seems tight enough at first, but the plate slips through my hands—and then through Josef's as he, too, tries to grab it as it falls—and finally it crashes onto the floor, shattering into pieces.

"Oh," I say uselessly as the shards settle around my feet.

"I'll get a broom," he says.

*Damnit.*

We sweep up the pieces, big ones in a trash bin, smaller ones wrapped in a cloth, and the only words exchanged—*Do you see that piece under the sink*—are practical ones.

I've ruined the moment, if there ever was one. On my hands and knees, I skim the floor with a wet towel to mop up the tiniest fragments. My dress is now damp and dusty at the hem, and my underarms are slick with perspiration. On my feet again, I wipe my forehead with the back of my arm. Josef sweeps methodically, head down, broom bristles scraping the floor.

"I think that's the last of it," I say. "Do you think we try to save this towel with the fragments, or can we just throw the whole thing away? Josef?"

He stops sweeping and raises his eyes to mine. "You look beautiful in your dress."

I startle. "You don't have to say it *now.*"

"You were beautiful in your dress at the wedding, and sweeping up broken dishes in your apron you're even more beautiful. You have to know that."

He extends his hand, and my face flushes until I realize he's

beckoning not for my hand but for the glass-filled towel, tossing it in the trash bin. "We'll throw it away."

"Josef."

"I'll finish the rest of the cleanup on my own." He plunges
his hands back into the soapy water.

"No."

"It's fine."

"*No*," I say, making a decision. "Let's go dance." He starts
to protest again, but I'm already untying my apron. "Enough,
Josef. Enough."

I'm saying enough with washing the dishes, but I'm also
saying enough with your pulling back. Enough with your
deciding when we're done talking and when you want to tell
me you prefer to keep to yourself and when you want to tell me
I'm beautiful. Enough with that. I won't put up with it anymore. I hold out my hand, firmly. "This is your last chance to
come and dance. If I put my hand down, I'm not asking again.
Ever. I'm not asking anything of you ever again."

He has to think about it; I see him calculating the price of
either move. Only when I've let my hand drop a centimeter
does he take his from the sink, soapy and dripping, and accept
my outstretched palm.

The water trickles from his hand down onto my own
knuckles, past my wrist, but I don't think it's the drip that
makes me shiver.

Back in the main room, the musicians have put away their
instruments, and someone's turned on a phonograph instead.
It's not traditional wedding music anymore, but band music,

bright and bubbly with the sound of brass horns. I don't know how to dance to it, but neither, it seems, do a lot of people. Two of the Canadian workers are giving a demonstration in the middle of the room, and then others clumsily follow their lead as best they can. Josef looks relieved; he'll be far from the only beginner on this dance floor.

He puts one arm around my waist as the Canadians are doing. It makes my skin jolt, but it's also awkward, trying to figure out how our bodies should fit together amid a sea of people while music blasts in the background. Josef, it becomes clear after a few minutes of dancing, has terrible rhythm. The steps are simple, but he can't seem to start on the right beat. I'm trying not to laugh at him, but then I can't help it. And instead of being annoyed, he's laughing, too, throwing his hands in the air and exaggerating every clumsy step.

Is this what a date would be like? Is this what it would have been like if I'd met Josef at school or a social club? Is this what it could still be like if we could have a relationship that wasn't colored by my pain or his?

"Come over here." I pull him to the corner of the room, behind a rack where people have hung jackets, where we won't bother anyone else. "Watch my feet," I say. "The third and fourth steps are quicker. It goes slow, slow, quick-quick."

He nods his head down to watch my feet, and then I nod my head down to offer more guidance, and then our foreheads bump together.

And suddenly we are kissing.

AS SOON AS OUR LIPS MEET, MY HEART JOLTS; MY HEAD FEELS dizzy.

And then Josef abruptly pulls his head back. For a moment I wonder if I've made a terrible mistake. *Does he not want this?* But then I feel his heartbeat, heavy against my chest, and realize it's just that he felt the jolt, too, and we're both overwhelmed. When he leans in again, it's with intention. He cups his hands behind my head and strokes my cheek with his thumb, and I lean forward. Our lips meet more softly this time, less clumsily, and so slowly time has stopped.

I've kissed someone before. The first time was at a birthday party when I was thirteen, when a boy named Lev and I were dared to go behind a dining room curtain. Lev and I spent the next two months occasionally sneaking off, him waiting for me after school with wilted bouquets of picked flowers. But this is different. It doesn't feel like kissing Lev did, like a pantomime or a rehearsal for the real thing. I can feel this kiss rushing through my entire body.

"Oops!" The coatrack moves—a man searching for his hat—and we both jump apart. "Oops!" the man exclaims again, cheerfully drunk. "Everyone is having fun tonight!"

The drunk man paws through the rack, giving me enough time to sober up and think about what I'm doing. Now is when I should suggest going back to the dance floor or getting a drink of water. Josef is looking at me, waiting for me to suggest that; he knows it's what should happen, too.

"Do you want to leave?" I ask instead. "Find another room where it's not so loud?"

He hesitates only a second. "Yes."

"Where do you want to go?"

"Where do you want to go, Zofia?"

"Let's go to your cottage."

This sentence carries a lot of things. I could have said, *Let's go see the new library room in the administration building.* I could have even said, *Let's go to my cottage, where Abek will return at some point tonight, and Esther, too, shoes in her hand, tipsy from wine.* But I know that Josef shares a room only with Chaim and that this afternoon Chaim did what Breine did: moved her belongings into a marital room they'll live in together. Josef's room will be empty all night.

I scan the dining hall. Esther and Abek have given up on dancing. But someone has produced a deck of playing cards, and they're sitting back at the table with Ravid and a few others. I catch Esther's eye and nod toward Abek. She nods back. *He's fine; everything's fine. I'll keep an eye on him for a while.*

I hesitate again, just in case, paralyzed for a moment at the idea of letting my brother out of my sight. But Abek is laughing; he seems to be having fun.

Outside the dining hall, Josef and I are suddenly shy, walking side by side like strangers. Josef apologizes for bumping against my hip, and I say nonsensical things about the stars. I say, "The stars are really bright tonight," even though they look like they do all the time. When we walk into Josef's cottage—when we pass Ravid's room in the front and go into Josef's in the back, and when I see the neat hospital corners on his bed—I'm suddenly even more aware of what I've done.

"That's Chaim's bed," he says unnecessarily, pointing to the mattress stripped of sheets. "I can sit there, or I can go find a chair if you'd be more comfortable."

"No."

"Should I offer you some water?"

"No."

"I haven't been inside a girls' cottage. Do they look—"

I cut him off before he can say more, putting my arms around his waist, crushing my lips against his. We're kissing again, only now we're breathing harder; I can feel his body start to respond to mine, feel the way my hands start out trembling but grow more certain, and then more certain than they've ever been about anything. I slide my hands under his shirt and then up against the bare skin of his chest, where his heart crashes against my palm. He gasps against my lips and then reaches for the buttons on my dress, lingering at the top one, near the nape of my neck.

"Can I—"

"Yes," I say, but then I have to do it myself when he can't work the button out of its hole. When I'm finished, he gently pulls my chin up using the tips of his fingers, and then he touches his tongue to the now-bare hollow of my neck.

My whole body shudders as he manages the next button on his own, and then the button after that.

I forgot that pleasure could feel this strong. After years of feeling nothing but perpetual, insistent pain, my body had begun to feel like an instrument of it. Like it was built to withstand things rather than experience them. And then when the war was over, when I was safely in the hospital, what I mostly felt was numbness, a protective anesthetization against my own feelings. I forgot that I could want something because I wanted it and not just because I was starving or cold.

"Zofia," Josef whispers, and his voice brings me back to this moment, to the gritty reality of this moment and of my body. How the door is thin, and unlocked, and could be opened any minute. How Aunt Maja told me what happens on wedding nights, but it was always put like that—*what happens on wedding nights*—and not what happens with a boy you've known only a few weeks.

I close my eyes, trying to block Aunt Maja's face, but now my body is warring with itself.

"Wait."

"What?" Josef says in between kisses on my neck, soft, slow kisses that make me melt.

"Josef, wait."

This time my arms move before my brain can think, and I push Josef away. He looks back at me, confused, raising his palms.

"I'm so sorry. I thought you were all right with—I must have misunderstood."

"I have only eight toes," I blurt out.

"What?"

"Eight. At the hospital, two of them were too frostbitten to save. If my shoes come off—I didn't want you to be repulsed if you saw my feet."

Josef steps back and studies me and then turns his back. I think this must mean he's disgusted, until he flips up the back of his hair. "Do you see it?" he asks. And I do; it's hard to miss: a bald spot the size of an apricot. "One winter, I got sick. My hair started falling out, and in this spot it didn't grow back," he continues. "And I don't think it ever will. I will be bald there forever until the rest of my hair falls out, too."

"Is that why you never comb your hair properly?" I ask, and start to laugh.

"That's exactly why. If I properly combed my hair, everyone would see how little hair I have left."

I roll up my sleeve: a spidery scar, running from my forearm up past my elbow. "A shuttle flew off the loom at my second camp," I tell him. "It didn't heal right. I thought if I reported the injury, they would send me to the sick barrack, and I would never come out."

"I'm missing my right molars." He pries his mouth open with his fingers, nodding at me to look inside, where two black holes replace what used to be teeth. "A soldier hit me with the butt of his rifle, and they flew out of my mouth."

"I have scars from flea bites," I tell him.

"You think you have flea bites? I itched mine until they bled; I couldn't leave them alone. Pockmarks, all up and down my legs."

He lifts one corner of his trousers. It's dim enough that I can barely see these alleged pockmarks, but I am laughing anyway, laughing and crying as we continue this tour of our bodies, of the secret, hidden things that are broken in them. Josef is laughing, too, as he lets go of his pant leg and puts his hand on the sleeve of his shirt.

"My shoulder was dislocated, and it didn't set right," he says. "I can't do even one push-up anymore. I have trouble holding myself up on my arms if I'm in a certain position. If I'm..."

He trails off. He's not laughing anymore. By the lamplight, I can tell that his face has turned red, and then I feel myself blush, too, because I can tell what he's trying to say: If I were on my back, and he was above me, it might not work, he might not be able to hold himself there.

"I don't mind," I say.

Josef hesitates. "Do I need to... should I go get—"

He doesn't finish, but I know what he was about to say. *Should he go get protection? Could this have consequences?*

"No." I'm overcome by a wave of tenderness and then one last wave of nerves. "I haven't—I haven't bled in a long time. Josef, when my clothes are off, you can count my ribs. Even after months in the hospital, I don't look very...womanly." *My breasts are gone*, is what I mean to tell him. My cycle is dried up. I am shriveled; I am a nothing-girl.

"I don't mind," he says, and reaches to turn off the lamp.

My final confession and this final darkness have liberated me. He knows every embarrassing thing about my body.

Outside, far in the distance, I can still hear music from the wedding.

I am thinking of Breine, having a wedding now to prove she is alive, to remind herself to never again wait on things that might make her happy. I am thinking of Aunt Maja and her wedding-night advice. But Aunt Maja isn't here to give me advice anymore; nobody is.

I reach down toward the button of Josef's pants, but before I can unfasten it, he grabs my hand.

"Don't," he says. "There's something else." Josef's voice is low and husky.

"That's enough maladies."

"Not something that's wrong. Something else about me. I haven't been able to think of a way to—"

"Please stop talking," I instruct him. And he does. He sits on the edge of the bed and puts his hands on my waist while I finish unbuttoning the rest of the buttons on my new purple dress and let it slip to the floor. I take his hands, and I put them on my flattened chest. From his sharp intake of breath, I can tell I am not too flat for him.

He puts his lips on my stomach, and I run my hands through his hair. I kiss the top of his head, and we remember that we are alive.

*HERE'S A PIECE OF MY MEMORY, OF MY DEAD-GHOST-MEMORY, come floating back to me. It seems like I should have a happier one, like doing something happy should also trigger happy memories. But that's not how this puzzle works, it seems. The pieces don't come in order. Each piece floats around the waste of my mind until it attaches itself to something random, obscure.*

*They didn't send my father to the left when we got to Birkenau. My father was already dead. My father was dead because, when he saw the German soldiers kick the old pharmacist, he went to help him, and so they shot him. First, one soldier viciously jammed his hand against my father's throat, knocking out his wind, and then they shot him. Casually, like their guns were flyswatters. He fell to the ground. His arm bent ragdoll-like behind him; I remember thinking his shoulder would be dislocated.*

*He wasn't the only person to die that day on the soccer field in the rain. The soldiers shot others who disobeyed orders. People who tried to sneak from one line to the other. A woman began screaming that her son was at work, that he had a dispensation; if she'd known she wasn't going to be allowed back to her house, she would have said goodbye to him. She tried to leave; they shot her.*

*There was so much death and blood that day, happening all at once. The rest of my family, I lost when we got to Birkenau, and maybe* it was easier for me to believe I had lost my father that way, too: to the left, all at once. Remembering that I had lost him a few days before then would mean that I had to have two battering rams of pain instead of just one.

Does it really matter, in the end? He's just as dead either way.

WHEN I WAKE UP NEXT, JOSEF IS STILL SLEEPING, ON HIS stomach, his hair tousled like beach grass. This is the position he fell asleep in, too, the position both of us did. Side by side on our stomachs, hands curled neatly near our chins, suddenly aware of each other's personal space and how it would be rude to impose on it. Before sleeping, my last memory is me asking him whether his shoulder hurt, him asking me whether I was too cold, me saying that I wasn't cold, but I *was* nearly naked, so I was going to keep my arms where they were, protecting my nakedness. Him laughing.

I meant to close my eyes for just a minute and then go back to Abek. But it's clear I fell asleep for longer. It's still dark outside, but the sky is a dark bruise instead of an inky black. Closer to sunrise than midnight. I fumble for the lamp by the side of Josef's bed and turn it on; it's just bright enough to see around the room and get my bearings. I'm half-dressed. Earlier, Josef wrapped a blanket around his waist while he searched in the dark for our underthings, passing mine to me before turning away to pull on his own—belated modesty that amused me. He must have gotten up again while I was still sleeping: A chair leans underneath the doorknob, safeguarding against anyone walking in. And when I went to sleep, my dress was in a pool on the floor. Now it's folded on his nightstand, with my shoes tucked underneath. Easy for me to find if I wanted to leave while it was dark.

His own clothes hang in the open wardrobe on a wooden bar with a piece of twine tied in the middle, to partition his half from Chaim's, I assume. Chaim's half is empty now, and Josef's has only one other shirt inside: the one he was wearing the day I met him, the one he's worn every other time I've seen him. Even when the donation boxes come, spilling over with linen and mothballs, he apparently never takes anything from them except for his new wedding shirt.

I tiptoe across the floor to take the shirt out of the wardrobe, cringing as the hangers clatter, but Josef doesn't wake. The shirt is the kind of faded gray that could have once been white or once been blue; sun-starched now, but carrying the washings and weight of a hundred other days pressed on Josef's skin. It smells clean like grass and the sun it dried in, and underneath, it smells like Josef himself, the smoky sweetness of his skin. Up close, I can confirm what I'd earlier noticed about Josef's handiwork with the buttons: They've been reattached, securely but without any eye to aesthetics. The pocket is still torn. It's not as necessary to the shirt, I suppose.

Quietly, I walk back to my dress and feel in the pocket. I'd tucked a needle and thread inside, just in case something went wrong at the last minute with Breine's dress. I don't think Josef will mind about the mismatched color.

Sitting on Chaim's empty bed, I prop the lamp next to me and fix the buttons first, snipping off the crooked ones and aligning them with the buttonholes. For the pocket, I turn to a basic whipstitch, the first stitch I ever learned, with Baba Rose carefully guiding my hand as I dragged the needle through two practice scraps of cloth. This isn't the fancy sewing reserved for the clothing at our factory. It's the private, family sewing I would use to hem my father's pants or to add a patch on Baba Rose's sleeve.

"What are you doing?" Josef is still half asleep, his voice low and cracked, a crease of pillow imprinted across his cheek.

"Go back to sleep," I say.

"Are you fixing my shirt?"

"Why don't you have more than one?"

"I have two," he mumbles.

"Well, *now* you have two, because you picked out a new one for the wedding. Why didn't you ever pick out another one before?"

"Other people need them more."

"Josef. You had *one shirt*."

"I like watching you work. You're very good."

"How would you know? Judging from the state of the buttons before I fixed them, you're very bad."

"I like watching you work." He's fading again, slurring his words together.

"Go back to sleep, Josef."

I wait until his breathing has steadied again, and then I make an extra fold in the fabric of the pocket. I cut off a bit of fabric from where it won't be noticed and quickly begin to stitch.

*Z is for Zofia, 1945, who fixed one of your shirts and tore the other off you.*

I twist the cloth between my fingers, as small a roll as I can make it, and work it into the extra space I'd created in the pocket, then I sew it shut. I'd be both mortified and pleased if he ever found it. My family thought it was sweet when I made these messages, but the few other times I did this for friends, I never told them. I could never decide whether they would think it was sweet or strange. Maybe it is strange. I barely know Josef.

*Today I am choosing to love the person in front of me*, Breine said, telling me that she planned to marry a man she hadn't even known for two months. Not that I am saying I want to marry him. Not that I am saying I love him.

But last night we were together, and even if Josef never finds this message, I like the idea of my name being close to his skin. I like even more the idea that there is a record of what happened last night, and something could happen to me, and something could happen to Josef, but there will still be that record because I wrote it down.

Almost back at my cottage, I see a figure slipping out the door: Breine in a dressing gown, clutching something to her chest.

She startles at my footsteps, then laughs when she realizes it's only me.

"What are you doing, just coming home?" She raises one eyebrow. "*Someone's* been having a good time."

"What are you doing here at all?" I tease back. "Aren't you supposed to live with Chaim now?"

She shows me the item in her hand. "Toothbrush. I forgot it. Chaim said not to bother, but who wants to wake up without a toothbrush the first morning next to their husband?" Her face turns pink at the last word. "Husband! Can you believe it?"

"It was a beautiful wedding, Breine."

"Wasn't it? I really think so."

"It was. And now I should let you get back to your *husband*. If you're away too long, he'll think you've changed your mind."

"Yes." She gives a little, silly curtsy, holding the edges of her dressing gown. "I'm glad I saw you, though, because I was going to look for you tomorrow anyway. I wanted to tell you something—Ravid isn't coming."

"To bed with you and Chaim? I hope not."

She laughs. "To Eretz Israel. Ravid is in contact with someone who has a boat. It can leave from Italy. But he and Rebekah aren't going to come with us. They told us after the wedding."

"Why wouldn't he come? He's organized all of you, hasn't he?"

"That's why. Ravid is staying behind to help organize more trips; he thinks he's more valuable this way."

"I'm sure it's hard for you to say goodbye to a friend."

I'm still not sure why we're having this conversation. I don't know Ravid well enough to have an opinion on whether he should go with the rest of the group.

But Breine's eyes are crafty; there's a complicated look in them as she grabs my hands. "That's what I wanted to talk to you about. Zofia, I'm wondering if you should come with us." She holds up a finger before I can protest. "I know you said earlier that you have your own plans, but now the invitation is real. There are two empty spots. You don't have to take them, but—listen. I'm grateful to you for making my dress, and I'm happy that you found your brother, and, well, I'm a little older than you, and I don't mean to sound bossy, but—it's been really comforting for me to move forward with life, not go back. If we went to Ravid before anyone else did, I bet he would give you the slots. You and Abek."

"I can't just...leave."

"Why not? You came here to find Abek, and you've found him. You've done what you wanted to do. Think about what happens next, though. All right? It's only a suggestion."

I slip my hands out of Breine's. Pretend I'm cold. Tuck my hands underneath my arms and look at the ground. "I'm not ready to decide anything yet. Abek *just* got here. I *just* found him. It's only been a few days."

"Does this have anything to do with Josef?"

My face burns hot that she would ask this, that she'd assume I might plan such a big decision around a boy I'd known only a few weeks.

"I apologize," she says in response to my silence. "I saw you dancing together and now you're coming home at four o'clock in the morning."

"It's not about Josef. It's about the fact that I already had a plan. Once I found Abek, we were going to go back home. That was the plan."

"Zofia," she says gently. She doesn't try to take my hands again, but she somehow makes herself shorter than I am so she can look up at my eyes. "What's there for you now? Tell me, Zofia. What's waiting for you back there at your home?"

"My friend Gosia," I start, but I know that's not an answer. Gosia would tell me to go be happy, wherever that was, and to send her postcards along the way. What else? My family's apartment? But I could leave that for Gosia as well. That home feels like part of my history, but it was new at one point, too. At one point, Baba Rose and her husband were young and newly married, and they moved into an empty apartment and started to fill it with furniture and make a new life.

What was special about that apartment before they moved in? Nothing. Everything special about that apartment was the family they built in it. Couldn't it have been any apartment?

I think about the last time I left my family's home. In the dead of night, while sweet Dima slept, on the same day I'd seen a Nazi flag in my neighbor's flowerpot and the same night a group of men had threatened me. My home had already been looted, destroyed, a shell of itself. I told myself that the place I'd grown up didn't feel right because my family wasn't there with me. What if it didn't feel right because it's not right anymore?

Abek didn't say he wanted to go home to Sosnowiec. He just said he wanted to go home.

"I just think it's better for all of us to keep moving," she repeats. "That's all."

"I'll think about it," I say. "I'll talk to Abek."

"Think quickly," she says. "If I tell Ravid you're interested, he might be able to hold off other people for a week or so. So think hard, but think quickly."

BACK IN MY OWN BED—WHILE ESTHER DOZES ON THE OTHER side of the room, and Abek is curled up in Breine's old spot—I toss and turn, trying to lull myself back to sleep by counting sheep, then by multiplying by twos and trying to recite countries of the world. My pillow feels hot and uncomfortable, and I can't stop thinking that an hour ago it was Josef's pillow my cheek was lying on. The sun is half up, filling the room with violet and then a burnt orange, and I reconcile myself to the idea that I won't sleep any more tonight.

Across the room, a mumble. Abek. I freeze, afraid that I've woken him with my tossing, but then the noise gets louder. Abek thrashes in his sheets. He's still sleeping. It's a nightmare: The noises he's making aren't words but yelps, desperate and scared. Immediately, I crawl out of bed and cross over to my brother. First, I stroke his forehead, making soothing shushing sounds, but when he doesn't settle, I shake his shoulder roughly.

"Abek. Wake up. Wake up now." His eyes slide open, out of focus at first, scrambling for purchase in the dim room, clawing at my wrist. "You're dreaming. You're just dreaming."

He shoots up, drawing in a breath. "Did I bother you? Did I say anything?"

"I barely noticed you making any noises," I lie, my heart breaking a little at the memory of his weak little yelps. "I was awake already, actually. And Esther—" I nod to where Esther is sleeping as she usually does, head buried beneath a pillow.

"Oh."

"And—and now that you're awake, too, let's get up and go for a walk."

"A walk?" he repeats, a touch of sleep still in his voice. "Now?"

"Yes, I wanted to anyway," I improvise, going back to my bed and looking for my shoes. Really, I just don't want to send him back to sleep and hear him make those noises again. "Come on, I have your shoes, too."

Vaguely, I know Foehrenwald is on the outskirts of an actual town called Wolfratshausen. Esther told me about it, how there are a few open shops, places to buy hard rolls or a cup of soup. I've never had occasion to walk through it, and now seems a good day to try. We don't have a wedding to prepare for. I don't have a dress to sew. I don't have a brother to find. If I don't plan something for Abek and me to do, the day will stretch in front of us at loose ends.

The sun is still rising when we leave the cottage. Abek walks behind me, rubbing the sleep out of his eyes with his fist.

"Isn't this nice?" I try as we pass the stables and the pond. "Being out, on our own? I thought that instead of going to the cafeteria for breakfast, we could go to a restaurant and have a cup of coffee. And I think there are castle ruins. We could go to those first."

But when we get to the castle ruins Esther mentioned, I see her descriptions were generous. A plaque informs us that the castle was demolished two hundred years ago, when lightning struck a turret storing gunpowder. Now there's nothing but a few loose rocks.

"Coffee," I say stubbornly. "Let's see if we can find real coffee. It's a special occasion, I can afford it this once. And maybe a pastry?"

But this idea doesn't work, either; we're still too early for any cafes to be open. There's hardly anyone else on the street. Plus, after last night's chilly weather, I chose to wear a sweater, but now the day is unexpectedly becoming a last gasp of summer. It's early morning, but as we dispiritedly turn back to camp, sweat pools under my arms. My dress clings uncomfortably.

"I wonder how Uncle Tootle is doing," I say, my voice falsely cheery, directing the comment to Abek's sagging shoulders ahead of me as he trudges down the narrow gravel road.

"Huh? Oh. Right. Ha."

But it's not as funny in the daylight. Even I know that. I was just hoping to recapture some of the silliness from the night before.

"Zofia." He stops in his tracks, jamming his hands into his pockets. "I'm sorry about the wine last night. Getting upset."

"You don't have to apologize," I say, motioning us to keep walking. "It was the end of a long day, and a lot happened this week."

"Still, I shouldn't have."

"It's fine," I insist. "And now I made you get up at the crack of dawn for nothing, it turns out, and it's boiling hot. But we're almost back to the camp; we can get some wet rags to put on our foreheads and cool off."

"Or," he begins slowly, "or, I was thinking we could do something else."

"Like what?"

"We could go for a bicycle ride."

"Ha," I say—my turn now to be sardonic. "Was there a bicycle in the donation box?"

"No, didn't you see them when we passed? There were a few outside the stables." We're at the borders of the camp now. Abek points ahead toward the whitewashed stables, where two rusted-out contraptions lean against the wall.

I realize now he hadn't been joking. He's excited, actually, as much as I've seen since he first arrived.

"But," I protest, laughing, "we don't even know how to ride bicycles." I was going to learn the summer the Germans arrived, then they made a law that Jews weren't allowed to have them.

"*I* do."

"You know how to ride a bicycle? When did you learn how to ride a bicycle?"

"Ladna's," he says. "The farm where I was staying. She had one; I could teach you, too."

My first inclination is to tell him he's mistaken. He doesn't know how to ride a bicycle. I feel as I did when he told me that he'd tried to read Charles Dickens, heartsick and bewildered at the idea of a life I know nothing about.

"It's too hot for that."

"It would be hot, but the wind would make us feel cooler. Please?" he asks, looking suddenly shy. "Let's both do it. It would be fun. To do something new together. Something we've never done together before."

"Like, a new memory?" I ask.

His face lights up. "Yes. A brand-new thing."

"I suppose."

The bicycles by the stables are rusted-out; the rubber of the tires looks cracked and fragile, and the brakes squeak. Abek makes a show of inspecting them—for me, I think, a sweetly chivalrous gesture—and pronounces them safe, "as long as we don't go very far."

"Swing your leg up," he instructs me, holding the back of the seat firm.

"I'm going to fall over."

"You're not."

He's already demonstrated for me, pedaling the bicycle

with his slender, gawky legs. He's explained that you only fall if you stop. The faster you go, the safer you'll be, he said.

"Are you paying attention, Zofia? You're not going to fall over," he reassures me again. "You're going to start with one pedal up and one pedal down, at about eleven o'clock and five o'clock. And then you press forward on the up pedal at the same time that you push off the ground with your other foot, and catch the down pedal. Does that make sense?"

"Can't we start on the grass?"

Abek shakes his head. "It's better on hard ground. It seems scarier, but you can build speed faster there, so there's *less* of a chance of your falling. Are you ready? I promise I won't let you fall."

The handlebars jerk in my hand; I know all I have to do is keep them straight, but they seem to have a mind of their own as I kick off the ground in my best approximation of the way Abek demonstrated. I can sense he's right. If I could pedal faster, I'd feel more balanced. But I can't make my legs move like that; the old, flat tires seem to hug every piece of gravel.

We try again and again, for short bursts at a time. Five meters, then fifteen, then twenty. Each time, Abek helps me stop the bicycle, reposition a difficult chain and then discusses what I should do next time: how I should sit farther back in the seat, how I might try starting with my right pedal up instead of my left one. He is, I realize with bittersweet pride, a good teacher. Even for someone so young. He's patient and thorough, and he insists on trying to teach me, even when I say I'd be happy to sit and watch him ride alone.

*He's a nice boy*, I realize is what I'm trying to formulate. He grew up to be such a decent, kind boy.

We must have been riding for an hour. Beside me, Abek has one hand on the bicycle seat and the other on the handlebars, keeping me from tipping over or steering off the road. I can see the muscles in his skinny arm tense so hard they're quivering. His knuckles have turned white, and he's panting harder than I am as he works harder and harder to keep up.

"We can stop," I start to call out.

"No, I have it; I'm not letting you fall."

"You're getting tire—"

"Zofia, watch the road."

But it's too late. When I turn to look at Abek, my body forgets it is connected to the handlebars, that turning myself will also turn the bicycle. Abek tries to right it again but can't. For a perilous moment, the bicycle hangs in balance, deciding which way to topple, and then Abek grabs my waist and pulls me toward him so we fall toward the higher ground instead of a ditch.

My knees skid against the grass, but it's worse for Abek. I've landed half on top of him, the heel of my shoe digging into his shin.

"Are you all right?" I ask, rolling to my knees, terrified that I've injured him.

"I didn't mean for that to happen," he apologizes, scrambling to his feet. "I said I wouldn't let you fall; I promised."

"You didn't do it on purpose," I assure him, relieved he's not hurt. "Unless you *did* do it on purpose because I made you get up so early."

He shakes his head, mortified. "I promise I didn't."

"Abek, I was joking. Of course you didn't do it on purpose. I had fun."

"Really?"

"I really had fun. You're a good teacher."

He gallantly offers his hand, helping me up, and then we both hear the sound of someone approaching from the stables.

"At least with the horses, they look sort of guilty when they throw you," the voice calls. I turn my head and see Josef, hands in his pockets. "That bicycle doesn't care at all."

He's wearing the shirt I repaired only a few hours ago, and thinking of this turns my stomach warm. I wonder if I was supposed to do something when I left—leave him a note or wake him again. I don't know the protocol for leaving a man's bed in the middle of the night.

"Those horses never look guilty," I say, feeling for any remaining grass in my hair.

"You're just not close enough friends with them yet."

Abek is looking back and forth between us. I'm glad I introduced them yesterday; I wouldn't know how to now. My friend Josef? My beau? He must have seen us leave together last night.

"The brakes squeak, right?" Josef turns to Abek. "That's what I heard someone say yesterday."

"They squeak. And this chain won't stay on."

Josef crouches down, and Abek kneels next to him, their heads close together as they examine the chain, hands growing greasy and dark.

"I don't really know anything about bicycles," Josef is telling Abek. "But, what if we tried just cleaning the chain? The grease is caked on."

"I should have tried that before we even rode them," Abek says.

"I'm sure it wouldn't have mattered. These bicycles are a mess."

They look so at ease with each other. I like how Josef talks to Abek, reassuring him that he wasn't at fault for the malfunctioning bicycles. I like how Abek listens.

*Family?* My heart asks the question before my brain can stop it. Is this what my future could look like, or some form of it?

"There are some clean rags in a pile in the stables," Josef tells Abek. "I can work on the chain, and then, if we wanted to try something for the brakes, the trade school building might have a kind of oil that would work. Do you want to go see? It's the A-frame building behind the dining hall."

Abek wipes his greasy hands in the grass before disappearing into the stables, returning a few moments later with a couple of soft flannels. "These?" he asks, tossing them over and then setting off in the direction of the building that Josef described, eyeing me quickly to make sure it's okay.

As Abek disappears from sight, Josef settles back into the grass and tries to work the chain off its sprocket. "Try there," I suggest, pointing.

"You know about bicycles now?" he teases. "Do you want to do this?"

"I know how to figure out machines when they break. I've reassembled sewing machines; I've fixed looms."

He colors—I told him this last night. I told him that the scar on my arm is from a shuttle flying off a loom. I told him that when I was about to be naked in his bedroom.

Following my instructions, he works the chain off and then lays it in front of him in the clean grass.

"I, um, was going to come and find you later," he says, picking up one of the soft cloths and beginning to clean the chain, link by link, of its caked-on grime. If I didn't know better, I'd think that Josef is as uncomfortable as I am, trying to figure out how to talk to me today. "You left something in my cottage last night."

Mentally I scroll through what I could have left; all I had with me were my clothes and shoes, and I know I didn't walk home naked. "What did I leave?"

"Reach into my pocket for me," he says, nodding to his messy hands.

*It's the note I left in his shirt*, I think, mortified. *Somehow he's found it already, and now he's going to tease me about it.* Josef catches my expression, but it obviously doesn't register to him what it means. "It's some thread," he explains. "Left over from when you fixed the buttons."

"Thread," I repeat in relief, and now I do slide my hand into Josef's breast pocket, skimming along his chest until my

fingers wind around the tangle of silk pooled at the bottom. It's
still thrilling to touch him in such an intimate way, but I realize with embarrassment that I've let my hand linger longer than
necessary. Quickly, I pull the thread out and stretch it in my
lap, working loose the knots it's tied itself into in Josef's pocket.

It's somewhat of a fool's errand to even bother with it.
There weren't more than four or five centimeters of thread left
over after I finished the mending. I can find a use for almost
anything: A slightly longer piece of thread could have been
used for sewing a solitary button, or as dental floss, or for tying
into a doll's hair bow. But this piece is so uselessly short, even
I could think of no use for it. I'd thrown it into a waste can in
Josef's room. Meaning, I realize with pleasure, that he fished it
out on purpose so he would have an excuse to talk to me.

"I'm sorry I left so early," I say, smoothing out the untan-
gled string in my lap. "I thought I should get back to Abek, and
I didn't want him or Esther to worry, and..."

*And I had no idea how to act*, I silently finish the sentence.
Because I've never been in that situation and never thought I
would be.

Josef stops my apology. "Of course, of course. I assumed
you wanted to get back. I was going to leave you alone this
morning because I thought you'd spend it with Abek." He pol-
ishes another link on the now half-sparkling chain. "How is
Abek? How is it being with him?"

"He's—" I stop myself because I was about to say, *He's
fine*, which is such an incomplete response for this situation.

Josef looks up at me and sets his work back down on the grass. He's actually interested in my response; he isn't just looking for something perfunctory. "He's been out here for an hour, teaching me to ride this stupid bicycle. Even though I'm terrible at it and the bicycle is terrible. And it's strange, because . . ."

I pause because I'm trying to formulate something out loud I haven't even had a chance to formulate in my head. "Because since he came back, the whole thing has been like a dream almost. Having him at the wedding, having him sleep in our cottage. But in an odd way, just now, this morning, is when I've felt most like I had a brother. Not just a memory. If that makes any sense."

Josef bites his lip, nodding. "I think it does. With my sister—there's a difference between loving a person and loving a memory of them. Or loving who someone is and who you want them to be."

"Esther says we even laugh the same."

"You don't."

His response throws me off guard, and I ball up my little piece of thread to toss at him. "Thanks."

He puts his hand up in mock defense. "I didn't mean to offend you; I'm just saying that I don't think you have the same laugh. Yours is more sly. I've seen it; you snort sometimes."

*"Thanks."*

"I mean it in a good way. You laugh like everything is a secret." He glances up at me, his mouth twisting a little in embarrassment, I think. "You laugh, and I'm never sure what's going to come out of your mouth next."

He's nearly done cleaning this bicycle chain, so I go to where the second bicycle is still leaning against the wall of the stables and walk it back. This one's chain is even more mangled than the first; it's why Abek and I didn't choose it to begin with. Laying it on the grass, I protect my hands with a clean cloth and remove it from the gears.

"Breine is trying to get me to come with them," I say.

His hand falters.

"They're in contact with someone who has a boat. It will leave from Italy, and there are still slots on it. They're going soon."

"You never talked about—I always thought you were going to—" He collects himself and begins again. "Do you want to go?"

"I'm not sure. I've barely had a chance to think about it. Do *you* want to go?"

He presses his lips together. "I'm not a part of that group."

"Neither am I. Breine just said they had some unexpected openings."

He's silent for long enough that I begin to think he won't answer at all. "I'm not going to go," he says finally.

"Why not?"

"I'm just not. It's not the place where I belong. I don't want to take a spot from someone who really wants it."

"Okay," I say. "Then what do you really want?"

"What do you mean?"

I know I'm treading into personal territory, but I press on anyway. I've been in this man's bed; it's not out of line for me to ask these questions. "Well, Breine and Chaim are here because they're learning to run a farm. Esther is learning stenography. And I'm here because I was looking for my brother. But, when we were in the wagon on the way to the Kloster Indersdorf, you said you were trying to leave as quickly as possible. Only, I haven't seen you trying to leave."

He tenses. "I take care of the horses."

"I'm not saying you're not being useful. I'm only saying that it sounded like you wanted to collect yourself and move on, but I've never heard you mention what you want to do next. I don't even know what you did *before*."

"Before, I lived with my family and learned to take care of horses."

"*During*, then. I have no idea what happened to you during the war."

He clenches his teeth. "During the war, I lost my teeth and gained a bald spot on my head."

"Josef. You know that's not what I—"

"I would be sad if you left," he interrupts.

"What did you say?"

He finishes with the chain and wipes his hands off on the rag. "I want you to go with Breine and Chaim if you want to. I know that I just met you, and I wouldn't ask anything from you. But if any part of you was telling me about Breine's invitation because you wanted to know my reaction...my reaction is, I would be sad."

I chew the inside of my cheek, trying to keep from grinning at what Josef just said. "I think I would be sad, too."

"So maybe until you decide," he says, "you can keep leaving little pieces of leftover thread in my room that I can keep finding excuses to return to you."

I retrieve the thread from the grass where it landed after I tossed it at him. "Do you want to just take this with you so you can give it back to me tomorrow?"

"I do." Solemnly, he takes the thread. "Can I kiss you now?" Josef asks.

"You can."

WITHIN A FEW DAYS, ABEK AND I HAVE COBBLED TOGETHER a routine. Breakfast in the morning. An hour or two of his trying to teach me to ride, an activity at which I'm relentlessly hopeless. And then after that—my alterations on Breine's dress have had an unexpected result. The evening after the wedding, a woman I've never seen before stops by the cottage with a skirt in her hand, asking if I can hem it. The next day, her friend brings in a jacket that needs to be nipped in at the waist, and a trickle of men bring in shirts with loose buttons, pants with dragging legs, suits needing patches at the elbows.

It's not difficult or inspirational work, but it's work. It's useful; it's something that makes me feel useful and normal. People have hardly any money to pay with, so I end up with other things: Resoled shoes for Abek. Candles, kerosene, a carved wooden box to keep supplies in.

And then, one evening I sit in my room and finish the

delicate embroidery on a handkerchief for a going-away gathering planned for that night. Miriam. She finally came back to our cottage a few nights after the wedding, but she soon realized that her reason for staying at Foehrenwald had disappeared. Now that she knows her sister won't ever be coming, she's decided to go back to Holland. She thinks she still has friends there. Breine and Chaim organized the gathering and asked me to make the gift. I stitched flowers around the edges, and then, in the middle, all our initials.

It's a heartbreaking party, a party that's trying to do a lot of different things. It seems odd to ask Miriam to remember her time in Foehrenwald when so much of it is defined by things she would like to forget. But I give her the handkerchief anyway, and she folds it carefully into her pocket.

"Do you know, my sister's name is Rose?" she asks, sadly running her hand over the flowers. "I will think she knows you made this for me."

After the dinner is over, I walk back to the cottage with Abek, thinking about Miriam going back to Holland, about beginnings and endings.

There's no strict reason why I need to be in Foehrenwald. I could take in sewing anywhere. I could do it in Sosnowiec, and that would free up two beds for the other refugees who continue to arrive every day. This place is not meant to be permanent.

"Do you want to try riding again before it's completely

dark?" Abek asks. "Or, I think some people are going to play cards later."

We're about halfway to the cottage, walking down the dirt path. It's chilly tonight, back to normal autumn temperatures, and I fold my arms in front of my chest. "Actually, I was thinking we should talk about the future."

"The future?"

"What to do now. You've been here a little while, and now that we've found each other, we should have a plan."

"Okay," he agrees. "What are the options?"

"Well, we could go back to Sosnowiec right now," I say slowly. "That's the first option. It's what I've always assumed we would do. We could live in our old apartment, and we could try to find our old friends. Do you remember your old room? I know Gosia would like to see you, and—"

"What else?" he interrupts. "You also said we could go with Breine and Chaim on their boat."

"We could go with them on their boat," I continue, a bit thrown off at how quickly he seemed to dismiss the option of going home. "Or, there are ships, I suppose, to anywhere in the world. We could go somewhere else," I blurt out. "We could go to—to Sweden. Or Argentina, or America."

"I wanted to go to Norway," Abek says suddenly.

"Norway? Since when?" I laugh. "Why?"

He looks down. "There was a man who was nice to me. He was from Norway. He told me there are all these—they're not rivers, but they're like that. And mountains."

"Fjords," I supply. "They're inlets, I think. Okay, we could add Norway to our list. Anywhere else?"

*Does Josef want to go to Norway?* a part of my brain wonders, but I quickly swat away the thought. This conversation is about Abek and me. It's not about Josef. "The thing that's most important is that you need to be back in school," I say. He makes a face. "You *do*. You probably haven't had steady lessons of any kind since Mrs. Schulman, when you were eight, and you've never been in a real schoolhouse."

"Can't you teach me?"

"That's not really a permanent solution. I need to be thinking about how to make money and take care of us."

"I could work, too," he offers.

"I don't want you to work. You're too young. I want you to still have a normal childhood. School was important to Papa and Mama; you remember."

He rolls his eyes. "I'm not a child." There's a testiness in his voice, like I heard when I wouldn't let him have the wine at the wedding.

"Well, I want you to still have a normal *life*," I amend my statement. "Normal twelve-year-olds go to school."

"Normal twelve-year-olds don't survive Birkenau by jumping into latrines to hide from the commandant every time there was a selection. It's too late for me to be a normal twelve-year-old."

"I don't care about *normal* twelve-year-olds," I say exasperated. "I care about my bro—wait. Wait, Abek, what did you say just now?" In my head, I repeat back what he's just said, trying to figure out why it sounds wrong to me.

"Nothing. Never mind."

"But your job was to work *for* the commandant. That was what I worked out for you. Why would you have to hide from him in latrines?"

"I said never mind. I just misspoke. Am I allowed to misspeak?"

"Of course you are, I just—"

"I don't like talking about the past," he insists, angry. "And you always want to talk about it."

"That's not true."

"About Papa's taking over the business, or what Mama used to say about something when we went somewhere at some time, or why Aunt Maja wasn't married, or what old friends would want to see me."

A chatting couple approaches, but they both quiet as they pass. We've raised our voices without intending to. The woman is watching us until she sees my noticing and then abruptly picks up the conversation again, in a louder tone than normal. "I don't mean to be doing that," I say, lowering my voice.

"You're always testing me to see what I remember and what I don't. Like you think there's something wrong with me."

"I'm not."

"It *feels* that way." Abek turns away, shoulders hunched protectively near his ears. "Why does it matter if I remember what lies you told?"

"Because it's our *story*. Because it's *important*."

"Because it's important to *you*. It's more important to you than I am."

"Abek!" I'm taken aback by the words coming out of his mouth and by the sudden vehemence with which he's saying them. "That's absolutely not true."

My first reaction to Abek's unrest is to tell him that he's just imagining things; of course I'm not doing what he says I'm doing. But even while I want to do that, I can't help but be confused and alarmed.

How did this conversation get out of control so quickly? I can't mark what made Abek so suddenly angry, and I can't help worrying that the anger is covering up something else. I don't like the way this conversation is making me feel. I don't like what it's pulling at, what it's teasing out of my brain.

*Why wouldn't Abek remember the deal I made for him to work for the commandant?* It seems so basic, such a basic piece of our story. Is there something he's not telling me? Something so awful he thinks I can't handle it? Or something he's not remembering? How could he not remember such an important detail of our past?

"Let's go back," I say, exhausted by the conversation. "Let's just go back to the cottage."

∞

"You're lost in thought."

A hand touches my arm gently, and I jump. It's Josef; he raises his hands in apology. "I've been calling your name for a few minutes. I didn't mean to startle you."

"You didn't—I mean, you're right. I was just lost in thought."

I've just left Abek at the cottage. When the awkwardness between us didn't seem to abate, I told him I needed to go for a walk. My feet took me immediately to the stables, where my feet have taken me several times over the past few days. I'm standing in the doorway, too distracted to go inside.

Josef walks back to his three-legged stool and recommences cleaning out some brushes and combs. Every time I've come here, Josef has been in the middle of something—mucking out a stall, fixing a tool—and he always greets me as though he's both surprised to see me and not surprised. In the beginning, I took this for indifference, but soon I realized he's just trying not to get his hopes up and expect me. I didn't see him at dinner. I still never see him at dinner.

I see him *after* dinner. I see him on midnight walks, when he stops and kisses me against the rough wall of the stables. I see him in the dark of his bedroom, when his hands no longer fumble at the buttons on my dress. But then, after, I sneak back to my own cottage. And I eat dinner with Breine, Esther, and Chaim. And what Josef and I have together seems both ill-defined and important, but he mostly stays apart from everyone but me.

Today, while Josef does his work, I take an apple from the burlap bag and hold it below Feather's nose. Her mouth is warm and fuzzy in the palm of my hand as she takes the fruit and nudges me for another one.

"Something's bothering you?" Josef asks.

"No, I'm fine," I answer.

But I guess I wait a beat too long before answering, because instead of nodding and moving along with the conversation, Josef looks at me with a raised eyebrow. "Is there something in particular you wanted to talk about?" There's trepidation in his voice. He's worried, I realize, that what's not fine might have something to do with him.

"I just had an odd conversation with Abek," I say. "He's said some things I don't understand."

Josef looks both relieved and concerned at the same time. "What kinds of things?"

"He was angry with me because he said I'm dwelling too much on the past. But I wonder if he doesn't want to talk about the past because he doesn't remember things—things that I feel he *should* remember. That are important to my family."

It wasn't only the story about the commandant, I realize. On our very first night, he couldn't complete the gaps in a story I was telling. And then at the wedding, he asked whether Papa had walked Aunt Maja to her chuppah, as if he didn't remember Maja wasn't married. I'd assumed it was just the glass of wine, but could it have been something else? Should I have thought it odd that he mixed that up? It, too, is a rudimentary detail about our family.

But then he *was* only nine when we were separated. How many strong memories did I have of the period before I was nine? Aunt Maja wasn't the only aunt I had. My father had a sister, too. She moved to London when I was six, married an Englishman, converted to Christianity for him, lost touch. I don't even know her married last name. But before all that, I have hazy memories of her coming over for dinner. Was she dating the Englishman at the time? Were they already married? Did she come to our house alone? I honestly can't remember.

"Such as, Zofia?" Josef nudges my foot with his own; I've spent a full minute staring into space without continuing my thought. The second apple in my hand is gone, too, and I wasn't even aware of Feather's eating it. "You said he didn't remember things."

"*Some* things," I correct him. "He has specific memories of some things...just not others."

I don't know why I'm being so coy, so reticent. When I give Josef my examples now, they come out haltingly, and they sound silly, even as I'm saying them.

"And, a few times, he's just gotten annoyed with me. Out of the blue, for reasons I don't really understand. And since I don't really understand why he's upset, I don't know if I should apologize. It's just...confusing."

While Josef listens to me, he picks up the tool he's just finished cleaning, a wooden-handled device with serrated metal teeth. If I'd seen it lying on a table, I would have thought it was a weapon or a torture device, but instead, he moves it gently over Franklin Delano Roosevelt's flank, loosening burrs and clumps of dirt, following the path of the comb with his hand to make sure he hasn't missed anything.

"Well?" I ask when I'm finished explaining my concerns. "Does it sound like something I should be worried about?"

He bites his lip, thinking. "I'm not sure you're listening to yourself."

"What do you mean?"

"You're worried that Abek doesn't remember things. But isn't that one of the first things you told me, the first day we talked? Your memory has holes. You don't remember things you should. You get confused about what really happened, and you're not sure what's real and what's not. Maybe he's just a little confused, too. The way you were."

"Do you think that's it?"

"I don't know. Does it sound like it could be right to you? People's brains don't work in the same way. Just because his memory lapses don't look exactly like yours, it doesn't mean they're not real."

Josef's theory could explain what's happening with Abek and also why I feel so viscerally concerned by it. Is he like me, a victim of the same memory holes? Do they run in our blood, all our lapses and blank spots traveling through our veins? Are we both sick; are we both broken?

My own memory has holes in it. Why should his be perfect?

"Zofia, Buchenwald is a horrible place," Josef says.

"We were all in horrible places."

"I know," Josef says. "But Buchenwald—I've heard there was a patch of woods called the 'singing forest.' It was called that because they would torture men there. Tie prisoners' hands behind their backs and then hang them from their wrists and leave them there. From the camp, you could hear the men screaming. The singing forest."

My stomach turns. Is this what my brother had to witness? Were these the sounds accompanying him to sleep every night? The sounds of tortured men begging to die?

Suddenly I'm ashamed. I've just spent this conversation worrying over whether Abek remembered the right things from before the war, and I've been ignoring everything that could have happened during it. Everything that could have torn him apart.

"I think you're right," I say slowly. "Thank you."

"Is there anything else you wanted to talk about?"

"No," I say. "I want to go find Abek again. I'll leave you to your work, and maybe see you later?"

"Wait. I was wondering something, too." Josef has stopped what he's doing. His hands lie loosely by his sides, and I notice he's turning pink around the collar.

"Oh?"

"I was wondering... if I could eat dinner with you tomorrow. If you'd rather I didn't, that's fine, of course, but if there was room, I wondered if I could eat dinner with you."

His shyness feels backward, just as everything about my interactions with Josef have felt backward, and for a brief second, I think about saying no—I don't want to risk disrupting what we have. But then, what I have is always changing, anyway. What more is there to disrupt?

"We meet at five thirty," I tell him. "And none of us will wait for you if you're late."

Abek isn't back in the cottage. I find him instead in the courtyard, just behind the administration building. In the twilight, he's watching a group of men play a soccer game, knees curled up to his chest, chin resting on top of them. I sidle up slowly, prepared to open my mouth and apologize, but he speaks first.

"Dobrotek." Abek still isn't looking at me; he must have spotted me out of the corner of his eyes. This word comes out of his mouth like a begrudging bark.

"What?"

Now he turns to look at me. "In the story you used to tell me. The one with Princess Ladna. His name was Prince Dobrotek."

It still takes me a moment to place what he's talking about: the conversation from his first night here, when he told me about staying with an old woman named Ladna, and when I reminded him that Ladna was also the name from a fairy tale we used to tell.

"That's right," I say. "The king told the prince that if he couldn't find his kidnapped daughter, he would be put to death."

"But Prince Dobrotek did find her," Abek adds. "And they inherited the kingdom and lived happily ever after. I remembered it."

He raises his eyebrows, as if to say, *Are you happy now?*

And I am happy. I'm relieved in a way that doesn't even fully make sense. *Problem solved*, my brain tells itself. *Calm down; you are worried about nothing.*

"Abek, I'm sorry." I carefully slide onto the bench with him but make sure to leave space, several inches, so he doesn't feel crowded. "I really am trying. I'm sorry if it feels like I'm trying to force something. It's just that I wanted to find you for a really long time. But in my mind, you were always exactly who you were before. And I should have realized you would be different. Because I'm different, too."

He fiddles with the hem of his pants. Twenty meters away, I hear the thud of a soccer ball, the cheer of a team scoring a goal. "I know you wish we could go back to how we were before," he says. "I know it's disappointing."

"No." I start to reach for his arm and then think better of it. "I mean, of course I do. I want the world to go back to where it was before. But not because of you. I'm so happy you're here. Are you? Aren't you happy you came here?"

He pauses long enough that I don't know what will come out of his mouth. I worry he'll say he's *not* glad, or he's leaving, or that I'm a disappointment to him. But finally he hunches his neck down into his shirt collar and says, "I am. I think I am."

*You are worried about nothing*, I repeat to myself. *See, everything is fine.*

THE NEXT MORNING, ONE OF THE FOEHRENWALD OFFICE workers brings me a note: Could I stop by the administration building that afternoon to talk about housing?

I can already anticipate the conversation. In the front room of the cottage, Miriam has left, but she was replaced almost immediately by two more girls, in a space that is now so filled with cots it's nearly impossible to maneuver around them. I know it's this crowded all over camp. Esther and I have been allowed such relatively luxurious accommodations because of Abek's presence. Esther has been kind enough not to complain about sharing her space with a boy, but they wouldn't assign other women into this situation. The administration probably wants to know what our plans are, whether they should reassign us to family housing or make different arrangements.

Before I can make it inside the administration building, though, I spot Breine on the edge of the courtyard, repotting some of the plants from the herb garden. She's proudly wearing her new ring, even as her nails and hands are caked in dirt. Chaim is just a row over; they work in unison. They already look like a matched set, and she waves when she sees me.

I owe her an answer about whether Abek and I will go with them. She told me I needed to think quickly; she told me there wasn't endless time.

The idea that there's not endless time seems crazy to me. For years, it seemed as if there was nothing but time, stretching out like a nightmare, days that felt like years as we all prayed for an ending and for reunification with the people we loved. Nothing happened at all, and now everything is happening at once.

I owe Breine an answer, but I can't give her one yet, so instead of stopping to talk to her, I return her wave from a distance and call out, "I promise I'll talk to you soon."

Inside the administration building, I pass Mrs. Yost's office, and the door is ajar. I hear paper rustling inside, and I step inside to say hello, but she's not at her desk. The rustling is coming from Mr. Ohrmann, the caterpillar-eyebrowed man from the aid organization. The desk in front of him is again piled with ledgers and composition books.

"Mr. Ohrmann! I'm sorry to disturb you; I'm here for an appointment with someone else, and I thought I'd just say hello to Mrs. Yost."

"She told me she's just running a few minutes late—a small fire to put out."

"I'll come see her another time," I say, already retreating through the door. "I didn't mean to disturb your work."

"Miss Lederman—it's Miss Lederman, isn't it? Wait a moment. Mrs. Yost tells me you have been reunited with your brother."

There's nothing accusatory in the statement, but it still makes me feel guilty. Mr. Ohrmann tried to help me with my search, and I can't even imagine how many cases he must be juggling. He looks exhausted, eyes red-rimmed. I should have found a way to leave word with him that he could take me off his list.

"I know; I need to contact organizations—yours, especially— and tell them they can close my file," I apologize. "It's just . . . it happened fast, barely a week ago."

He's already waving me off, unbothered. "I don't get to hear nearly as many happy stories as I'd like, much less in person," he says. "I'm just glad this is one of them. Have you decided what you'll do next?"

"We're trying to figure that out now. That's partly why I'm in the building."

"I wish you the best. I'll tell Mrs. Yost you stopped by."

I've already walked through the door when I hear Mr. Ohrmann calling my name again. When I step back into the office, he's holding aloft a single sheet of paper with just a few typewritten paragraphs on it.

"Miss Lederman? If I'm going to close your file, I don't suppose any news relating to Alek Federman is relevant now, is it?"

"Alek Federman? I suppose not. Thanks for checking."

I start to leave again, but this time it's me who stops myself. "Why do you ask?"

Mr. Ohrmann is already sliding the letter back into a folder. "We found some news about him. But obviously not news that concerns you. The name similarity must just be a clerical coincidence."

"Just out of curiosity, though, what is the news? Is he... alive?"

"I believe he is," Mr. Ohrmann affirms. "It turns out he wasn't in any of the records—death, transfer, or liberation— because he'd actually escaped a few months before liberation. He and another boy."

"So you've talked to Alek?"

"My colleague talked to the other boy. They didn't stay together after the escape—it hadn't been planned, and they didn't even know each other before it. They were both assigned to work outside the camp, and the truck left them behind. They thought splitting up would give them each a better chance of surviving. The other boy didn't know where Alek is now, but it answers the question of why he wasn't in any records."

"I didn't know anyone escaped," I say.

Mr. Ohrmann nods. "It's incredibly rare."

"How did you learn about it?"

"I happened to be talking to a colleague about your search, and he remembered an interview he'd conducted months ago. The notes were still in a file. The young man—Alek's escape partner—mentioned Alek's name. The young man was looking for him, too."

"But his name was really Alek," I confirm. "It wasn't a misspelling; his name was really Alek after all, not Abek?"

Mr. Ohrmann looks pained. "We believe so. It's a little complicated. The interview was conducted through an interpreter. The boy was Romanian, a language none of us speaks. He was getting confused by the foreign names.

"Anyway. This isn't your concern now," he finishes brightly. "Yours is a file I can close."

"But it sounds like Alek Federman's is one you'll have to open? Will you still find him? Is anyone looking for him?"

"You can't get caught up in everyone else's searches," Mr. Ohrmann warns me.

"I know; I'm just wondering. Will anyone find out where that boy is?"

"Believe me, this is a lesson I have to employ myself." Mr. Ohrmann shuffles more papers, a stack that never seems to get tidier despite his attempts to organize. "You just have to tell yourself: Yours is a file I can close."

THE HOUSING OFFICE IS EMPTY WHEN I STOP BY TO ASK ABOUT my note. There's time for me to go back to the cottage before dinner, but I find I don't want to do that. I'm having trouble concentrating after my conversation with Mr. Ohrmann; I feel unsettled.

Ahead of me, two girls carrying books emerge from the library room; it must be open now. That seems like a soothing place to be for a troubled mind—a quiet room, nothing but the sound of turning pages.

Even now, with everything unpacked, it's apparent that "library" was an optimistic designation. Along two of the walls, just a few warped shelves contain hard-backed volumes emitting the vague scent of must and mildew. Someone has gone so far as to arrange them by language, but otherwise they're a jumble: A bird-watching guide is tucked between a historical biography and an encyclopedia for the letter *N*. Mismatched chairs are pulled up to a solitary table; I'm the only one here.

I pull over one of the chairs to sit on while I look through the Polish section, which is full of mostly boring titles that make me suspect these books had sat unread in people's attics for a long time before ending up in this camp.

I ought to try to find something, though. I used to like reading, sometimes—my mother would pass on her fantasy novels. Now, I can't remember the last time I read a full book cover to cover. In the hospital, words swam in front of my eyes. The other girls and I would lie on our backs sometimes and listen to poems the nurses would read during rest times.

Maybe I could handle something basic now, though. I page through the only two books that look promising: a romance that turns out to be courtly and dry, and what looks like the second volume of an adventure series. Without the first volume, though, the plot is confusing, and I can't keep track of the characters. Maybe I'm not ready to read anything yet after all.

As I pull the chair back to where it belongs, I spot another Polish book, already sitting on the table: *The Good Ferryman and Other Classic Stories*. This one is a children's book, the pages are half illustrations and all dog-eared. A donation from a family, maybe, whose children had grown, who didn't need fairy tales anymore. I open it to the table of contents.

"The Princess of the Brazen Mountain." "The Bear in the Forest Hut."

I page past illustrations of dragons and children turned into birds. At the beginning of the next story, a picture of a man whose beard swirls into a great cyclone, I start to read.

*In a far-off country, beyond the sea and the mountains, there lived a king and queen, with a beautiful daughter. A great many princes came to woo her but she liked only one of them.*

My eyes travel mindlessly over the next few sentences before I slowly register what I'm reading. It's *The Whirlwind.*

It had taken me a few paragraphs to piece together what I was reading because I've never seen it written down before. My parents always recited it as a bedtime story when I was little, and I learned it from them. The details changed a little depending on who was telling it—Mama emphasizing the fantastical adventures, Papa the victory of good over evil, and the story transformed a little over time, as my family created a version that was all our own.

But here it is, the official version. In print. In a library just a few hundred meters from the cottage where my brother is probably getting ready for dinner.

"His name was Prince Dobrotek," Abek told me.

*Abek couldn't remember the prince's name. Until he could. Until out of nowhere, he said he suddenly remembered after all: The prince's name was Dobrotek. And I was so happy. I took that memory as a sign. I took that memory to mean something important.*

My fingers have grown cold. I'm still turning the pages, but I'm barely paying attention to what's on them.

Had Abek really remembered the name? Had he remembered it out of the blue?

Is it just a coincidence this book is sitting here on the table instead of on the shelf, as if someone was only recently read-ing it?

Beneath my hands, the cover falls closed.

What is the real question I am trying to ask? What is the theory I am trying to prove? What is the thing that keeps nudging against my brain?

If this book is sitting on the table because Abek came in yesterday and was reading it, then why wouldn't he have just mentioned to me he'd done it? He could have just said, *Guess what? I went to the library and found a book of fairy tales, and it had the name of the character we couldn't remember; isn't that interesting?*

Unless it wasn't actually remembering the prince's name that mattered, but *showing me* that he remembered. Showing that he had memories of our reading the story together. That he had memories of me before the war. Proving something.

*Proving what?*

This means nothing, I tell myself. This is all useless specu-lation. I don't even know if Abek looked in this book, and it wouldn't matter anyway, because this book is here to be looked at, and Abek is my brother, and he is here, and that is what means something, and this means nothing, because this is all useless speculation, and I don't even know if Abek is the one who looked in the book, and even it wouldn't matter anyway, because this book is here to be looked at, and Abek is my brother, and he is—

*Brrrrrrr. Brrrrrrrrr.*

My thoughts are pierced by a loud sound, metallic and shrill. My knees give out. My brain is on fire.

Before I can process what the sound is, my body has

reacted. I'm on the floor. I'm under the table on my hands and knees, and I'm shaking and can't control myself.

*You're in the library in Foehrenwald*, I tell myself, but I tell myself louder, *Run*.

*Breathe*, I instruct myself. My mind hasn't gotten caught in a loop like that in more than a week. Not since Abek arrived. I'd hoped that meant I'd moved beyond it. I'd hoped I was better. I'm dripping with sweat.

*There's nothing to be scared of*, I repeat.

From under the table, I see a pair of brown men's shoes appear in the doorway. The shoes pause, and I shrink away from them, fighting back screams.

Then the body attached to them lowers.

The face that appears is kind. A young man I've never seen, watching me shake under the table. *You're in Foehrenwald. You're safe.*

"Are you all right?" the man asks.

I shake my head.

"Stay there; I'll get help."

I shake my head again, and a whimper comes out of my mouth. *Don't leave.*

"Did you fall? Do you need help getting to your feet?" He stretches out his arms, and I reach mine out, too. He puts his hands under my elbows and helps me stand. "Are you sure you're all right? You look a little pale."

"A noise." My voice comes out scratched and wavering. I clear my throat to start again. I haven't let go of this man's arms. I'm still clutching them, and I know it must seem strange, but

I'm also afraid if I let go, I won't be able to stand steadily on my own. "I heard a noise. It startled me."

Recognition dawns on his face; he pulls on a silver chain looped around his neck. "It was me. This whistle—I was testing it out to use with workers in the fields at mealtimes."

"For workers," I repeat.

"To call them back for dinner. I'm sorry it scared you. I shouldn't have tested it inside."

A whistle for workers in the fields.

But that's not what I heard. I heard the whistle of helmeted guards as the train pulled into Birkenau. I heard a thousand screams that were all the same scream, I heard myself whispering, *It will all be okay*, when really I was screaming inside.

"It's fine," I repeat. "I was just startled."

"Should we get you checked out?" the man suggests, helpful. "Would you like me to walk you to the nurse?"

"No! I mean, no, thank you. I think I'll go lie down."

It's so silly, but really I just don't want to be near his whistle. His whistle is part of the door that I don't want opened, part of the path I don't want my brain to walk down.

"It's so silly," I tell him out loud now. "I don't know why I was being so silly."

When I let go of the man's arms, I make sure I'm leaning against the table in case my legs don't support me. The table squeaks a bit on the floor under the burden of my weight, but I manage to not fall. Then I cautiously wave a hand to show him, I'm fine, I'm fine, I was just overreacting, silly me, and finally he leaves, looking once over his shoulder.

Slowly, I pick up the book of fairy tales from the table and shelve it. Then I stand in front of the bookcase, straightening the spines, evening up the rows. It's a pointless task. I'm sure that after the dinner hour, when the library room would be at its busiest, the shelves will quickly become messy again. I know what I'm really looking for is a mindless task for soothing and distraction. In the hospital, we would sometimes slip skeins of wool over our hands, roll them into balls of yarn. It was better to have that to focus on than whatever was tormenting our brains.

I do not want to think about the train whistle.

I do not want to think about a book of Polish fairy tales.

I do not want to think about why my brother might not have remembered one, or why he might have felt the need to pretend that he did.

I do not want to think about what I've been scared to say out loud, what I have been afraid to think to myself.

I do not want to think about how he might not be my brother.

I'M OUTSIDE THE ADMINISTRATION BUILDING AND NOT EVEN sure how I got there. I blink into the sunlight, vaguely aware of the sound of voices, the rustle of fabric as people move past me on their way to dinner. I walk with them because it's easier than fighting the crowd and walking in the other direction and because I don't know where I would go anyway.

Why would I let myself ask that about Abek? How far am I letting my imagination run? As I repeat these questions to myself, they slowly transform into the same question I've been asking myself since the war ended. Not *am I crazy* but *how crazy am I?*

Near the closed doors of the dining hall, I see familiar faces. Breine and Chaim. Esther, waiting for the doors to be opened, putting her eyeglasses back on after wiping them clean on her skirt, waving for me to join her in line. And Josef. Josef is also there, because this is the night he asked if he could join the rest of us for dinner. He raises his hand and smiles. He expects I'll be happy; I can barely nod in his direction. His face falls, but I don't have time to worry about his feelings.

Abek is standing in the group, too. Hidden behind Chaim; I don't see him until I'm nearly there. He and the young woman next to him are playing some kind of word game on a scrap of paper, passing it back and forth between them. He looks up and sees me, and his face breaks into a smile.

*Ruffle his hair*, a voice inside me instructs, so I do. I tousle his hair and say, "Do you even know how to comb it anymore?" because that seems like the kind of sisterly thing I would say to Abek.

He laughs and turns back at his game.

Is this my brother or isn't it? When he first arrived, showing up at this very spot, I'd noticed things about him that looked different. He was taller, but of course he was taller. His hair was darker, but of course it was darker.

But could I take that same information and use it to reach different conclusions?

For the hundredth time, I wish I had a photograph. Something I could analyze to make comparisons. A photograph, or the cuts of hair my mother kept from our first hair trims, tied with ribbon and tucked in her wardrobe. I wish I had my mother here, who could talk about this with me, who could surely look at this boy and say for certain whether he was her son.

There's nothing, though. Everything was taken away from us, and so there's nothing left to compare the present with the past. Nothing that can help me measure how crazy I am. *Is it crazier to believe someone is your brother who really isn't, or to find a person you've been trying to find for years, only to convince yourself they're not the right person after all? To throw away your chance at happiness?*

The dining hall doors open. A mundane sigh of relief rises from the crowd. *So hungry*, people murmur. *Hope the cabbage is better today.* I walk in with everyone else, line up in front of the giant vats, accept the food ladled onto my plate, sit down at the place at the table that has somehow become mine. Put my napkin on my lap.

I didn't even think to arrange it so I could sit next to Josef. He's kitty-corner from me, still eyeing me, certain now something's wrong but not sure what it is.

*If this boy isn't Abek, what could he possibly want? Money?* I don't have any. If he's hoping I'll take him back to a house filled with nice furniture and comfortable rugs, he's about five years too late.

*What else could he want? Passage somewhere? A first-class ticket somewhere?* I don't have that, either. I have Breine's offer of a rickety boat, but I didn't even have that when Abek first arrived.

*Does he just want to torment me?* Because that's the only explanation I can imagine right now. He's a con artist who takes pleasure in seeing a gullible, crazy girl parade him around, stupidly happy to have found him.

"How was your day, Zofia?" Esther, to my right, asks pleasantly as she passes me a water glass.

"I went to the library." I eye Abek to see if he has any reaction to this. But his focus is on his plate, slicing the potato in front of him.

"I was going to go there later," a boy at the other end of the table offers. "I was going to see if they had an—"

"I went to the library and I found a book of Polish fairy tales," I continue loudly.

"Oh, really? That sounds—"

"The book had lots of ones my family used to tell when we were little," I say even louder.

Around me, the previously cheery conversation settles into an awkward quiet as people exchange glances, wondering if something's wrong with me.

Beside me, Esther also looks concerned but responds carefully. "That's nice," she says. "Do you want to tell us about them? I wonder if there are any stories all of us would recognize."

"The book looked like someone else had been reading it," I continue, plowing over Esther's attempt to guide my unhingedness. "It was sitting there, open, like someone else had just been reading it before me."

"Well. That *is* the way libraries work," Breine says. She's laughing, but now she has to work harder to make the laughter sound like a joke and not a bundle of nerves. "Unless the ones where you're from are a lot different from mine. Right?"

She addresses the question to the whole table, and almost everyone takes the opportunity to look at her and laugh.

Now I think I've seen something. Abek looks up from his plate. At me and then back at his plate again.

*Is it because he's worried about how strangely I'm behaving, or because he was the one reading the book?*

Next to me, Esther keeps her head down and her voice low as she leans over. "Are you feeling all right?"

"I'm fine," I say shortly, not wanting to engage in a conversation that would force me to take my eyes off Abek. But he doesn't meet my gaze again. I want to bang my fist on the table, make a noise that will force him to look up. But what would that accomplish, besides alarm everyone else at the table?

What is any of my behavior accomplishing? My stomach is filled with dread. My stomach is filled with so much ill-defined, terrified dread.

"Please excuse me," I say, rising abruptly, dropping my napkin on the table. "I'm going to go lie down."

"Do you need any help?" Esther sets down her own napkin. "I can walk you back."

"It's just a headache coming on." I improvise, trying to sound reassuring. "A migraine."

"Oh, *oh*. My mother used to get those. They're terrible." Esther and the rest of the table make clucking sounds of sympathy. But also, I think, relief at having an explanation for my odd behavior. "I'll definitely walk you."

"No, I think I just need to be still." I hold up my hands, preventing her from accompanying me. "In a very quiet room," I add, hoping the last sentence will signal that I want to be alone and she and Abek shouldn't come check on me. "I'll lie down for a few hours, and then I hope I'll feel better."

"You don't have a headache, do you?"

I jump at the hand on my arm. Josef has followed me out of the dining hall, appraising me knowingly.

"I think there's something wrong with my head." It's the truest statement I can make.

He measures what I've just said. "Do you want to talk about it?"

"Not right now."

"Is it about—"

"It's not about you," I interrupt. "It's about something I need to figure out." I continue on before he can offer the help I can see he's about to offer. "And you can't help me figure it out, and I don't even know if there's a way to figure it out. I just know I need to do it alone."

He removes his hand from my arm. "I'm not sure how to do this," he says.

"Do what?"

"I'm not sure if I'm supposed to just let you go, or if I'm supposed to insist on helping you because we've—because we're..."

"You're supposed to let me go this time, Josef," I say, looking anxiously down the path toward my cottage. "Maybe not every time, but right now you're just supposed to let me go."

Reluctantly, he steps back. I can see him struggling with

himself, wanting to listen to me but still certain something's wrong. Finally, he forces a smile on his lips. "All right. But you'll tell me if you need anything? I think I've proved that I will commit violence on your behalf. And that was before I liked you. Now I'm willing to be even more brutal. I'm willing to punch all the latrines."

He leans in and kisses me. And for a moment, I kiss him back; for a moment, I consider that this is what I could do instead. I could stand here and kiss him back, his fingers tangled in my hair, his lips urgent against mine. We could go back to the dining hall, and I could behave normally around Abek. Tonight I could kiss Josef again, and life could just continue. Moving forward, as Breine suggested it should. For a moment, this version seems like a possibility. For a moment, my life goes in two different directions.

But then I pull away. Put my hand on Josef's heart and step backward. I don't think this version is a possibility. No matter how deeply and desperately I want it, I don't think it's ever been a possibility for me.

THE COTTAGE IS TIDY AND EMPTY. OUR THREE BEDS ARE neatly made. Esther's stenography book rests on her night-stand, opened to where she was studying for a test, and my sewing supplies are on mine. Nothing is on Abek's. He hasn't collected any personal effects since he arrived.

*What did he come with?* I try to remember. He was holding a bag when he first appeared in the dining hall. I thought it was a pillowcase at first, but up close I later realized it was a satchel. Dirty, but well made and canvas. He was protective of it. He didn't let me carry it when I offered.

On the other side of his bed, there it sits, propped against the wall.

After only a moment's hesitation, I unbutton the flap and empty out the contents: The shirt he was wearing when he arrived. Two spare sets of underthings. A spare pair of socks. A crumpled piece of paper with painstaking handwriting providing directions to Foehrenwald.

Another sheet of paper, which I unfold. The handwriting on this one isn't familiar, either, but the words are: It's the notice about Abek I composed for Sister Therese at the Kloster Indersdorf. I can't tell whether this is her handwriting, or whether it's one of the copies she promised to dictate to personnel at the other facilities for children.

Did I ever even ask Abek exactly which one he'd come from, which one he'd seen the notice at? I don't think I did. I don't think I wanted to ask too many questions. I remember physically blocking the doorway with my feet because I was so afraid he'd leave. I needed so badly for this story to end the way I wanted it to.

The bag is empty. There's nothing else inside. I turn it upside down to be sure, shaking and shaking it, sweeping my hand over the bottom lining to be sure.

*The lining*—could something be sewn into the lining?

I rush to my nightstand and open the drawer, tossing all my belongings onto the floor until I find my scissors, leaving the drawer open as I take them back to the satchel. I hold the scissors aloft. I'm about to stab through the canvas when I stop and picture what I must look like. Hair wild. Breathing heavy. Scissors held in the air.

What am I hoping to find? What evidence could possibly answer my questions either way? A detailed confession letter? A diary? None of that would be sewn into a lining. There's nothing. *What am I doing?*

*What am I doing?*

What am I falling back into? My body feels, all at once, the way it did in the hospital months ago. My heart is heavy with nothing. My brain is aching with nothing. I have nothing, I weigh nothing, I am nothing except for the weight and grief I've been carrying around for what feels like forever.

I slump against the wall, sliding to the floor, my head scraping against the plaster.

And that's when I see it: a dingy triangle. A scrap of cloth, peeking out from between the mattress and frame of Abek's bed.

I crawl over to it on my hands and knees and take it between my fingers.

Muslin. I immediately recognize the material as muslin. But it's older, tattered, dirty. White at one point, now rust-colored and stained. When I pull it out, I see it's a much bigger piece of fabric than I expected. The bundle looked tiny because it was rolled into a small tube. I spread it flat on the ground and begin to unfurl it.

*Happy birthday, my little snail! May you never forget who you are; may you always find your way home.*

*A is for Abek, the youngest Lederman, the spoiled son of Helena and Elie, and younger brother of Zofia, who is making you this magnificent present . . .*

*B is for Baba Rose, the grandmother whose fingers are nimble and whose mind is more nimble, who holds the family together with patience and love in the beautiful apartment where we all live. She is the best seamstress in the city, and also the most exacting one . . .*

*C is for Chomicki & Lederman, the company that will be yours*

*one day, which makes the most beautiful clothing in Poland. It was*
*founded by Zayde Lazer, and his best employee was a young man*
*named Elie, whom he invited home for dinner one night. That's the*
*night when he first met—*

It goes on. It goes on, all the way to *Z*. It's my whole family
story. More detailed than I remembered it. Everything about
my family that a person would need to know. I forgot how
small and pretty my handwriting could be, how much I managed to fit on that one piece of cloth.

I don't know exactly how this fabric ended up under this
mattress.

All I know is this: The morning before we left for the
stadium, I took this fabric from the wall where it had been
hanging, and I quickly sewed it into the lining of Abek's jacket.

I sewed it into his jacket, and then a few hours later we
left for the stadium and a few days after that, the Nazis made
us remove all our clothes and put on new, shapeless ones that
didn't fit. And all our old clothes were placed in a pile, where
they were checked for money or valuables and then sold or
repurposed.

The point is that Abek would not have been in possession
of this cloth. That's why I don't have any of my old clothes
or photographs or mementos—because we weren't allowed to
keep anything at all after that day.

The point is that the most likely person to have discovered
this letter is the prisoner with the job of sorting through the
clothes, of ripping our lives apart at the seams, stitch by stitch.

"I BROUGHT YOU SOME TEA."

I gasp at the sound of knocking and, without thinking, ball the cloth into my fist. But it's not Abek; it's Josef standing at the door, knuckles still on the frame.

"I told you, you didn't need to come with me," I manage, bringing him into focus, his curly hair, his sharp eyes, his slender frame.

"And I promise I won't make a habit of thinking I know better than you what you need," he says. He sets his mug of tea on the nightstand. "But in this one instance, I really wanted to make sure you were all right."

"Am I...all right?" I cannot even begin to think of how to answer that question. A sound comes out of my mouth, something between a yelp and the emptiest laugh in the world.

"Zofia?" Now he senses something must really be wrong. He crosses the room and kneels beside me on the floor. I feel the heat of him, just inches away, and I'm glad he's here. I want him here, the reality of another body.

"Hold me," I say. I don't mean it in a romantic way. I mean it like, *Hold me together.* I mean it like, *Am I really real? Is any of this really happening?* Josef doesn't take it in a romantic way, either. When we climb onto the bed and he puts his arms around me, it's with the urgency you would use to warm someone with hypothermia. Or someone who'd had a bad shock. The kind of holding you do when your goal is to keep them alive.

He wraps his arms around me tightly enough that it's almost hard to breathe, and this discomfort is inexplicably comforting. It reminds me that I'm here, tethered to this earth. The labor of my breathing reminds me that I have a body at all.

"Something happened, something you're not ready to talk about," he says. Mutely, I nod. "I'll stop talking. I'll stay here with you until you want me to leave, but I'll just remain silent."

He wedges his chin over my head, firmly and deliberately. I feel as though he's burrowing in for a storm with me, readying us both against the wind. I try to steady myself against the beat of Josef's heart. I try to match my breaths to his. I try to feel grounded by this, the comforting pressure and weight.

I try to feel grounded, but the feeling of Josef's arms right now is competing against six years of misery swirling around my head with nothing to drown them out since Josef has promised to remain silent.

*Remain silent.*

A *is for Abek.* B *is for Baba Rose. They'll be gone soon, Baba Rose said about the Nazis in their tanks, but then they weren't, they weren't, they stayed for years. Remain silent. My neighbor Mrs. Wójcik's dogs barked in her apartment, and the Nazi dogs were barking at Birkenau. I unloaded the pellets of Zyklon B, and Bissel fell out the window, and I sewed Breine's wedding dress, and I sewed the Nazi uniforms, and my arm was throbbing from the shuttle, and I worked every day because we all worked every day because we didn't want to die, except some days I wanted to die. Some days I did.*

*I walked to the soccer stadium because we weren't allowed cars. I walked from Neustadt to Gross-Rosen in a frozen, frozen winter, when I could not begin to fathom how one foot was continuing to go in front of the other. And my toes were amputated by a doctor in white, and my father ran to help the pharmacist in the mud. And the soldier used his hand to break my father's windpipe. Remain silent. I ate a plum with Josef, and I plucked a plum-colored dress from the donation box, and I buried a turnip in the ground, except maybe I didn't, maybe I didn't do that at all.*

*I waited in lines. I waited in lines to be discharged from the hospital. I waited in line for moldy potato skins. I waited in line for bread. I waited in line to get on the train for Foehrenwald. I waited in lines with all the other Jews of Sosnowiec to learn our fate on the twelfth of August in 1942, and my father ran to help the pharmacist in the mud, and Josef punched Rudolf's windpipe in the courtyard. And the soldier punched my father's windpipe in the soccer stadium, except that neither of them were punches, they were slices at the throat with the meaty L of a hand. Remain silent.*

I slip back into focus. The room slips back into focus. Josef slips back into focus, his arms still wrapped around me.

"Silent killing," I whisper.

"What?" Josef asks. But his breath catches; I'm close enough to be able to tell.

My voice is unnaturally calm. "It's what the German soldiers called their combat training. Silent killing."

*Stilles toten.* The German Army had its own hand-to-hand fighting style. Just the basics, the dirtiest of basics: A knee to the groin. A jab in the eyeballs. Or, hand flat like a knife, a vicious stab to the throat, before your enemy was paying attention, before he even knew you were fighting. It's what brought my father to his knees in the stadium. When he tried to help up the pharmacist, a soldier jabbed him in the neck, then they shot him.

I had never seen fighting to kill until the German Army arrived in Sosnowiec.

And I had never seen it anywhere else until I arrived in Foehrenwald and saw Josef do it to the man in the courtyard on the morning I arrived.

"You weren't in a camp," I whisper.

"Zofia."

My skin begins to crawl. I slowly ease out of his arms. "That's why you don't like to talk about where you were during the war."

"Zof—"

"You're not Jewish; you weren't in a camp; you were in the German Army."

I'm still edging away on the bed; he reaches out to pull me close again, and I move farther.

"Were you in the German Army? Just answer my question."

The words are a command, but my voice comes out as a plea. I'm waiting for him to tell me it's not true; I'm just confused. He doesn't.

"Say it, Josef."

"Zofia." He says my name for the third time, a name that I have loved hearing him say before, whispered in the dark. But now my name only sounds like Josef not wanting to tell me the truth.

And I already know the truth.

I back away more quickly now, stumbling over the desk chair, nearly falling. Josef rises to help me, but before he can take half a step forward, waves of nausea roll through my stomach. I lurch for the washing basin and heave into the bowl.

"Don't you dare come near me, you sick, *sick*—" I heave again, my hands tight on the bowl, and Josef finally stops in his tracks. "Why didn't you tell me? You wanted to torture me some more? You didn't think I'd been through enough?"

"I swear it wasn't," he says, stricken. "Zofia, I swear it wasn't that."

"You were just looking for someone to take to bed? You thought what Rudolf did when I arrived—that maybe I'd fuck for a scrap of bread?"

"I tried to stay *away* from you. I was going to tell you, I *tried* to tell you, that night in my room. I should have," he says. "I should have told you."

I straighten up again. "What you *should* have done is turned yourself in."

A bitter bark of a laugh comes from Josef's mouth. He

spreads his arms wide and looks around the room. "Turned myself in to—*where?* I didn't commit any crimes, Zofia. I was an eighteen-year-old boy who was drafted to fight."

"And now you're a twenty-two-year-old man."

"And I'm *different* now than I was then."

Outside, I hear a peal of laughter, a group returning from dinner. The noise rouses me enough to realize I want to get out of here. Finding my footing, I push past him toward the door. "I will tell everyone. I will tell every single person here who you are."

"Tell them."

My hand on the knob, I turn back to see if Josef's last sentence was a dare, if he doesn't believe I'll actually do it.

"Tell them," he says again. "Please."

The Josef behind me is a Josef I've never seen before, wild-eyed and desperate. "Please, tell them. I haven't known how to for months. Tell them; do whatever you want to do. But could you listen to me first, just for one minute?"

He rushes on, without giving me a chance to refuse. "I *was* in the army. But after a while, I knew I didn't want to be. I was a deserter, do you understand? I ran away. In the middle of the night, I just left, with the clothes on my back. I slept in empty barns, in the cellars of old women. The SS would have shot me if they'd learned who I was; I was a deserter, an enemy to them, too."

Everything is falling into an awful place. Josef isn't Jewish. When he said he didn't want to dance at the wedding, it was because he didn't know the wedding dances. When he said he didn't belong on the boat with Breine and Chaim, it wasn't because he'd lost his faith, it was because he never had it to begin with.

I reel against the doorway, glad my hand is already on the knob, because I need it to hold me up. *Is there any way this isn't happening? That's what I'd prefer. That this conversation we are having right now isn't happening. That I am sitting in another room somewhere while my brain is having this delusion. I would prefer my brain spin. Let me be broken. Let me be broken; I would prefer it.*

"But you showed me," I yell at him, my voice breaking in tears. "Your injuries. You showed me where your teeth had fallen out because the soldier hit you."

"The injuries—they're all true," he says quickly. "The soldier did hit me. I saw him harassing a girl, and I tried to stop him. He hit me with the butt of his rifle, and my teeth flew out. It happened; it just didn't happen in a camp. I did have flea bites. I did lose my hair. My shoulder was dislocated because some men beat me for not handing over my food. I suffered like you did."

"You *haven't*, Josef. Suffered like I did. I nearly died. Everyone I knew was tortured and starved and beaten, every day, for years. *Years.*" My voice is trembling at the audacity of his comparison. "You cannot imagine suffering like that. Was your whole family ripped away from you and led to slaughter like mine? Is your whole family dead?"

"Whether or not they are dead, I would be dead to them," he says. "They supported the Reich; they believed in it."

*Klara.* He told me after his sister died, his family became something he didn't recognize. Is this what he meant?

"They must have been so proud," I say. "So proud of their soldier son."

He takes a cautious step toward me.

"Zofia, I swear, I've thought and I've thought about what I could have done differently, but I did the only thing I could do—I left so I wouldn't be a part of it. I didn't try to refuse my conscription, and you're right—it had to do with my parents. But I started thinking clearly almost immediately, and then I left so I wouldn't be a part of it."

He's looking at me, with his deep, beautiful eyes and his hungry expression, and he's begging me to understand.

*Can I understand?* Was leaving enough? Was deserting enough? What would I consider enough? Would I have asked him to shoot his superior officers before he deserted? Go into hiding rather than enlist at all? Try to spy for the Allies? What's the minimum expectation I have for human decency in a war that was entirely inhumane?

For a minute, I'd like to rewind the clock. I'd like to go back an hour when Joseph followed me from the dining hall and kissed me. I'd like to feel that again. Or I'd like to find an entirely different timeline: one where I accept Josef's explanation that he did the best thing he could think of in what he saw as impossible circumstances. I'd like to forgive him.

For a minute, I feel my grip loosen on the handle. Josef draws in a quick, hopeful breath.

*But he never told me.* I keep coming back to that.

We have lain on our stomachs in barely any clothes in the dark of his room, and we've talked and we've laughed and he never once said, *I'm not who I've led you to think I am.* The memory of these nights brings on a new wave of nausea, a new depth to my horror. This man has kissed me. This man has been *inside* me.

"Zofia." He reaches a hand out to touch me, and I shrink back, my resolve steeled.

"No."

*"Please."*

"You are never allowed to touch me again," I hiss. "You lied to all of us, to every single one of us, because you knew that would make it easier for you. And that was more important to you than—" Here, my voice begins to shake with emotion. "Making life easier for you was more important than understanding that it was hell for us."

"You're right. You are," he says softly. "I was a coward."

I feel like I'm not even looking at Josef anymore. I'm looking at someone who slightly resembles someone I used to know, and I'm realizing the whole thing was a disguise.

"Go away," I say finally, removing my hand from the doorknob, realizing something. "You should be the one to leave now; it's my cottage."

"Zofia—"

"Go *away.* Don't ask me to forgive you."

"I'm not asking you to forgive me," he says bitterly. "I probably shouldn't even forgive myself."

"You shouldn't," I say. I hold the door open for him, and when he leaves, I finally cry.

THE LAST TIME I SAW MY MOTHER WAS UNSPEAKABLE AND SAD.

The last time I saw my father was unspeakable and sad.

The last time I saw Baba Rose and vivacious Aunt Maja was unspeakable and sad.

The last time I see Josef is unspeakable and sad. I think that was the last time. How could that have been anything other than the last time?

I am exhausted by unspeakable sadness, by wearing it like a cloak.

The first time I saw Abek, he was seven pounds and four ounces. My father and I paced up and down the street outside our house. He said we could walk to buy ice cream, but we never made it to the shop. Every time we reached the end of the block, he would decide we should run back, quickly, in case there was news. We would get back to our building, and then Aunt Maja or Baba Rose would lean out the window and shake their heads. *Not yet.*

*Were you this nervous when I was born?* I asked Papa. *I was too young to be nervous,* he said. *With you, I was only excited. I couldn't wait to meet you.*

The third or fourth time we returned from our failed ice-cream mission, Aunt Maja leaned out the window and said, *Don't leave again; we think it will be soon.* Then she leaned out the window again and said, *It's a boy,* and then we both ran inside and all the way up the stairs, to where Abek was redder and smaller than I'd imagined his being, wailing like a kitten, wrapped in white. My mother passed him to my father, who gave Abek his pinky finger to suck on, and I watched him to figure out what to do when it was my turn.

*Make a cradle with your arms,* Mama told me as Papa shifted the small, hot bundle into my awkward, outstretched hands. *This is your brother,* she said as I stared at his wrinkled fingers and the fine smattering of hair covering his scalp. It's your job to protect him, she said. That's what big sisters do; they protect their little brothers and sisters from the beginning to the end.

I tried, Mama. I tried, Papa and Aunt Maja and Baba Rose. I am so sorry I failed.

*The last time I saw Abek wasn't when I left Auschwitz-Birkenau, gripping his fingers through the barbed wire fence. It wasn't when we walked toward the showers and I told him not to worry about taking off his clothes, because he was going to be issued new ones. It wasn't*

*when I left him a turnip and he left me a mud drawing in return. Those*
*things didn't happen. They never happened.*

By the time we arrived in Birkenau, the old and the sick among us
had died on the trip. Baba Rose had died on the trip. She was in the car
with Abek and me; my mother and Aunt Maja had been shoved into
the next one, and I didn't know if they were alive or dead.

Abek was begging me for water. I don't have any, I kept saying. I
wish I did, I wish I did. The cough he'd caught from Mama, the one
that was just a tickle when we were in the stadium, had gotten worse
and worse. It racked through his body—violent coughs. He coughed up
bile, and then he coughed up nothing. He cried because of the pain it
caused his ribs, and I knew his ribs must be broken.

And then he wasn't begging for water with his voice, he was only
begging with his eyes. He'd become too weak to talk.

A bucket of water was finally shoved in, but by the time it reached
us in the back of the car, it was empty.

And then he wasn't begging at all.

He could barely lift his head. I said his name, and he blinked,
slowly. I don't even know if he registered me. He disappeared so fast; he
became unrecognizable so fast.

A second bucket was finally shoved in, but by the time I spooned
some through Abek's mouth, it dribbled back out his chin. He wasn't
able to swallow.

A hundred years passed in that moment, in realizing my brother was
too weak to swallow, and I didn't know how I could make him. I must
have been thirsty myself; I must have been in pain, but all I can remember
is that my brother couldn't swallow and I lived a century in that moment.

There were slats toward the top of the car. I could see through the *slats what was happening. I could see a guard line up three people, front to back, and shoot a bullet through them all at once to use only one bullet. I could see, in my mind, the memory of my own father receiving a bullet to the head, and the soft way he crumpled to the ground. How long would it be before they shot us?*

*I could see the future. They would finally open the door to our car. They would unload us, and I would have to carry Abek out because he couldn't walk. And I would be carrying him to his death. I would be laying him at the feet of the Nazi guards who would separate him from me and then kill him alone.*

*I knew that his ending, at that point, was inevitable. He was too weak. His death was the finishing stitch on a garment that is mostly complete. The only control I had in the matter was what kind of stitch should be used.*

*I'd taken off Abek's jacket to use as his pillow, and now I bunched it up in my hands. I started to tell his favorite stories. I put the jacket over his nose and mouth. He didn't struggle. He wasn't conscious anymore. I don't even know if he was alive anymore. He might have gone already; he was so still, I could no longer see his chest rise and fall.*

*It still took away pieces of my soul with every passing second. It was still, I think, a mercy.*

*That's what I told myself, what I had to believe was true. It was a mercy. It was protecting him. It was an impossible thing that was more horrible than every other choice in the universe, except for the choice of letting the guards do it. At least this way, he wouldn't be alone.*

*When it was finished, I made a space for him on the floor of the train car. I kissed his cheeks. I covered him with his best jacket, because we had all worn our best clothes, and I had sewn my best message into it. It was Abek's life story, written in my smallest, neatest handwriting: my name, and our parents' names, and the songs we sung, and the stories we told.*

*But of course he wasn't allowed to be buried in peace. Of course he wouldn't have been allowed to go into the earth draped in an expensive-looking jacket that the Nazis could have sold or stolen or searched through. Someone would have had to undress him, to take and sort those clothes. Another prisoner.*

*Another prisoner who was also a little boy. My brother was gone, but in the end, his story wasn't.*

*I left pieces of myself in that car. I left pieces I will never get back. I left them unwillingly, as my mind forced itself to block away those impossible, impossible minutes. I left them willingly for my own protection, because remembering that story would have demolished every reason I had to survive.*

*And beyond all reason, beyond any possible explanation, I still did want to survive.*

He's in the library. I wondered if he would go here. It's where I would have gone if I were him, after what happened at dinner. The book of fairy tales isn't out anymore. But Abek is sitting there, at the little chair at the little table, his hands tucked underneath his legs. It's the seated position of a little boy. His face looks like it could be a hundred.

"Abek," I say, and then immediately qualify it in my mind. The boy I keep calling Abek. The boy who cannot actually be Abek. I don't have anything else to call him.

That's what I should ask him: *What should I call you? Where did you come from? What is your real name?*

He looks up at me with dull, heavy eyes. "I thought about leaving," he says. "After you said you'd come here and found the book, I thought maybe it would be better if I just left right away."

"Why didn't you?"

"I don't know. I should, though, right? I should just go?"

Now is when I should say yes. He should go. This boy should go away and leave me. But I am exhausted by so much unspeakable sadness. And so, when I open my mouth, what comes out is, "Tell me a story."

He looks at me, confused. "From the book of fairy tales?"

"No."

"What, then?"

I pull up the other chair, sit down in it, scrape it to the table. My first impulse is to fold my hands so they won't shake, but I worry that will look too businesslike. Instead, I lay them flat on the table. Palms up. I have nothing left to hide.

"Tell me a story you make up," I say. "One that I haven't heard before, a new fairy tale. Tell me—tell me a story about a little boy that has a happy ending."

We stare at each other. I think he can tell what I'm asking, but I'm not sure. I think I know what I'm asking, but I'm honestly not sure of that, either.

"Once upon a time," he begins, but his voice is thin and wavering, so he clears his throat and starts again. "Once upon a time, there was a boy who lost everyone."

He looks up at me. *Is this what you wanted?* his eyes ask, and I nod. *Go on.*

"The boy saw everyone he loved die in front of him. A mother and a grandfather who were killed as soon as they got to Birkenau. An uncle who one day couldn't get up to work and the next day didn't get up at all. A father who screamed in pain for days before he finally closed his eyes. And the boy wondered, was bringing his father water while he was sick the right thing to do, or did it only keep him alive longer; did it only make his suffering last?

"And finally—and finally, the boy lost his sister."

He tries to blink back tears, and his voice catches, and then he doesn't try to hold back the tears, he just lets them come.

"He lost an older sister. Before she died, she still managed to send notes to him from the other side of camp. She still tried to save rations for her little brother, even when keeping them might have saved her. She stayed alive so much longer than it seemed possible, so long it seemed like she might survive. But she couldn't survive. In the end, she just couldn't. The last note he got was from her bunkmate saying she was gone."

My own eyes are prickling because it's not my story but it is my story. It's unfamiliar and familiar all at once. He starts again.

"Once upon a time, that boy, who was all alone, heard of another sister, and he wondered if maybe two people could be family again. He read a story about the Lederman family. He read it, and he thought it sounded like his own family. And the whole time he was in the camps, he would think of the

Ledermans. He would take out their story and read it, again and again. He would pretend that maybe they had survived even though his family hadn't, and he could go be a part of them. Maybe what he realized is that all families are very similar, the ones who love one another. He thought, the Lederman sister who had written the story must love her brother very much.

"And so once upon a time, after all the rest of his family died, that boy decided that if he lived through the war, he would try to find this family."

"So he did," I whisper.

"So he did." He furtively wipes a tear from the corner of his eye.

"If that sister had found her own brother, he would have left her alone," he continues. "If the Lederman family already had one another, he wouldn't have bothered them. He didn't even expect it to work. It was just a quest, just a reason to keep going.

"And then, as soon as he succeeded, he started to realize what a mistake he'd made. How dangerous it had been, and how stupid, and—and how unfair it had been. But then he didn't know how to tell the truth without making things worse, because for such a long time, thinking about finding a new family is what had kept him going. And he thought that the sister might feel the same way. She might have been as alone as he was."

This boy wasn't trying to torment me. He wasn't trying to get money from me. He wasn't trying to get a passport from me. He was trying to get a family from me. He was trying to grab onto something small that would make his days the smallest bit more bearable.

I look at the defeated boy, sitting on his chair in the library, and I see choices spreading out in front of me.

The muslin cloth from Abek's jacket is tucked in my pocket. I could pull it out now. I could shake it at him, angrily, or throw it in his face. I could get up and leave, or I could tell him to.

But as we are sitting here at this table, two desperately, desperately lonely people, what I keep thinking is this: It is its own kind of miracle. For the boy who found my muslin letter, years ago, to have managed to keep it all this time. And for him to then come and look for me, after the war. And for him to then hear about another letter that I wrote, three years later and hundreds of miles away, that I pinned on a board in the middle of a camp where all the children were looking for something.

For me to have met the nun in a convent who happened to be in charge that day, who happened to remember a boy that sounded like my brother. For me to have met a Russian commander who told me about the existence of Foehrenwald. For me to have invited an old family friend to that dinner, who spoke Russian and could help translate.

To bring me to this moment, a hundred things had to happen in order, and they all happened.

None of these are the miracles I was looking for. But they're miracles nonetheless.

The boy in front of me looks at me with such desperate, hungry eyes.

I swallow. "What was the boy's name? In your story, what is his name?"

His mouth sets in a firm line; he barely hesitates before he answers. "His name is Abek."

"Before that. Before that, what was his name?"

"His name used to be Łukasz. But only at the beginning of the story. By the end of the story, it is Abek."

"It's not really a happy story," I tell him.

"You didn't say it had to be a happy story. You just said it had to have a happy ending."

"A happy ending," I repeat.

The boy in front of me is still waiting for an answer, and here is what I find myself thinking:

I am thinking, I have done it, without even meaning to. I thought after the war was over, I would find my brother and we would find a new home, and only then, after all that, would we begin to build our family again, we would complete our alphabet.

But I ended up building it on the way. Most of it, I completed along the way.

*A* is for Abek.

*B* is for Baba Rose. *No. B* isn't for Baba Rose any longer. Baba Rose is gone. *B* is for—*B* can be for Breine, effervescent and hopeful, planning her beautiful wedding inside a refugee camp. And *C* is for Chaim, her timid Hungarian groom.

*D* is for Dima, who saved me, taking me to the hospital and then taking me home to Sosnowiec.

*E* is for Esther, kind and steady, applying rouge to the cheeks of her protesting friend.

*F* is for Foehrenwald, where Esther and Breine and all of them were forced to live, and where none of them had been before, and where all of them tried to make it a home anyway.

*G* is for Gosia, Aunt Maja's friend, who survived, and who will always be a connection to my past.

*H* can be for Hannelore, the little girl loved by the family she calls stepparents, and *I* can be for Inge, the mother she'll never stop looking for.

*J* is for Josef.

*K* is Commander Kuznetsov, bringing a bottle of vodka, sending me to Foehrenwald.

*L* is for the Lederman family, the Chomickis and the Ledermans, and all the people in the family, because even though they are gone, I will carry their name and history forever: my mother, my father, beautiful Aunt Maja, Baba Rose.

*Ł* is for Łukasz. A boy who was not part of the Lederman family. Who eventually wished he was.

*M* is for Miriam, whom I barely knew but who was also looking for her own sister, who wrote letter after letter after letter.

*N* is for the nothing-girls, trying to become something again.

*O* is for Mr. Ohrmann, traveling the continent, trying to sew families back together as best as he can.

*P* is for Palestine, Eretz Israel, which could be our future.

*R* is for Ravid, trying to organize his people to go there, even when it seems impossible.

*S* is for Sosnowiec. I will make *S* always be for Sosnowiec, because you can't erase where you've come from, and nobody else can erase it, either, even when they change the name and tear down the street signs.

Ś is for Uncle Świętopełk, an old man who can carry memories of the past, from long before this terrible thing happened to us, and who can say he is still alive after the terrible things finally ended.

*T* is for Sister Therese, the nun who gave me hope.

*U* is for Nurse Urbaniak, the nurse who gave me bread.

*V* is for Mrs. Van Houten, an old woman who volunteered to walk a young woman she barely knew to her groom on the evening of her wedding, and who represents the tiny, tender kindnesses we have tried to give to one another. *V*, even though it doesn't even exist in the Polish alphabet, typically, and neither does Q and neither does X, but I am meeting people who exist outside of my alphabet now; my alphabet is new.

*W* is for the Wölflin family, who represent the larger, heroic kindnesses. The people who took in children, who risked their own lives.

*X* is to x things out. To cross out the things I'll forget on purpose. Some things are okay to forget on purpose.

*Y* is for Mrs. Yost, trying to run Foehrenwald. And for all the other people trying to run all the other places in this terrible land after the war.

*Z* is for Zofia.

Here is what I am thinking, sitting in this makeshift library across from a boy whose life has been every bit as hard as mine.

I think we must find miracles where we can. We must love the people in front of us. We must forgive ourselves for the things we did to survive. The things we broke. The things that broke us.

I choose my next words so very, very carefully.

"Maybe I could meet Łukasz one day," I say. "Not right now if he doesn't want to. But one day. Maybe one day he can tell me more of his story." I stand and extend my hand.

His face fills with the most fragile hope. "Does that mean—"

"Yes, Abek." My brother's name, spoken out loud, carries so much in it now. It's an offering, it's an acceptance, it's a lie, it's a goodbye. I clear my throat and start again. "Yes. It means that for now, we should go home."

# Epilogue

## London, 1946

IT'S ALMOST TIME. ABEK AND I HAVE SAID THIS ENOUGH TO EACH other that it's become a joke. *Don't worry; we're almost there*, he said when we rode in the back of the truck and I was desperate to use the bathroom, and then we ended up being in the truck for nearly three more hours as we were driven through Germany and then through France, past checkpoints and through demolished cities. *Don't worry; we're almost to the front of the line*, I consoled him as we waited for hours to have our papers processed, but then the aid workers changed shifts and we had to keep waiting. Now *almost* has become the joke for "never," and we say it all the time. The tire is almost fixed. I would almost eat a live octopus.

But now we really are almost there, I think. Because as we stand near the dock, smelling the brininess of the air while the salt chaps my lips, the ship has begun sounding its horn.

The people around us—the hundreds of other people clutching suitcases—hear it, too, and they all begin to chatter.

Ottawa. This is the name of the place we're going, the place where the local Jewish federation has sponsored us and the other families lucky enough to be selected in the lottery. We'd pulled out a map, traced our fingers along the southern border of Canada, found the city in the east, on the border of a province called Ontario.

"How are your feet?" I ask Abek, because his shoes are too big for much walking, it turns out, and we didn't layer on extra pairs of socks soon enough to prevent them from blistering.

"Almost okay," he says.

"Really, almost?" I ask, concerned.

"They're fine, I promise," he reassures me.

I wish I'd taken some of the things from the closet in my family's apartment when I left Sosnowiec—the sewn mementos, the memories of a previous life. I would have, if I'd realized I was leaving for good. Now in my valise, I have changes of clothes, and needles and thread, and a new pair of sewing shears that someone, incredibly, sent over in a donation box. Nicer, even, than what my family's factory once had, with blades of clean, polished steel. We're all traveling light. We're all carrying just enough energy to start over.

Maybe one day I can write to Gosia and ask her to send the heirlooms. Maybe one day I'll have a new life that will allow me to make space for the previous one.

In my valise, I also have a square of graying cloth, cut out from a shirt that I'd found on the doorstep of my cottage in

Foehrenwald the morning after my last conversation with Josef. I'd spent the previous night trying to decide what I was going to do. How do you measure forgiveness—who deserves it, who can dispense it? How do you measure whether someone is punishing themselves enough? I debated whether I was going to tell Mrs. Yost, or whether it was possible she already knew. Whether I'd tell Breine and Esther, at least.

But I woke up that morning, and the shirt was on my doorstep, and Josef wasn't. He'd left. So I didn't have to decide whether to forgive him. I only got to decide that his absolution wouldn't be my job. It made me relieved, and it makes me sad.

I think about him more than I wish I did. I wonder where he is and if there's a world in which I'd see him again.

I kissed Breine and Esther and Chaim goodbye several weeks after that, as they left to find their own new start on their own boat. I had explained to them why we wouldn't be joining them. Abek and I wanted something brand-new, something we'd chosen entirely on our own. A new decision for a new family.

And in a way, we found the most comfort in choosing something the most unknown. A place we knew almost nothing about, where there would be no reminders of pain and no expectations to live up to or down to. We read a book about ice hockey. We asked one of the Canadian volunteers at Foehrenwald to sing us the national anthem.

The boat is an ocean liner with three smokestacks, the size of a floating town almost. The gangway is long and zigzags up the side, and at the beginning, passengers stop and hand over papers, waiting to be checked off a manifest.

Abek walks onto the gangway ahead of me but turns back when he realizes I haven't followed. "Are you coming?"

"Almost," I say, and then, quickly, "I mean, yes."

I take his outstretched hand and move forward. The boards sway a little under my feet, but I keep moving forward.

# A Note on History and Research

I WROTE THIS NOVEL, MY THIRD SET IN THE WORLD WAR II ERA, because after five years spent researching those horrible years, I realized that most of the books I'd read and documentaries I'd seen all finished at the same place: the end of the war. They ended with the liberation of a concentration camp. The disbanding of an army unit. A celebration in the streets. There was much less about what happened in the weeks and months after the war, when an entire continent had to find a way to recover from the suffering it had experienced and the atrocities it had committed.

Several years before, on a somber vacation, I'd taken a long, meandering train ride from Germany through the Czech Republic and into Poland. The trip began in Munich, where I visited the site of the Dachau concentration camp, and it ended in Kraków, where I visited Auschwitz-Birkenau, the most infamous Nazi death camp of the Holocaust, where more than one million people were murdered.

Late one night I realized, sickened, that my comfortable passenger train was following a route that a different train could have followed in 1941 or 1942, packed with terrified people heading to their deaths. My train made a brief stop in a city called Sosnowiec, and the name stuck in my brain. I came home and read a little about it, and when I began writing this book, I set about trying to re-create, as best as I could, what might have happened to a young woman who had been taken from that town at the beginning of the war, and who now had to return to it.

Germany invaded Sosnowiec in 1939, and life changed immediately for the Jewish people who lived there. They were banned from work and from attending schools and made to live in a ghetto. They were used for forced labor for the Nazi regime. First, forced labor in the streets—snow shoveling, road cleaning—and then, forced labor in factories because Sosnowiec, being an industrial city, had many factories that the Germans took over for their own production.

Finally, Jews were used as forced labor in concentration camps. In August of 1942, thousands of Jewish families were ordered to report to the soccer stadium, where they were told they'd receive new identification but they were instead sorted into lines and then deported to camps.

I read somewhere that one of the reasons writing fiction about the Holocaust is so complicated is because the atrocities were so vast and so horrific that writing about true things can end up sounding like fiction. Our minds simply don't want to process that these things happened; we assume the author must be exaggerating for effect. I'll say only that the details I included about the camps were true. Including the "singing forest" of Buchenwald, where tortured prisoners were left to scream and die. Including the chaotic arrival scenes, where prisoners described having their infant children ripped from their arms and slaughtered by hand. In the middle of the war, a small group of young women with sewing skills were taken from Birkenau, forced into slave labor at a textile factory called Neustadt, and then later forced to march, in the winter, to the concentration camp Gross-Rosen to evade the approaching Allies. I patterned Zofia's imprisonment off that journey.

Before the war, the Jewish population of Sosnowiec was twenty-nine thousand people. After the war, only seven hundred returned.

And what they returned to was, in many cases, a persecution that was less systematic than it had been under Nazi occupation, but no less hateful. Anti-Semitism was still rampant; the war didn't end people's prejudice.

Several incidents from Zofia's return to Sosnowiec were inspired from Polish survivor accounts: Sala Garncarz wrote of trying to board a train to her family's home of Sosnowiec, only to have the conductor tell her that Jews weren't welcome on his train or in his country. When she finally reached her family's apartment, it had been taken over by strangers who showed no sympathy. Michael Bornstein recounted the story of being woken from bed as a young child by the sound of drunken men banging on the door because they'd heard a Jewish family had returned. The family was saved only because Bornstein's cousin had spent the war hidden in a Catholic convent: She could recite enough prayers to convince the men that the family was Christian.

Postwar Europe was still a terrifying place to be Jewish. In 1946—a year after the war ended—in the town of Kielce, Poland, forty-two Jews were murdered by an angry mob of police and civilians. Massacres like these weren't isolated, and they all had the same intent: to make it clear that Jews were not welcome to return. And so, after enduring years in death camps and concentration camps, survivors now found that their nightmares still hadn't ended. Poland no longer felt safe, and many set about starting over in new homelands. In the months and years after the war, a web of displaced-persons camps sprung up around Germany. Some of the people who went to them had no other choice: Their own homes had been demolished or had new families living in them. Their own families were gone. Their homelands had become foreign places to live. In search of safety, they came to these camps, located in convents, office complexes, and sometimes in the very concentration camps they had just been liberated from.

Foehrenwald was a real place, on the repurposed grounds of the I.G. Farben pharmaceutical factory, famous for making Zyklon B. It was one of the most prominent camps, holding thousands of people at the peak of its existence, and incorporating trade and language schools. The Kloster Indersdorf was also a real camp, for children, run out of a convent and populated by children who needed to be retaught to eat and sleep peacefully. An estimated 1.5 million children died in the Holocaust.

I used Foehrenwald and the Kloster Indersdorf as rough templates for *They Went Left*, but changed some details and also incorporated details from other camps. There were several, for example, that functioned mostly as training farms for young Jews who planned to emigrate to Israel and were learning to work the land. One of the most famous was Kibbutz Buchenwald: A group of prisoners took the patch of land that was meant to be their destruction and instead turned it into their salvation. Many of them did ultimately take ships, some sanctioned and some secret—*Aliyah Bet*—beginning in the fall of 1945.

The first book I read about displaced-persons camps was *The Rage to Live: The International D.P. Children's Center Kloster Indersdorf* by Anna Andlauer, a moving testimony of postwar life for children. For other accounts of postwar life, I recommend *The Hidden Children: The Secret Survivors of the Holocaust* by Jane Marks; *We Are Here: New Approaches to Jewish Displaced Persons in Postwar Germany* by Avinoam Patt; *Life Between Memory and Hope: The Survivors of the Holocaust in Occupied Germany* by Zeev Mankowitz; *Kibbutz Buchenwald: Survivors and Pioneers* by Judith Tydor Baumel; and the documentary *The Long Way Home*, directed by Mark Jonathan Harris.

I am again indebted to the United States Holocaust Memorial Museum (USHMM) in Washington, DC, and especially to its priceless collection of oral histories. To name a very small few: Bella Tovey, Sonia Chomicki, and Zelda Piekarska Brodecki all gave richly textured descriptions of what it was like to grow up in Sosnowiec during the occupation. Hana Mueller Bruml described the liberation of Gross-Rosen. Regina Spiegel spoke of learning to become a seamstress at Foehrenwald. Writings by Henry Cohen, who served as Foehrenwald's director in 1946, described life in the camp: the fact that there was a library, for example, and a Jewish police force, and that residents were allotted three ounces of canned meat a day. He also wrote of black markets, camp tensions, and other facets of the time and place that I didn't have a chance to illuminate.

And, a story I have thought of again and again while writing this book: Alice Cahana spoke of her sister Edith. She spoke of how the two of them, as teenagers, survived selection together at Auschwitz-Birkenau when the rest of their family was sent to the gas chambers. She spoke of how she and Edith managed to stay together through the entire war, when they were transferred to Gross-Rosen and finally Bergen-Belsen. They celebrated liberation together. And then, Edith, weak and sick, was taken away in an ambulance to recover. Alice watched the ambulance drive away with her sister, and she never saw her again. She never saw her again, but never stopped looking.

The USHMM has an online database that allows researchers to look up Holocaust victims by various criteria: by name, by age, by the camp they were placed in, or by the city they were born in. All my characters' first names came from these records, from the lists of real people who were born in Sos-nowiec, or who were imprisoned in Dachau and Auschwitz, or who were, like Zofia, eighteen years old in 1945, trying to start life anew with ravaged hearts on a ravaged continent, in a ravaged period of time in which the entire world seemed to have gone crazy.

Besides those accounts, I've read probably a hundred Holo-caust memoirs in my lifetime, and I know I carried pieces of each of them into this. I know, for example, that the idea for a prized bottle of Coca-Cola came from Thomas Buergenthal recounting his first sip of the strange foreign drink after sur-viving Auschwitz as a young boy. I know that Gerda Weiss-man described the surrealness of a neighbor asking to borrow ribbon so she could sew a swastika onto a flag. I offer a blanket debt of gratitude to any survivors who found ways to tell their stories, and for the journalists and historians who facilitated that storytelling.

I filled this book with sadness because there was plenty of sadness. I ended this book with hope because, improbably, there was plenty of that, too, in the camps for displaced per-sons: romances, babies, new starts, new life. Some of my favor-ite photos to look at while researching *They Went Left* were the photos of weddings that happened in displaced-persons camps. I looked at image after image of optimistic brides and grooms, dressed in whatever clothes they could make or borrow, surrounded by the new friends they had made into a family, getting ready to face the future together.

I don't know which is more unfathomable to me: the base evil and cruelty of the Holocaust, or the undying hope that survivors managed to take out of it. I don't know which is more unfathomable, but I do know which we should aspire to.

# Acknowledgments

This book, like many of my creative projects, came into existence because of my agent, Ginger Clark. Over the course of a single afternoon, I sketched out via email the vaguest concept of a plot. She kept writing back— *And then what? What about this?*—until the characters became people and the vague outline became a story I was desperate to tell.

Lisa Yoskowitz has been my editor through three books now, and by this point I should cite her as a coauthor. Her incisive notes make every paragraph better; I feel lucky every day to work with her and with the rest of the team at Little, Brown Books for Young Readers.

Magdalena Cabajewska patiently answered my many questions about the intricacies of the Polish language.

My seamstress-equestrian mother, Dawn Dannenbring-Carlson, fact-checked my descriptions of sewing and horses.

My dear friend Rachel Dry gave thoughtful feedback on an early draft.

My husband, Robert Cox, gave me love, laughter, and everything else.

# Monica Hesse

is the bestselling author of *Girl in the Blue Coat*, *American Fire*, and *The War Outside*, as well as a columnist at the *Washington Post*. She lives outside Washington, DC, with her husband and their dog. Monica invites you to visit her online at monicahesse.com and on Twitter @MonicaHesse.